"Why did you lock the door?" she asked.

"To ensure we won't be interrupted." Jonus spoke from behind her as his hands captured her shoulders.

"I'm not going to have an affair with you," Polly said with desperate bravado. But her body had turned traitor, and she was powerless to break away from him.

He tightened his hold until, weakening, she leaned back against him. "But we're so right for each other...." His arms loosened, and his hands rose to gently cup her breasts. "Don't you need to have a man touch you?"

"No," she whispered desperately through the excruciating pleasure.

"I don't think your body agrees with you...."

Dear Reader,

Welcome to the Silhouette **Special Edition** experience! With your search for consistently satisfying reading in mind, every month the authors and editors of Silhouette **Special Edition** aim to offer you a stimulating blend of deep emotions and high romance.

The name Silhouette **Special Edition** and the distinctive arch on the cover represent a commitment—a commitment to bring you six sensitive, substantial novels each month. In the pages of a Silhouette **Special Edition**, compelling true-to-life characters face riveting emotional issues—and come out winners. All the authors in the series strive for depth, vividness and warmth in writing these stories of living and loving in today's world.

The result, we hope, is romance you can believe in. Deeply emotional, richly romantic, infinitely rewarding—that's the Silhouette **Special Edition** experience. Come share it with us—six times a month!

From all the authors and editors of Silhouette **Special Edition**,

Best wishes,

Leslie Kazanjian,
Senior Editor

CAROLE HALSTON
Courage to Love

Silhouette Special Edition

Published by Silhouette Books New York

America's Publisher of Contemporary Romance

For my mother,
a career homemaker,
and my precocious niece Rebecca

SILHOUETTE BOOKS
300 East 42nd St., New York, N.Y. 10017

Books by Carole Halston

Silhouette Romance

Stand-in Bride #62
Love Legacy #83
Undercover Girl #152
Sunset in Paradise #208

Silhouette Special Edition

Keys to Daniel's House #8
Collision Course #41
The Marriage Bonus #86
Summer Course in Love #115
A Hard Bargain #139
Something Lost, Something Gained #163
A Common Heritage #211
The Black Knight #223
Almost Heaven #253
Surprise Offense #291
Matched Pair #328
Honeymoon for One #356
The Baby Trap #388
High Bid #423
Intensive Care #461
Compromising Positions #500
Ben's Touch #543
Unfinished Business #567
Courage to Love #642

CAROLE HALSTON

is a Louisiana native, residing on the north shore of
Lake Pontchartrain, near New Orleans. She enjoys
traveling with her husband to research less familiar
locations for settings but is always happy to return
home to her own unique region, a rich source in itself
for romantic stories about warm, wonderful people.

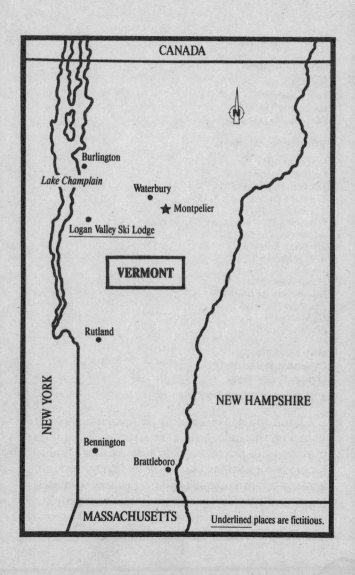

CANADA

Burlington

Lake Champlain

Waterbury

★ Montpelier

Logan Valley Ski Lodge

VERMONT

Rutland

NEW YORK

NEW HAMPSHIRE

Bennington

Brattleboro

MASSACHUSETTS

Underlined places are fictitious.

Chapter One

It isn't as though you're desperate for a job.

Sitting behind the wheel of her compact station wagon in the parking lot of the Logan Valley Ski Lodge, where the steep mountain highway wound to a dead end, Polly Dearing reviewed her state of finances in order to calm her panic before she went inside for her interview.

There wasn't enough money from the sale of the farm and Brad's life insurance for her to live on it indefinitely, but fortunately she wasn't in the position of having to worry about finding immediate employment. Naturally she wouldn't want to deplete her bank account and not keep a nest egg to fall back on. Without a college degree, she wasn't going to find it easy to accumulate savings on the kind of salary she could expect to earn.

Now that she was all settled after her move to Vermont, she was ready to get out and find something to do to occupy her time, as well as support herself. Still, there was no urgency.

It wasn't crucial that she impress the owner of the lodge in her interview today. Working at Logan Valley seemed ideal to her, since she lived just ten minutes away in a rented chalet, but several small towns and villages were within easy driving distance. After some searching, she would surely find employment in the immediate area. As a last resort, she could commute to Burlington or Montpelier on the interstate.

Polly was open to almost any type of job that was within her capabilities. She might not have impressive qualifications on paper, but she was basically intelligent and confident that with some on-the-job training, she would catch on quickly to what was expected of her. At twenty-nine she wasn't too old to learn new skills and adapt to a working-world environment.

There was little doubt in her mind that she would turn out to be a valued employee, given the chance to prove herself. She possessed the all-important good character traits: honesty, dependability, personal pride, and willingness to work hard and put forth her best effort. She had always been a friendly, outgoing type and got along well with people. That should be an attribute in any job.

Polly's best bet today was to look upon her interview as good experience, no matter how it turned out. There was no reason she should have high expectations. In addition to not having any previous employment record to speak of, she was a newcomer to Vermont. In competing with the locals for available jobs, she would naturally be at a disadvantage, especially when the employer was a native Vermonter, like the owner of the ski lodge, Jonus Logan. Logan Valley had been named after his grandfather and namesake, according to the brochure Polly had tucked in her purse.

"Relax. This is not a matter of life and death." She spoke aloud to herself in a stern voice as she got out of her car and slammed the door. "You're just here to apply for a job. There's nothing really important at stake."

The deeper truth behind Polly's pep talk to herself brought a wave of sadness. She sighed, her mood turning bleak, as well as calm. Nothing important was at stake, because no one except herself would be affected by the outcome of the next thirty minutes.

And even she wouldn't be seriously affected, whether or not she got a job. She wasn't laying herself on the line. Her self-esteem wasn't at risk, because it was safely protected forever by her memories. Polly had already succeeded at her chosen occupation of homemaker and wife and mother.

That occupation had ended tragically three years ago when she had buried her husband and child in a cemetery in southern Illinois. Never again would she have the heart to take on those same demanding and rewarding roles, which had fully utilized all her talents.

Any job that Polly got would be just that—a job, something she did for a paycheck. There would be no ultimate, binding commitment. There would be none of the deep satisfaction that reached down into the very core of her being. And it wouldn't matter greatly if the job carried no promise of permanency.

With her anxiety gone, she stood for a moment in the parking lot, gazing at the lodge. A couple of weeks earlier she had driven up to Logan Valley out of curiosity and been rather taken aback to see a modern two-story structure with clean, simple lines and expanses of glass. She had been expecting something more rustic.

Somewhat to her surprise, she had found herself approving the overall effect. Normally, modern architecture didn't appeal to her, but the lodge, stained a pale silvery gray, was in harmony with its setting. And what a glorious setting it had, ringed with mountain slopes that now, in late October, were ablaze with gold and orange and red. The fall foliage was in full color, so that the eye hardly noticed the dark green of evergreen trees.

Polly could easily imagine how breathtakingly beautiful this same view would be after the first big snowfall when the mountainsides were carpeted with downy white. Her vision made her wistful. She did hope that there would be a job opening for her at Logan Valley Ski Lodge.

Aside from the convenience, it would be a treat just to come to work each day during the various seasons. According to the brochure, the lodge stayed open year-round, though its busiest times were fall and winter.

Polly had never done any downhill skiing, and she was looking forward to trying it this winter. Employees probably got a break on the price of lift tickets, or maybe they even got to ski free during their off time. That would be another benefit.

Feeling some of her earlier anxiousness returning, Polly took a deep breath and headed for the lodge entrance, walking with her long athletic stride. She wore low-heeled, sensible shoes. At five foot eight, she didn't need any extra height, and the shoes went with her outfit, a brown-and-black plaid skirt, beige blouse and brown corduroy blazer.

After deliberating long and hard over how to dress for her interview, she had decided that it wouldn't be appropriate to show up in her Sunday best to apply for a job. She didn't really own any fashionable business clothes, and her practical instincts ruled out going shopping in Burlington for an outfit that would be more professional, a chic tailored suit, for example.

Why spend good money on clothes that she might end up having no use for? And besides, Polly was afraid she might feel self-conscious, wearing new clothes that weren't her usual style. Her best bet was just to be neat and presentable. To *be* herself, a forthright, down-to-earth type.

After all, she wasn't applying for an executive position. It wasn't really clear in her own mind what her job options were. When she had called and set up the appointment, she had been intentionally vague about the type of work she was seeking, preferring to explain in person that she was willing to do almost anything as long as there was opportunity to advance to more responsibility and higher pay.

Polly was expecting to enter and find herself in a lobby with a front desk where guests checked in and out, but instead she walked into a spacious foyer with a stairway leading upward and curving out of sight. In keeping with the lodge exterior, the decor was modern yet understated, with soft gray the dominant color.

Taking in quick impressions of rough-textured wood paneling, rugged tile flooring and wonderful photographs of scenes from nature, Polly found herself reacting again with an instinctive approval that surprised her. She usually found the contemporary look in interior decorating much too sophisticated for her taste.

The slick, shallow element was lacking here, though. While there wasn't a cozy, homey air about the lodge, either outside or within, there was none of the commercial atmosphere of a chain hotel. She sensed that thoughtful attention had gone into the design and the decorating decisions.

It seemed safe to assume that the owner, Jonus Logan, had taken a personal interest in the development of his inherited property and that the lodge reflected his personality. He apparently did his own hiring and firing of employees, since he was interviewing Polly today.

How old was he? she wondered, feeling her first glimmer of curiosity about her prospective employer. Was he in his prime, undertaking an ambitious business venture, or was he nearing retirement age and just getting around to a pet project?

Polly would soon find out, if he didn't keep her waiting. Polite voices drifted through an open entryway on her right. She headed for it, feeling her nerves tighten, but then stopped involuntarily as a little girl of about seven or eight came into sight, descending the stairs slowly. A very unhappy little girl, judging from her posture and expression.

The smile Polly had been preparing to summon to her lips came naturally, along with a flood of warm sympathy and a simultaneous pain in her heart. Her Jennifer would be about the same age, if she had lived.

The little girl's parents must have taken her out of school to go on vacation with them, Polly reflected, obeying her instincts and standing there, waiting to speak a few comforting words. Perhaps they had punished her for some misbehavior, and she was feeling all alone in the world.

Showing no evidence of shyness, she surveyed Polly glumly, not smiling back and not quickening or slowing her pace down the stairs.

"Are you looking for your mommy and daddy, sweetie?" Polly inquired as the little girl reached the bottom.

"I don't have a mommy anymore. She died," came the ready answer in a despondent, resigned voice. "And my daddy's in his office, where he almost always is." Her face brightened suddenly. "Are you here to see him about a job?" she asked shrewdly.

Polly was slow to reply, adjusting to both the little girl's identity and her rather peremptory manner with an adult. Apparently she was the lodge owner's daughter and had sized Polly up immediately as a job applicant, not a guest.

"If your father is Mr. Jonus Logan, then I do have an appointment with him," Polly said in a gentle but firm voice.

"You can call him by his first name," the little girl said, giving her regal permission. "Everybody else does who works for him. I'll show you where his office is. Just come with me."

"That would be very helpful, thank you." Polly spoke with exaggerated courtesy to her small guide's back. "Why aren't you in school today, dear?'' she inquired when she had caught up in a few long strides.

"I had a bad stomachache this morning."

"Did you have to go to the doctor?" Polly asked sympathetically, and got a quick guilty look.

"No. My daddy was going to have somebody take me, but I got better. Not *well*," she clarified. "But it just hurt a little bit."

Polly had been shepherded through the entryway into a reception area, where an elderly couple had evidently just finished checking in to the lodge. A young blond woman behind the registration counter was handing them a key and giving them instructions for finding their room.

"Tell them to wait a minute, and I'll show them the way, Donna," the little girl interrupted to order bossily. She ignored the blonde's irritated glance, adding as she headed for a closed door, "After I take this lady in to see my daddy."

"Jennifer, your father is talking long-distance on the telephone. Don't go barging in there," Donna warned, keeping her voice under careful control.

She might as well have saved her breath. The little girl didn't even seem to hear. She marched officiously up to the door and rapped a couple of times with the knuckles of a small fist. She looked over her shoulder to speak to Polly, who had come to a standstill.

"You need to tell me your name so that I can tell my daddy you're out here," she said.

Since the name Polly had given her own daughter wasn't uncommon, this wasn't the first time during the past three years that she had met a little girl named Jennifer, but it was never easy. Today, hearing the woman Donna address the lodge owner's daughter brought a familiar shock of pain, followed by the inevitable sadness.

Despite her emotion, Polly refused to be bullied by a headstrong child, who was obviously in need of being taught better manners.

"I can introduce myself to your father, Jennifer, when he's ready to see me," she told the small girl in a kind tone that boded no argument. "You've done your good deed by bringing me here."

The door behind Jennifer swung open, and she tipped back her head with an uncertain smile to look up at the man who appeared. Polly looked at him, too, with a feminine interest that caught her unprepared. He was no older than about thirty-five and well over six feet tall, with ruggedly handsome features and sandy-colored hair.

His rangy, broad-shouldered build was all the more noticeable because he wasn't wearing businessman's attire. A dark green corduroy shirt was tucked into gray twill pants, and his suede boots were well broken in. Except for his unsmiling expression, he could have stepped out of the pages of a catalog selling quality clothing to the outdoorsman.

It was clearly evident that he didn't welcome the interruption by his daughter. There was no hint of fatherly indulgence in his manner as he frowned with a kind of exasperated patience down at Jennifer. She spoke up hurriedly before he could question her.

"Hi, Daddy. I brought this lady for her appointment with you."

Seeing how eager the little girl was for her daddy's approval, Polly wished that she'd gone along with her request a moment earlier and given her name, so that Jennifer could have performed introductions and bolstered her case for having acted responsibly. The sense of regret became disconcertingly personal as he turned his gaze on her. Polly was sorry that she hadn't worn a more becoming outfit, sorry that she hadn't taken more pains with her appearance.

Immediately she felt defensive and self-conscious, afraid he might be able to read her feminine reaction to his virile good looks.

"I'm Polly Dearing," she said crisply, walking closer. "I'm here to make a job application." She smiled warmly at Jennifer. "Your daughter was kind enough to act as my guide and help me find your office."

He stepped forward, extending his hand. "Jonus Logan. I'm pleased to meet you, Polly."

His eyes were a wintry shade of blue gray and keenly observant. Polly felt as though a searchlight were trained on her face as she shook hands with him. His clasp was cordial, but businesslike. Embarrassed by her own rush of pleasure at the strength of his fingers, she pulled her hand away abruptly.

"I don't mind waiting for a few minutes if you've been interrupted in the middle of something important," she said with dignity.

"No, I'll see you now. Please come on into my office," he requested, turning to lead the way. Polly followed with lagging steps, fighting her female appreciation of his tall, rangy physique. In comparison to the span of his shoulders, his hips were narrow and his legs long. He carried himself with an easy athleticism that left little doubt that he was probably an expert skier.

Jennifer stood to one side of the open door, looking crestfallen rather than relieved that she'd escape a scolding. Polly stopped, welcoming her rush of empathy for the little girl. Jonus Logan wasn't showing much sensitivity as a father. It wouldn't hurt him to give his daughter a little attention before he shut himself up in his office again. Couldn't he see how hungry she was for his approval?

"Thank you again, Jennifer," Polly said. "I know your father must appreciate your trying to be a big help to him."

The none-too-subtle reproof in her tone wasn't lost on the lodge owner, who had also halted and was waiting to close the door. Polly met his keen, bleak gaze squarely, standing her ground as Jennifer's champion. The fact that she wasn't getting her job interview off to a good start was of no concern. The idea of herself as an employee at Logan Valley Ski Lodge wasn't very feasible, anyway, now that she'd met its owner.

"Jennifer was too ill today to go to school," he said sternly, glancing from Polly to his daughter and then back to Polly again, his expression oddly thoughtful. "She is supposed to be playing quietly and resting."

There was no underlying message for Polly to mind her own business, even though there was the suggestion that she might first find out the facts before she started making judgments.

Jennifer was inspecting her shoes, avoiding her father's eyes. "I'm feeling almost well now, Daddy," she mumbled. "Do I have to go back to my room?"

He sighed, his face gentling and mirroring his inner struggle between wanting to relent and wanting to be firm. It wasn't the first time he'd fought the same losing battle with himself, Polly sensed, far too involved in the exchange between father and child.

"Just mind your manners and don't make a pest of yourself," he threatened gruffly.

"I won't, Daddy," Jennifer promised, edging away.

Polly ached for one of them to make a move and break through the restraint that kept them from ending the scene with a show of affection. The little girl would only need some slight encouragement to go to him to have him pat her on the head or spank her lovingly on the bottom. For just a second, Polly thought that he was on the verge of saying something more, but then he gestured for Polly to enter.

She took a breath and strode past him. His office was a moderate-size room, sparely furnished and decorated in keeping with what she'd seen so far of the lodge interior, but more masculine in tone. His desk was situated so that he could see out through the large windows that formed most of the outside wall.

In the forefront of his view was the lodge parking lot. If he had been looking out, he could have seen Polly arriving minutes earlier. The realization only made her feel more ill prepared for the interview.

"I could fill out an application form outside and leave it," she suggested. "That might save us both some time." And save face for her. In addition to everything else, all her lack of confidence about job seeking had flooded back.

"It shouldn't take long for either of us to find out what we need to know," he replied, going around behind his desk. "Please. Have a seat. That is, unless you've changed your mind and are no longer interested in a job at Logan Valley Ski Lodge now that you've gotten a look at it." He glanced out the window and added frankly, "I saw you drive up and come in. You seemed to be having doubts from the outset."

Polly remembered how she'd sat in the car, working up her nerve to get out, and then how she'd stood and gazed at the lodge, killing her nervous tension with the cruel reality that she was a woman stripped of everything precious in life except memory. Observing her from his office, Jonus Logan had made the wrong interpretation of her state of mind.

"I was having doubts, but they were about my chances of being hired," she told him honestly. Her poise had returned along with her sense of her identity: Polly was and would always be Brad Dearing's widow and Jennifer Dearing's bereaved mother. Nothing could change that.

She went on matter-of-factly, "I haven't ever been employed except for a part-time job in a drugstore when I was in college. I don't have a degree. I dropped out in my sophomore year to get married. That was nine years ago. My husband and I had a farm, and I did all the bookkeeping and took care of the office work, but that's the extent of my business experience. I've been a mother and a wife," she summed up with no note of apology. "As you can see, my qualifications don't look that good on paper."

Her background information about herself had come as no surprise to him. He nodded, as though in agreement with her concluding statement, but then he indicated the chair nearest her. "Why don't you have a seat?"

Polly had been fully prepared to make a proud departure. She hesitated, coping with a strong reluctance to stay. Impatient with herself, she sat in the chair, keeping both feet on the floor and her back stiffly erect.

He dropped down into a swivel chair behind the desk, his manner completely businesslike. "What kind of hours did you have in mind?" he asked.

Polly didn't answer immediately, finding it odd that he had started off with that question. "The usual eight-hour day, I suppose," she said.

"You're interested in something full-time?"

"Why, yes."

"Is it a problem for you if you might be needed to work some evenings?"

"No," she replied slowly. She hadn't given any thought to the fact that a ski lodge with overnight guest accommodations, like any hotel, would have a night shift as well as a day shift for some of its employees, such as those who manned the reception desk and handled incoming telephone calls. "That wouldn't be any problem for me."

"Are you sure?" he pressed, seemingly not convinced. "It would mean being out on the road at night, maybe as late as eleven o'clock."

"I just live several miles from here," Polly pointed out, taken aback that she apparently struck him as a woman who would be afraid to drive at night.

He looked thoughtful and definitely interested. "Where exactly?"

She explained the location of her rented chalet, mentioning landmarks, since the paved road that led off the highway didn't have a name.

"I know the place," he said. "Ned Beechamp owns it." The fact that Polly was renting it evidently surprised him for some reason. "What are the ages of your children?" he asked. "They're in school, I take it."

His whole line of inquiry was suddenly clear to Polly. He had been operating under the misconception that she was still a wife and mother and was going to work to supplement the family income. Correcting him was painful, even after three years.

"I guess I should have explained," she began, and stopped, confused at his expression, which was suddenly apologetic.

He glanced at her hands, holding tightly to her purse in her lap, as he remarked, "If your husband is looking for work, too, I can always use an extra man on my outside crew. We're clearing ski trails at the present. With his experience operating farm machinery, he can probably drive a bulldozer with no problem."

"My husband passed away," Polly told him with as little emotion as she could manage. "He and our only child were killed in an automobile accident several years ago."

Compassion mixed with anguish crossed his face. Then his expression closed up and became bleak and distant. "I'm sorry— I had no idea," he said with a kind of formal sympathy.

Jennifer had said that her mother was dead, Polly remembered. From Jonus Logan's reaction, Polly's disclosure of her tragedy had been a jolting reminder of his own loss.

"You couldn't have known." She excused him with a gentle note. "I didn't make my situation very clear."

"I just assumed that you were a married woman with children when I saw you drive up in your station wagon."

He explained his error, looking out the window. "Then I saw the way you related to Jennifer and noticed your wedding ring. Please forgive me if I caused you pain."

Polly twisted the broad gold band on the ring finger of her left hand. "It's not the first time someone has made the same mistake. Wearing this does mislead people."

He rearranged papers on his desk, picked up a pencil and put it down, then resumed interviewing her as though the personal interlude hadn't occurred. "Where are you from originally, Polly?"

"Decatur, Illinois."

"I thought I detected a Midwest accent," he commented, nodding briefly. "Did you move recently to Vermont?"

"Yes. I've been here about a month and a half."

"Do you plan to stay through the entire winter? I'm not interested in hiring people who will up and leave in the middle of ski season."

"I'm planning to stay indefinitely," she stated, and didn't elaborate further, rebuffed by his whole manner. It was plain he wasn't interested in anything about her except what pertained to his decision of whether or not to offer her a job.

"You have friends or relatives in the area?"

"No, I don't."

"You've done some skiing here in the past?"

"I've never done any downhill skiing at all. I thought I'd try it," she informed him.

He frowned slightly at her tone and left an inquiring silence for her to fill with her own explanation.

"I didn't come to Vermont for the skiing. I'm here because I wanted to relocate to an entirely different area of the country. What I'm looking for is a year-round position, something with a future. The pay could be minimum wage starting off, as long as there's room for advancement and the promise of a salary increase once I've learned the ropes." She stopped, seeing that her words weren't getting any positive reaction from him.

He shook his head and sat back. "I'm afraid we're wasting each other's time. I can't offer you a job that has the kind of potential you want. You're thinking more in terms of starting a career. At the risk of being pessimistic, I doubt you're going to find anything promising in this immediate area. More than likely, you'll need to go to Burlington or Montpelier."

And she should be prepared for disappointments, Polly thought he was adding mentally. "I don't exactly want to start a career," she corrected him. "I just want to do some kind of challenging work that will allow me to support myself comfortably. Just in case I would be interested, what job openings do you have that I might fill?"

"I'm extremely short of help in the dining room," he replied. "I was hoping that you had experience waiting tables. I'm also taking applications for additional housecleaning staff and front-desk personnel, but the latter are required to be familiar with operating computers." A requirement he was assuming she didn't have, his tone candidly implied.

"You were interviewing me for a job as maid?"

Polly didn't try to keep her voice free of her indignation. While she didn't look upon any honest labor as degrading, she couldn't help feeling insulted that he had been putting her through the third degree to determine whether he should hire her to clean toilets and make beds.

"I was thinking more of hiring you as a waitress on a trial basis," he admitted bluntly. "Only because I am so shorthanded. Normally I wouldn't consider turning an untrained waitress—or waiter, for that matter—loose in my dining room when the lodge is booked to capacity, as it is now. Plus, we've been getting more than our usual number of outside dinner reservations." He sighed, preoccupied with the problem he was no longer hoping Polly might help him solve.

"You make it sound as though there's something difficult about waiting tables," she remarked, no less irked. "What is there to it other than taking people's orders and bringing them their food? You serve from the left and take away from the right and try not to spill anything on anyone." She shrugged. "Unless the menu is awfully fancy with dishes that have to be specially prepared at the table and served with a lot of fuss, I don't see why you shouldn't be able to hire any normally intelligent person who isn't clumsy and train them in one night."

"Our menu isn't elaborate, but we offer full-course meals with soups and appetizers at both lunch and dinner. There is considerably more involved than just carrying a plate of food from the kitchen and setting it down on the table," he replied. "Our guests are by and large sophisticated people who are used to dining in good restaurants. Quite a few come from New York. They're patient up to a point, but expect their waiter or waitress to be attentive, to notice when more butter is needed and to respond promptly to requests for a condiment or an extra napkin. It takes presence of mind and the ability to coordinate tasks to wait on half a dozen different parties in various stages of a meal."

"Those are common abilities for a woman," Polly pointed out stubbornly. "No housewife and mother can survive with a one-track mind."

"Working in your own home and pleasing your family aren't the same as being employed and dealing with the public. There are different pressures involved." But he wasn't going to argue the point with her.

"How much could I expect to make?" she asked.

"With salary and tips combined, you could easily earn between a hundred and two hundred dollars per evening shift between now and spring. Business slacks off then and is slower through the summer. To help make up the difference, I increase the hourly pay for my bartenders and wait-resses who want to work during the off-season.''

Polly's eyes had widened at the amount of money that he had mentioned. She didn't have to stop and do calcula-tions to figure out that she could live on that kind of in-come with no trouble.

"I had no idea that a waitress earned that much." Nor was she altogether convinced he wasn't exaggerating.

"Not every waitress does, just those who are good enough to work in a first-class establishment, which is what I'm running.''

"It would certainly be convenient for me to come to work up here," Polly said, thinking aloud. "I would rather not have to commute a long distance. Since you need someone so badly, I could help out temporarily and see whether I liked being a waitress. I could come back to-night," she offered.

He surveyed her thoughtfully and nodded. "Would a one-week trial period be fair enough in your opinion?''

Polly lifted her chin. "A week should be more than enough time for me to decide, but I'll work that long any-way to help you out."

It was going to give her no small amount of satisfaction to prove herself to him her first night on the job. By the end of a week, he would be sorry to lose her, if waiting tables wasn't her kind of work.

Chapter Two

"I'll show you where the dining room and kitchen are. You can go directly there when you come back at five o'clock." He rose to his feet.

Polly stood up, too. "What shall I wear?" she asked, and held herself more erect as his gaze ran down her tall figure. She felt dowdy and plain in her plaid skirt, blazer and sensible shoes, and yet conscious of her body. "I don't own any sort of waitress uniform."

"You won't need one. A black skirt and white blouse will be fine. Or black slacks, if you prefer. Once ski season starts, ski clothing is acceptable, in the appropriate colors, either black or red with white. The majority of my employees come to work dressed in ski clothes during the winter," he added, reacting to Polly's surprised expression.

"I guess it adds to the atmosphere," she remarked. "Do your waitresses wear red only in the winter?" He hadn't

suggested that she might wear a red skirt or red slacks tonight.

"No, any season. Not a maroon or brick red, but a true
primary red," he clarified on his way to the door. "It's the
color that my wife and I chose originally for waitresses'
outfits, but we decided on black as an option so that there
would be more room for personality differences."

Polly opened her mouth to inform him that she had
bright red in her wardrobe, since her husband had liked her
in vivid colors. She pressed her lips together without
speaking, disturbed to realize how much it seemed to matter that he had the wrong impression of her, as a drab
woman who wouldn't wear red.

His mention of his wife gave her an opening to make a
sensitive inquiry, mentioning the information his daughter
had revealed, but he ushered her from his office before she
could word one. Walking along beside him, Polly was all
too conscious of his height and his rangy, athletic build. It
required effort on her part to pay strict attention to his
words and not let the woman in her listen to the masculine
cadence of his voice.

During the brief tour of the dining room, kitchen and
cocktail lounge, which also functioned as a service bar for
the dining room, out of self-protection Polly avoided
looking at him and making eye contact, afraid she might
give away how he was affecting her. Fortunately he seemed
totally unaware of her struggle not to be attracted to him.

Or maybe it wasn't fortunate. If Polly had detected the
slightest hint of male egotism, she might have marshaled
her defenses more easily. Instead he was direct and earnest, treating her as though she were an intelligent equal.

She could have handled her female response to him on
the purely physical level. After all, she had always been
partial to the rugged outdoor type. Brad hadn't been as tall,
but he'd had a muscular, powerful build and had also carried himself without any swagger.

Polly wouldn't even have minded liking Jonus Logan. She got along well with men. Just because she didn't intend ever to get deeply involved with a man again, she could still enjoy contact with the male personality.

What alarmed her was that she felt a strong emotional pull toward the lodge owner, who quite obviously wasn't happy. Every time she glanced up at his sober features or connected with his steady, bleak gaze, she felt a tug at her heartstrings, in addition to the female reaction of her body.

He didn't smile once, and yet her instincts told her that he wasn't a dour, unfriendly man by nature. Behind his reserve and aloofness, there wasn't a cold detachment. The ring of enthusiasm, though missing from his voice, must have been there at one time, because he apparently put a great deal of himself into running his ski lodge.

Without knowing the details, Polly had had enough experience with grief to surmise that he hadn't recovered from the death of Jennifer's mother. In his own stoic way, he was coping with devastating loss and either didn't welcome sympathy or else still found it too painful to talk about his tragedy. Otherwise he would have taken the opening during their interview to share his own sad story. Polly had been through those stages herself and ached with empathy.

She had stumbled upon what wouldn't be a healthy working environment for her. Jonus Logan wasn't what she needed in an employer, even if he didn't have a small daughter named Jennifer. The fact that he did all but ruled out any possibility that Polly could take the waitressing job permanently. She was bound to encounter the little girl at the lodge and would have to battle the mother inside her, the same way she was having to battle the woman when confronted with the little girl's father.

The wise thing for her to do was back out of her temporary contract, make her departure and resume her job search. After all, she wouldn't be leaving him in the lurch.

Several times Polly opened her mouth to say that she'd had an about-face, but the words didn't come out.

As she made her exit, she tried to soothe deep misgivings with the knowledge that she hadn't really made any commitment, other than to work for a week.

Her chalet was like a safe refuge as she turned into the driveway. Tears came to her eyes as Sandy, her collie, came to meet her with his sad expression, wagging his tail halfheartedly. After three years, the family pet still acted as though he missed his little playmate and his master. *Where are they?* he seemed to be asking her.

"Hi, old fella," Polly greeted him huskily, and dropped down to hug him around the neck. Her emotion came as a relief. It helped to restore, once again, her sense of who she was.

Inside she was greeted by a plaintive meow from a marmalade cat who leapt down from the rocking chair Polly had bought at a flea market soon after she learned the good news that she was pregnant with Jennifer. Brad had refinished it for her. She hadn't been able to part with it or the afghan draped over the back, which had pulled threads and showed that it had been through many washings. Polly had knitted it during the month before she had given birth, when she had been huge and uncomfortable and filled with almost more happiness and contentment than she could stand.

"Have you been a good cat, Precious?" Polly inquired in a crooning voice, and got another meow for her answer. Reaching down, she gently scooped up the cat and cradled her in her arms as she moved over to the fireplace. The cat purred contentedly while Polly stood and gazed at the collection of small photographs in old-fashioned frames on the mantel.

The pictures were all of Jennifer at various ages, one of them of her with a fluffy marmalade kitten with a big bow tied around its neck. She had begged for a kitten as a present for her third birthday and had insisted on naming the kitten Precious, one of Polly's endearments for her.

She had been a sweet, loving child, but strong willed right from the first, and rambunctious. Polly had had her hands full. That was one reason she had postponed having a little sister or brother for Jennifer. Polly and Brad had planned to have three or four children. They had stopped using birth control a couple of months before he had taken Jennifer to town on an errand with him, and both of them had been killed in a head-on collision with another vehicle.

In her anguish, Polly had wished with all her heart that she had dropped what she was doing that day, gone along and met her death with them. During her blackest moments the first week or two following the accident, she might have considered suicide, except for the possibility that she could be carrying a life inside her.

But she hadn't been pregnant. By the time she knew, she had reconciled herself to living, not taking the coward's way out, which Brad wouldn't have approved of. He would have wanted her to go on with her life, to remarry in time and have another family. Polly loved him that much more in memory to know that he wouldn't have begrudged her happiness with another man.

It had been her decision to go to her grave as a widow, and not ever make herself vulnerable again by loving deeply.

Polly did want to meet people and make friends. She had already started attending church services in Waterbury, a nearby small town. Working at Logan Valley Ski Lodge, she would have an opportunity to get to know the employees who were local residents. Plus, she would come in contact with guests and seasonal employees.

Things had been rather quiet today at midafternoon because, as Jonus had explained, some guests hadn't arrived and most of the others were out driving or taking nature walks, enjoying the fall foliage. When ski season began, the lodge would be a beehive of activity. One of Logan Valley's big selling points was that the ski lifts were located just outside the building. There was no necessity for a guest to leave the premises during his or her ski weekend or vacation.

Polly probably wouldn't see that much of Jonus Logan or his daughter. He would have his hands full as owner-manager, and surely he didn't allow Jennifer to get underfoot in the dining room and kitchen and lounge, Polly's territory. Polly might encounter the child occasionally, but if she didn't encourage Jennifer with any attention, there shouldn't be any danger of becoming overly attached to the little girl.

Surrounded by her pets and her photos and her precious mementos from the past she'd brought with her to Vermont, Polly reasoned away her fears and took a positive attitude toward her new job. She was a little nervous as she got ready to return to the lodge, but also eager and basically confident. Waiting tables just couldn't be all that difficult.

The idea that she could wear her own clothes, rather than a uniform, appealed to her. Tomorrow she would go shopping for a ski outfit, she decided as she reached to take a black skirt off the hanger and then passed over it to locate a pair of black slacks.

But her hands moved on, without removing the slacks, to the far end of her closet, where she had hung the bright-colored outfits she hadn't worn during the past three years. Polly had considered discarding them when she was packing, but then her practical instincts had won out. The clothes were still perfectly good and had lots of wear left in them.

Besides, she hadn't resigned herself to wearing only dull colors for the rest of her life. It had just become a kind of habit she couldn't seem to break. In a new location where she wouldn't constantly be reminded of the past, she might regain some of her former pleasure in looking her best, even if she wasn't interested in turning men's heads.

Tonight she would be starting a new job and meeting coworkers for the first time. Why not make a cheerful statement and boost her own morale? On impulse, Polly took a pair of red slacks off the hanger and chose a white blouse.

Getting dressed had become a mechanical process. It felt odd now to strip and change and be attuned to her body. She was almost embarrassed to catch herself glancing at her reflection in the mirror and noting the generous proportions of her figure.

As a young teenager, Polly had been a tall, gawky bean pole until suddenly she had bloomed and become full-breasted, with rounded hips. It had taken her a while to adjust to her new voluptuousness and lose her self-consciousness over the notice she attracted from boys who'd treated her like a sister before.

Then she'd taken the physical changes in stride. Being a teenage siren just wasn't in her personality. She had enjoyed flirting and had her share of dates, but she'd also gone out for the girls' basketball and volleyball teams. Having fun and being friends with classmates of both sexes had mattered more to her than attracting an undue amount of masculine attention and being an object of jealousy. She had never seemed to find the time to spend hours in front of a mirror, experimenting with makeup and different hairstyles, the way some of her girlfriends did.

Basically Polly had maintained the same sense of values in womanhood, the same attitudes about her appearance, the same grooming habits. It wouldn't even occur to her to wear plunging necklines or tight sweaters to emphasize that she filled out her C-cup bra. Nor did she make any effort to be a fashion plate, even though she admired women who dressed with flair. Looking fantastic simply wasn't a priority.

Aside from the expense, Polly was out of her element when it came to putting together an outfit with accessories and accent jewelry. She stuck to basic styles, shirtwaist dresses and separates she could safely mix and match, clothes that were practical and comfortable, as well as becoming.

For similar reasons, she wore her brown hair in the same simple hairstyle year after year, keeping it essentially the same length as it had been in high school, several inches longer than shoulder length, and combing it back from her face and fastening it at the nape of the neck. Once in an adventurous mood she had it cut short, but then had grown it back when, no matter how hard she tried, she couldn't seem to get the same effect as the stylist. Too much time was involved fussing with it, and every few weeks she'd had to go to the beauty parlor for a trim.

When she wanted to go to a little more trouble, she used oversize hot rollers to get a softer look with loosely curling ends. Seldom had she bothered during the past three years, but this afternoon Polly got the rollers out. The five or ten minutes it took for them to heat up was sufficient for her to apply her usual minimum amount of makeup—a liquid foundation, powdered rouge brushed lightly on her cheekbones, mascara on the tips of her lashes, and lipstick. She had several shades of eye shadow, bought during the same period she'd had her hair cut, but she had abandoned any effort to learn how to apply the cosmetic skillfully, and emphasize her brown eyes.

She looked nice enough. That was the familiar conclusion that Polly came to as she inspected herself critically when she was ready to go. Not beautiful and not homely, just a tall, pleasant-looking brunette with a figure that was slightly too full.

Before leaving, she fed her pets and explained where she was going and when she expected to return, as though they could understand. It was habit to talk to them, and they seemed as comforted by the one-sided conversations as she was.

"You two behave yourselves and get along with each other," she instructed unnecessarily. The collie had been patient and tolerant from his first introduction to a spitting, frightened bit of marmalade fluff.

Arriving at the lodge a few minutes early, she parked in the employees' section of the lot, which was farther away from the entrance and on a lower level. The outside crew that Jonus had mentioned were evidently knocking off for the day. Men dressed in jeans and work shirts, most of them carrying thermoses and lunch buckets, were piling into pickup trucks and sturdy four-wheel-drive vehicles.

Polly received some politely curious glances as she got out of her station wagon. Another woman, driving an older car, had just pulled in ahead of her and exchanged greetings with several of the men as she walked toward the lodge. Hearing her addressed as Diane, Polly hurried to catch up with her and introduce herself. Jonus had mentioned the names of the other two waitresses working that evening, and the more experienced of the two, Diane Cutter, would be training Polly.

"I'm pleased to meet you," Diane responded with old-fashioned courtesy. "Thank heaven you came along. I've been threatening to quit if Jonus didn't get us some help. Of course, he knows me better than that."

"Maybe he did take you seriously," Polly replied ruefully. "That could be why he took a chance on hiring me. I've never worked as a waitress before," she confessed.

The two women chatted and got acquainted as they walked along. Diane showed polite interest in the sketchy background information that Polly provided, but didn't pry, displaying the lack of inquisitiveness Polly had already come to expect of Vermonters and appreciate. The veteran waitress volunteered that she had been born in the area and had lived there her whole life. She was married and had three boys, seventeen, fifteen and ten. A note of pride crept into her brisk voice as she mentioned them.

Polly was able to surmise that Diane fit into the category Jonus had mistakenly placed Polly in—a housewife and mother working outside the home to supplement the family income. It came as no surprise, when they both took off their all-weather coats, that Diane was wearing a black skirt and a prim tucked-in blouse.

The other waitress, Carol Otis, was a cute, petite blonde who looked no older than nineteen or twenty. When she showed up in a black skirt and white blouse, too, Polly regretted her own choice of outfits, but there was nothing she could do except try not let the fact that she was the only one of the three in red bother her.

Diane took charge, explaining to Polly the preliminary preparations to be done in the dining room and kitchen, and the procedure to follow when dinner guests were seated. She introduced Polly to her fellow employees. A shy youth called Nathan was the busboy. Reigning over the kitchen was the head cook, Kurt, a scowling, bald-headed man in his forties. His two assistants were a married couple in their early thirties, Lucille and Raymond Trace.

Lucille had long black hair braided into a single thick plait that hung down her back. Elaborate earrings of hammered silver dangled from her ears. Raymond was bearded and had the abstracted, gentle manner of a poet or an artist. Polly guessed that neither of the pair was a native Vermonter even before it was mentioned they were from California.

The bartender on duty in the lounge, Willie Travers, was a pleasant man of average height and build, about Jonus's age, she judged. The cocktail waitress working with him, Joan Whitter, might have been Polly's age, or younger or older. It was hard to tell. Heavily made up with streaked blondish hair and an air of hard sophistication, she wore a low-cut, tight-fitting red dress that made Polly feel understated, almost demure.

Joan and Diane conferred about Jonus's instructions that the cocktail waitress help out in the dining room again that evening, as she had done the previous night, by serving drinks, if she wasn't busy in the lounge. Apparently all his employees did call him by his first name, Polly reflected, remembering Jennifer's remark. But they definitely referred to him with respect.

"Who acts as hostess and seats people?" she asked Diane when they were returning to the dining room, ready to begin work.

"Oh, drat it! There's that hardheaded child, making trouble as usual," Diane muttered, not answering Polly's question as they both caught sight of Jennifer Logan.

The little girl had entered the dining room during the past few minutes and apparently had taken it upon herself to change the table settings. She was walking around a table, moving the red cloth napkins, which were folded into pyramids. Nathan followed, putting them back in the same place and pleading in an exasperated voice, "Stop it, Jennifer." He spotted Diane with relief, complaining helplessly, "Diane, she's messing up all the tables."

Jennifer glanced up, undeterred by the sight of the two women. She moved on to another table, busily rearranging as she explained, "I told Nathan that the napkins only get in the way, sitting where the plates should go right in front of people. He called me a spoiled brat and said I need a good spanking," she tattled. "I'm going to tell my daddy on him."

Nathan gave Diane a stricken look of guilt.

"Your daddy isn't going to like it if I tell him that you kept Nathan from doing his work," Diane told the little girl sternly.

"But I didn't!" Jennifer protested, immediately worried about the bad report. "I was only trying to help and make things better. Don't you think it's better to have the napkins over on the side like this?" she inquired of Polly earnestly.

Her eyes were a deeper blue than her father's, but she resembled him and had inherited his strong bone structure, too. She wasn't an unattractive child, but not pretty or dainty, either. It occurred to Polly that she may have overestimated Jennifer's age because of her size. Polly's daughter, too, had been big for her age, causing strangers to jump to the conclusion that she was older and should be better behaved.

"I don't think so," Polly replied, keeping her voice objective. "I think it works just as well, but probably looks nicer the other way. The napkins don't really interfere. Usually people put them in their laps as soon as they sit down."

Jennifer gave glum consideration to the answer and then set the napkin she'd just moved back in its original place. "I just wanted to help," she said, sighing. "Nobody ever wants me around."

Polly glanced at Diane, who had murmured, "Well, glory be," at the little girl's sudden docile turnabout. There was a motherly compassion in the other waitress's face and a gentle note beneath her gruffness as she answered.

"You just have to understand, Jennifer, that we are all employees, paid by your father to do a job. When you get underfoot and refuse to mind, it's hard for us to get our work done. In another half hour, for example, the dining room is scheduled to be open, and the tables aren't ready because you interrupted Nathan." Diane then addressed the youth, who was still standing nearby. "You need to get busy, collect all the vases and put fresh flowers in them."

"Yes, ma'am." He moved off.

"Polly, why don't you give him a hand out here to speed things up? Double-check to see that all the salt and pepper shakers are full, too, would you? I'll go help out Carol in the kitchen." Diane bustled away, leaving Polly to deal with Jennifer, as well.

Rejection was written all over the little girl's face. She clearly expected to be dismissed. Polly tried to harden her heart against a melting rush of sympathy, but it was a futile effort. There was no way she could send the child away feeling useless and unwanted.

"Nathan and I could use your help, Jennifer, if you can follow directions and do exactly what you're told," she said, against all her better judgment.

"Oh, I can!" Jennifer assured her, lighting up with eagerness. "You'll see. I'm good at not dropping things. My daddy says that I'm very well coordinated for my age."

"And how old are you?"

"Six. I just started first grade. I'm the biggest girl in my class," she stated without pride.

Polly had misjudged her age. She was a year younger than Polly's own Jennifer would have been.

"I was always the biggest girl in my class when I was growing up," Polly told her. "You get used to it."

"My mommy was tiny when she was a little girl, and pretty," Jennifer confided wistfully. "I wish I looked like her."

"My mother always told me that pretty is as pretty does. I never believed her, either," Polly added lightly, smiling at the small girl's disconsolate expression. "Now, let's put you to work. I'll set a tray over here on this stand, and you pick up the little vases from the tables, one at a time, and put them on it."

"I could pick up one in each hand," Jennifer suggested. "That would be faster. Here. Watch me."

Polly watched and agreed to the revised instructions when the little girl proved to be as adept as she had claimed. Jennifer worked diligently, following directions to a T, although several other times she pointed out ways she might accomplish her assigned task more efficiently. The child's mind was much too active and she had too much initiative to follow a routine unquestioningly.

Her teachers at school undoubtedly had their hands full, Polly reflected, smiling to herself. It was a delight being in the little girl's company, observing her and carrying on conversation. Yet the pleasure was edged with poignancy.

Aside from her own private sadness over all those joys of motherhood she was missing, Polly's heart ached for Jennifer, who was being deprived of the maternal love and attention she deserved and needed. She was much too serious a child, insecure beneath her streak of willfulness.

The best thing that could happen for Jennifer would be for her father to remarry, choosing a wife who would be a loving mother, someone who would bring fun into Jennifer's life and foster her playful, imaginative side, a side that Polly hadn't even glimpsed.

Polly doubted that such a match was in the making. If Jonus Logan were involved in a steady relationship, it would have been natural for Jennifer to make some mention of the woman. Furthermore, Polly's intuition ruled out the chance that he currently had a romantic interest.

It disturbed her how certain she was that he was completely unattached, still emotionally bound to his deceased wife, just as she was still bound to Brad. After all, she had only the sketchiest information on which to base her insight.

For all she knew, he may not even have been devoted to his wife. She might learn that he had been an unfaithful husband and was suffering from guilt. Maybe before she had died Jennifer's mother had run off with another man because Jonus was a workaholic and neglected her. There was any number of possibilities.

Whatever the circumstances of his tragedy, Polly and Jonus weren't soul mates. However much they had suffered in common, he was far more fortunate. He hadn't lost all his reason for living. He still had his little girl.

Polly hoped that he realized just how lucky he was.

Chapter Three

Promptly at six o'clock two older couples entered the dining room, accompanied by Jonus. Polly couldn't help staring at him. He had changed clothes since she'd seen him earlier in the day and was even more good-looking than she remembered, in dark slacks, a white turtleneck and a dark tweed jacket.

"Daddy!" Jennifer called out, then took an impetuous step, in her excitement bumping into a chair and jarring a table. Minutes earlier, she had agreed without argument to leave as soon as the first dinner guests arrived, and she'd been standing with Polly, the other two waitresses and Nathan, being a well-behaved child.

"Careful," her father cautioned.

Jennifer made her way toward him more slowly, saying eagerly, "Daddy, I helped Polly and Nathan take up all the vases and then put flowers out on the tables. I didn't spill a single drop of water. Did I, Polly?" She glanced back at Polly, managing to walk and still avoid another collision.

Jonus looked at Polly, but not for verification. He took in her appearance.

"Jennifer was a big help," she said, self-consciously aware that she was dressed differently from Diane and Carol. Looming almost a head taller than either of them, she felt like an Amazon.

"This is your little girl, Jonus?" one of the women inquired.

Polly relaxed ever so slightly, relieved to have his attention shift away from her. Even from across the room, she reacted physically to his gaze.

Observing him as he introduced Jennifer, Polly was far too involved in the byplay between father and daughter, just as she had been that afternoon. The same dissatisfaction welled up inside her when once again he restrained himself from an open display of parental affection, although he did touch Jennifer this time, cupping the back of her head as she stood close to him. Polly felt a strange tension in her stomach at the gentleness of his big hand.

"Go upstairs now and have your supper," he instructed. "Mrs. Allen is waiting for you. Jennifer and I have our own apartment here at the lodge," he explained to his companions, who apparently weren't close friends, or they would have known.

"Good night, Daddy. Goodbye, Mrs. Wilson. Goodbye, Mr. Wilson. Goodbye, Mrs. Orson. Goodbye, Mr. Orson." Jennifer prolonged her leave-taking, displaying a faultless memory for connecting strangers with their names. Then she turned with reluctance toward the door, obviously wishing she could stay longer.

Indignation filled Polly. There was no reason in the world that the child couldn't have eaten dinner with her father. She was old enough to have good table manners, and the two older couples gave every indication of liking children. It was insensitive of him to send her upstairs to have her meal with a baby-sitter.

"Polly?" Jennifer had stopped and was looking back.

"Yes, sweetie. What is it?" Polly's voice vibrated with warm sympathy.

"I could help out again tomorrow afternoon."

"That's good," Polly said, "because I couldn't have asked for a better worker."

The little girl glanced at her father to make sure he had heard.

"Go straight upstairs now," he told her. "No detours. And mind Mrs. Allen."

"Yes, Daddy."

He watched her for just a second as she walked away with much less reluctance than a moment ago. Then, after a thoughtful glance over at Polly that she couldn't read, he inquired of the two couples, "Would you care to sit near the fireplace?"

He was suggesting they take one of the choice tables. The dining room, like the outside reception area and the cocktail lounge, had a handsome wood-burning fireplace made of gray brick and large enough to accommodate logs. The fire Nathan had lit half an hour ago crackled cheerily.

The response from Jonus's dinner companions was unanimously favorable. He got menus and led the way to a table for four, where he seated the two couples and handed around menus, while he remained standing. Apparently he wasn't dining with them, Polly realized, but had just escorted them, in which case he could have gone upstairs and had supper with his little girl in their apartment.

"I hope you enjoy your meal," he was saying. "The rack of lamb is our specialty, but I can personally recommend everything on the menu. Polly will be serving you. She's new with us." He motioned for Polly to come over.

She stood rooted to the spot, completely taken by surprise. The possibility hadn't even occurred to her that she, not Diane or Carol, would wait on the first party into the dining room. And these people must be special guests of his, judging from the VIP treatment he was giving them.

"Here you go," Diane encouraged, handing her a notepad and pen.

Polly took them, thanking her, and mustering her dignity, crossed to stand on the opposite side of the table from Jonus.

"How are you this evening?" she greeted the foursome with a smile that didn't include her employer. She hoped that he would take the hint and leave her to do her job. She didn't need him looking on, making her twice as nervous. Thank heaven, he did start to move away. "Could I get you a cocktail from the bar?" she asked after the ripple of polite answers.

A discussion ensued between the two women, who mentioned names of exotic mixed drinks, including some Polly had never heard of. Out of the corner of her eye, she saw that Jonus wasn't making his exit from the dining room, but was headed in the direction of Diane and Carol.

"I wonder if your bartender knows how to mix an apricot stone sour. Why don't you go and ask him," either Mrs. Wilson or Mrs. Orson—Polly wasn't sure who was which—suggested.

"Why, certainly. I'd be happy to," she agreed.

A surreptitious glance revealed that Jonus was in conference with the other two waitresses, giving them directions that, no doubt, concerned her. She could feel the eyes boring into her back as she left the dining room and regretted, once again, that she'd worn the red slacks. They weren't too snug-fitting, but she was conscious of her hips and long legs.

"Sure, I can make an apricot stone sour," Willie, the bartender, assured her. "Do you mind if I give you a tip, Polly? As in hint," he added jocularly.

"No, I'd appreciate it," she replied.

"No matter what oddball drink somebody orders, don't bat an eye. Act as though you've served hundreds of them. If the bartender draws a blank, then you can go back and get more information or ask for a second choice. You'll save yourself a lot of steps and wasted time."

"Thanks, Willie." His suggestion made such obvious good sense that she felt rather foolish for not having thought of it herself.

Hurrying back into the dining room, Polly was glad to see that more guests were on their way in. With other tables occupied and the other two waitresses busy with their own parties, she wouldn't have the sensation of being an actress on a bare stage.

And Jonus was leaving finally. That was a major relief, too, to know that he wasn't watching every move she made. Not wanting to pass too close to him, Polly veered to her right, but he changed his path to intersect hers, giving her no choice but to stop. He obviously meant to have a talk with her before he left.

"Is there a problem?" he asked.

"No. No problem," she denied. "Everything is fine so far." If he would just move aside and let her get on with her job.

"You should wait for your drink order, especially if the bartender isn't busy," he instructed.

"I didn't order any drinks yet. I wasn't certain whether Willie was familiar with the drink the women wanted, so I went to ask him," Polly explained with a patient note. He obviously wasn't going to be satisfied until he knew the whole story behind her trip to the bar.

"Always just assume that the bartender can fill your order."

"Willie just gave me that same advice. From now on, I'll follow it," she told him shortly.

He frowned at her tone and opened his mouth to say something, but then glanced behind her. The people she had seen strolling into the dining room were glancing about, waiting to be seated. Stepping around Polly, he went to greet them by name. She hurried on to her table, smarting with a resentment she knew was a case of overreacting. He hadn't been sharp with her and had every right, as her employer, to supervise her on the job.

After that, one party after another appeared, and Jonus stayed, continuing to play host and assign tables. It dawned on Polly finally that he was there to act as his own maître d' and ensure that everything ran smoothly.

Her common sense told her that he wasn't keeping a constant surveillance on her, but every time Polly glanced his way, she seemed to catch his eyes on her. If she hadn't been so frantically busy attending to her tables, she might have been even more bothered by the knowledge that he was watching her like a hawk.

He gave her fewer tables than the other two waitresses and had them take care of all the larger parties, but Polly was still constantly on the move without a moment to catch her breath, never once feeling she had matters under control. There were simply too many things that needed doing at the same time.

At any one moment she could have a table waiting for desserts and another waiting for salads. While she was getting both courses loaded on her tray in the kitchen, Kurt would inevitably bark at her because her entrées for a third table were ready to be served and were getting cold. She didn't dare try to load the entrées on her tray, too. On her trip back into the dining room, she would be stopped along the way to be reminded that a party wanted their check, still another had requested after-dinner drinks fifteen minutes earlier and needed refills on their coffee. And would she please bring more cream?

What took priority? Did she dash to the bar, go back to the kitchen, or grab the coffeepot? What Polly would most have liked to do was walk out to her car and drive back to the peace and quiet of her chalet. Jonus Logan was right, as much as it pained her to admit it.

Being a waitress wasn't an easy job. It apparently did require special aptitude, which she was ready to concede she didn't have. After tonight, she would call it quits.

But that didn't mean she was going to apologize for doing her best. Nor would she take abuse from anyone, not the kitchen staff, the people she was serving, or Jonus Logan. "I'll do it when I can get around to it," she snapped at him several times when he tracked her down or stopped her to call her attention to something she needed to attend to at one of her tables. He gave the frown that said he didn't like the way she spoke to him, but he held his tongue.

Later Polly would surely be called on the carpet for her bad attitude, and not just toward him. She lost her temper when she took a filet mignon back to the kitchen to have it returned to the grill and Kurt raised his voice at her, accusing her of having gotten the order wrong.

"I ordered it rare because that's the way the gentleman said he wanted it," Polly yelled back at him. "But he's decided that he would prefer it medium rare!"

"Okay, okay," Kurt muttered, and gave her no further argument on the matter.

"I do hope you've enjoyed your meal," she managed to say in a pleasant voice when she brought the bill to the man who had sent the steak back, but she didn't add any words to the effect that serving him had been a pleasure. It definitely hadn't been. He had acted as though she should devote herself full-time to him and his party, and then had showed no appreciation. Polly didn't care if he didn't tip her. She wasn't going to play the hypocrite.

He didn't leave money on the table, and Polly had no way of knowing whether he'd written in a gratuity, because he got up abruptly, taking his bill with him, rather than signing it and leaving it for her to take to the cashier at the front desk. He stopped and talked to Jonus as he was leaving, and Polly could guess from his manner that he wasn't handing out compliments. Without a doubt, she was coming in for her share of criticism.

It infuriated her when Jonus nodded agreeably and, as he replied, gave no impression that he might be defending her and putting the obnoxious man in his place. Polly glared at Jonus as he looked around for her and caught her eye.

He frowned and gave his head a shake. If Polly had had a moment to spare, she would have gone over and informed him that he needn't worry. Neither her attitude nor her ineptitude was going to be a problem for him after tonight.

Finally, the dining room began to empty. There was a wonderful sense of relief, bordering on euphoria, as the number of Polly's parties dwindled, and she saw the end in sight. It felt incredibly good not to be under constant pressure, not to be rushed, to be able to give full attention to her remaining tables.

Jonus disappeared at some point and she could relax, knowing that he was gone. The camaraderie with her co-workers was nice. She and Diane and Carol and Nathan all shared anecdotes out in the kitchen. They made her feel good, telling her how well she'd done, especially for not ever having worked as a waitress before and being new on the job.

"You were a godsend," Diane declared.

When Polly pointed out that she hadn't been able to carry her load and wait on her share of tables, Carol's answer was, "Just imagine what it was like last night, with just Diane and me."

Polly didn't have the heart to voice her intention of quitting, and in truth she wasn't nearly so sure now that she wanted to quit, even though she was dead on her feet by the time they were finished putting the dining room in order. She couldn't believe how much money she'd made in tips, either, when she combined what she'd picked up in cash with the amount she collected from the cashier at the front desk for gratuities that had been written in on credit card bills and charges to room tabs.

Jonus hadn't exaggerated when he'd given her an estimate of what she could earn waiting tables there. Polly felt well paid for her night's labor, even after she'd given Nathan a percentage and deducted what she would give Joan Whitter, the cocktail waitress, for her much-needed help serving drinks.

"How about a drink on the house, ladies?" Willie offered when she and Carol and Diane went to the bar, looking for Joan. "You deserve it."

Diane refused and so did Carol, who took some teasing from the bartender about why she was in such a big rush to get home. The pretty blonde was a newlywed, Polly had learned, married to a young man who was a construction worker during temperate weather and a ski patrolman at the lodge during the winter.

"What about you, Polly? Joan and I could use some company," Willie said hopefully, leaning his elbow on the bar.

"That's for sure." Joan spoke up in a bored tone, but kept her voice low enough that her one table of customers over in a far corner of the lounge couldn't hear. "This fall-foliage crowd is early to bed and early to rise. They're all tucked in by now." She patted the bar stool next to her. "Stay and have a drink, Polly, if you're not in a big rush to get home."

Polly hesitated, tempted. She wasn't in the habit of sitting down in a bar and having a drink, but the place was almost empty. Despite her tiredness, she didn't feel at all sleepy, and there was no one to talk to at her chalet, except her pets.

"Maybe I will rest my legs before I make that long trip to the parking lot," she told the other two waitresses who said their goodbyes and left.

"What can I make you?" Willie asked.

"I'm really not much of a drinker," Polly admitted. "How about a whiskey sour? Or, no, maybe I'll try an apricot stone sour."

He grinned, needing no explanation of why that particular drink had come to mind. "One apricot stone sour coming up."

While he was mixing the concoction, Polly took out a five-dollar bill and laid it on the bar. She intended to pay for her drink, preferring not to accept anything gratis from the owner of Logan Valley Lodge, with or without his knowledge.

Willie served her and gave the bill a little push toward her. "Put that back in your purse. It's on the house."

"Thanks, but I'd feel better paying for it."

He made a negligent motion with one hand. "The boss runs a tight ship, but he's no skinflint. He doesn't begrudge his employees having a free drink every now and then, if that's what you're worried about.'

"Yes, but I'm not one of Jonus's employees," Polly corrected. "We had an agreement that I would work for a week on a trial basis." Jonus would probably consider her behavior tonight reason enough to back out of the agreement.

"Had? Past tense?" Willie queried.

He glanced beyond her, his whole demeanor undergoing a subtle change that alerted her, even before he wisecracked, "Coming in to see what all the noise is about, Jonus? We're having a gay old time in here tonight."

Polly froze, every muscle in her body tensing, as Jonus sat on the stool next to hers, saying in a tired voice, "Fix me a scotch on the rocks, Willie." She quickly took a sip of her drink, swallowing very carefully so as not to strangle herself on the tart, yet sweet liquid.

Jonus leaned back to see around her and addressed the cocktail waitress. "Joan, you can go ahead and leave any time."

Joan slid immediately off her stool. Willie had busied himself making his employer's drink. Polly had little choice but to turn her head and acknowledge Jonus's presence, which she could feel in every pore. He was disconcertingly close, his shoulder and elbow almost touching hers.

"I'm glad I caught you before you left, Polly," he told her, his wintry eyes searching her face. "I wanted to talk to you."

Willie put Jonus's drink in front of him and moved off toward the end of the bar. Joan had gotten her purse.

"Good night, all," she said. "Polly, I hope I'll see you tomorrow night again."

As much as she appreciated the sentiment, Polly could hardly respond to it. A minute earlier she might have said, "I hope I see you here tomorrow night, too, Joan," but now she was filled with ambivalence.

"Good night, Joan," she called after the other woman, who strolled out, swinging her hips.

Jonus took a swallow of his scotch, set the glass down and massaged his neck muscles with the same hand. "I overheard you mentioning our agreement. I won't hold you to it, of course," he said wearily.

Polly pondered his words, not certain of his meaning. "I won't hold you to it, either," she replied.

He frowned, looking puzzled. "As far as I'm concerned, the job is yours, if you want it. There's no doubt in my mind after tonight that you have the makings of a top-notch waitress."

She stared at him, as thrilled as she was dismayed. "But I ran around tonight like a chicken with its head cut off. People had to wait for their food. I don't have the right kind of personality to be a waitress. I yelled back at Kurt. Even though I did manage to control my temper in the dining room, I had to bite my tongue on a number of occasions. It must have come across that I didn't appreciate being treated like a servant." Not to mention the obvious, that she'd been very testy with him, her employer, all but telling him to stay off her back.

"Considering the amount of pressure you were under, you handled yourself remarkably well," he said. "Kurt was favorably impressed with you, you may be surprised to know. Diane and Carol both made a point of putting in a good word of recommendation, and not a single one of your parties complained about their service."

"Not even that huge, bald-headed man?" The man who had sent back his steak and, on leaving, had conferred with Jonus at some length.

"You're referring to Bratton. No, he was as complimentary as he ever is. He's the CEO of a large corporation and is just used to ordering people around. His only words of criticism were for me, because I was understaffed in the dining room and working my waitresses too hard." Jonus shrugged. "I could only agree with him and say that I was trying my best to rectify the situation."

"I'll work again tomorrow night and the rest of this week, like I promised," Polly stated. She sipped her drink, mainly for some excuse to look away from him. His gaze felt like a searchlight trained on her profile.

"You're under no obligation. If waiting tables isn't the kind of work you want to do, it wouldn't be fair of me to ask you to postpone your job search."

"But I feel obligated," she insisted. "I gave you my word. And I hate to let Carol and Diane down. They were both so sweet to me. As busy as they were tonight, they helped me as much as they could and gave me a lot of moral support. So did Joan and Willie. Just as you promised, the money is very good, too."

"But you don't like the work." His statement was a question.

Polly answered honestly. "I don't mind serving food and drinks to people. I was just disappointed in myself that I wasn't more competent. Whatever kind of work I do, I want to be good at it."

"Don't you think that you're expecting quite a bit of yourself to walk in and be competent at something you've never done before?" he asked.

"I suppose I am," she admitted.

"But there's more to it, isn't there?" he said with quiet perception. "Am I wrong in sensing that I got off on the wrong foot with you somehow and that you have reservations about me as your employer?"

"I was expecting the owner of Logan Valley Lodge to be older than you are," she evaded.

"Believe me, I'm a lot older than my thirty-five years. Sometimes I feel like a hundred." From the fatigue in his voice and face, he was feeling that old at the moment. "I think you'll find that the consensus among the people who work for me is that I don't have any patience with laziness, but I'm fair and don't turn a deaf ear when someone comes to me with a problem, either job-related or personal."

"Everyone seems to respect you," Polly hastened to tell him. She went on, choosing her words carefully, "There are personal reasons—which I would just as soon not go into—that make me doubt I would be happy working at Logan Valley Lodge."

He took a large swallow of his scotch. "You had these qualms from the outset, when you took the job on a temporary basis?" It was almost a rhetorical question.

She nodded. "But I would like to go ahead and work this week, as I agreed to do."

"Then I'll depend on you." He downed the rest of his drink as though that was the end of the discussion. But he didn't get up. "May I ask you one question?"

"Yes."

"Your child you lost . . . was it a daughter or a son?"

Her throat muscles constricted, making it impossible for her to speak for a moment. "A daughter. She would have been seven now. Her name was Jennifer."

He flinched visibly, but his voice was formal as he said, "I'm truly very sorry." Abruptly he got to his feet. "If you decide tomorrow not to come to work, I'll certainly understand. Willie." He addressed the bartender, who immediately hurried over. "See if Polly would like another drink. On the house. Don't take her money."

He walked out, leaving Polly in a state of turmoil.

Willie looked after him and then eyed Polly with a concerned expression. "Shall I mix you a fresh one of those, or would you like to try something different?" he inquired gently.

She pushed her watery unfinished drink toward him. "Could I just have a soft drink, please? Then I'll be going home."

"Coming right up."

"How long have you worked for Jonus?" Polly asked as Willie placed a fresh napkin and a tall glass in front of her.

"Going on five years. I've been with him since the lodge opened." The bartender shook his head sadly. "He was a different man, then. You wouldn't believe the change in him since he lost his wife, Trish. He worshiped the ground she walked on. It doesn't look like he's ever going to get over her."

"How long has that been?"

"Let's see. It was August two years ago that Trish was killed. Auto accident on the interstate. She had Jennifer with her. The car was totaled. By some miracle that little girl came out of it with just a slight concussion and bruises."

"Thank God for that," Polly whispered. Her blood was running cold in her veins. She couldn't bear to hear any more. "I have to go, Willie," she managed in a strangled voice as she got down from her stool.

"Polly, you look like you've seen a ghost. Are you okay?" he asked anxiously.

"I have to get home and let my dog out, poor old guy." Polly conjured a picture of her collie and tried to hold it in her mind as she sucked in a deep breath and took a step on numb legs.

"Here. Don't forget to take your money."

Polly didn't stop. It didn't seem in her power. Her voice sounded strange to her own ears as she bade him good night, adding, "Thanks for everything, Willie."

"Will you be working tomorrow night?" he called after her. "I'll stick the fiver in the cash register for you."

Polly didn't answer. If her life had depended on it, she couldn't have given him a yes or no. She was incapable at that moment of predicting her own actions. Some cruel fate seemed at work, sending her blundering into the aftermath of a tragedy with chilling similarities to her own.

All she asked for was to have a tranquil existence with sweet, nostalgic memories. Not happiness, just contentment. Was that unreasonable, considering what she'd been through?

She had borne her grief alone, accepting that grief was a solitary affair when the loved ones dearest to the heart were gone. Was it fair that she should be forced to share the anguish and despair of another human being who had suffered the same devastating loss?

No, it wasn't fair, but Polly felt utterly powerless as to what to do to protect herself. From the very first sight of Jonus Logan, she had seemed to lose control over her body and her emotions.

She couldn't even blame him. He wasn't knowingly at fault. Polly knew with disturbing certainty that he wouldn't want to disrupt her peace of mind. Nor would it please him to realize that he awakened a woman's needs in her that he had no desire to satisfy.

Jonus looked in on Jennifer, as he did every night before going to bed. The lamp on her chest of drawers cast a dim light in the room. The base of the lamp was a ceramic ballerina in a classic dance pose. It touched off a flood of memories that he kept dammed up because they hurt so intolerably.

Trish had wanted a little girl, even though she had insisted all through her difficult pregnancy that she would be just as happy bearing a son. Holding Jennifer in her arms in the hospital, she'd chattered on happily, making future plans for enrolling her in dance classes and taking her on shopping expeditions and doing all the things that a mother did with a daughter.

A vivid picture rose before his eyes. Trish pale and drained from the long hours in the delivery room, but still looking fragile and beautiful. "The next one will be a boy for you, darling," she'd told him.

Jonus hadn't spoken the thought in his mind, not wanting to spoil the moment for either of them. There wouldn't be a second pregnancy for her. He wouldn't risk the danger to her health. The past nine months had been pure hell for him, worrying about her and cursing himself for putting her at risk.

As an only child himself, Jonus had always wanted to be the father of at least two children, maybe three or four. He'd grown up envying friends in large families. In his ignorance, he hadn't taken into consideration that bearing children could be so hard on a woman, or at least on a small-boned woman like Trish.

And Jennifer had been a big baby, weighing eight pounds, Jonus remembered as he walked noiselessly over to his daughter's bed. She lay curled up into a fetal position and looked so vulnerable in her sleep that sick fear clutched at his heart. Very carefully he pulled the covers up and bent to touch his lips to her cheek.

Then he eased out of the room, leaving the door open and the night-light on, illuminating the golden-haired ballerina frozen in graceful motion. Jonus sighed. Trish would have wanted him to have their daughter in dance classes, but Jennifer resisted. When he consulted the woman who ran the dance school, she had recommended against forcing the issue.

Jennifer should be playing with other children, having her little friends over to spend the night, going to birthday parties. She wasn't doing any of those things and seemed to balk at any of Jonus's efforts to arrange normal childhood activities for her. To his disappointment she wasn't taking to school at all. He had hoped that the contact with classmates would be good for her.

Jonus knew that he was failing her, providing for her physical needs but not for the nurturing of the small total person. He felt inadequate as a father, too strict one moment and too permissive the next. Perhaps he might have coped better rearing a little boy single-handedly, he reflected wearily as he stripped off his clothes in his bedroom, leaving the door to it open, too, so that he could hear Jennifer if she had a nightmare and called out.

With the room plunged into darkness, he continued the train of thought as he got into bed. What Jennifer was lacking was maternal care. But how could he fill that void without remarrying? A paid nanny or baby-sitter was no substitute for a mother.

Jonus didn't even have any interest in dating. He had ample opportunity to meet attractive unattached women. Without being conceited, he was aware that the majority of them issued invitations. The problem was that he couldn't rid himself of the feeling that he was being unfaithful to Trish, even though his rational mind told him that he wasn't. On the few occasions during the past two years when he had taken a woman to bed, he had found the sex empty and unsatisfactory.

Everything in him rejected the idea of another woman as his wife. It was inconceivable that he would ever be able to speak wedding vows a second time and mean them. Yet how could he hope to give Jennifer a mother without being a husband?

Jonus sighed, flinging one long arm across the empty space beside him.

As many times as he had grappled with his dilemma lately, he didn't know why he was letting his mind travel down the same path again tonight and reach the same mental dead end. That wasn't quite honest; he did know.

Disappointment was the reason.

With her appearance at the lodge today, Polly Dearing had seemed to embody everything that Jonus could have asked for in a substitute mother for his daughter. He had seen her arriving for her appointment with him and classified her as a young matronly type with a husband and children.

The scene with Jennifer outside his office door had strengthened his snap judgment. Noting the way Polly rose to the defense of his little girl at the risk of antagonizing him, Jonus had decided on the spot that he would hire her in some capacity.

It stuck out all over that she was one of those women who loved children, and not just her own children, which was the case with some of his employees who were mothers, he'd learned. Polly wouldn't be railroaded by a willful child, though, his instincts told him. He couldn't keep Jennifer confined to their apartment, and one of his constant concerns was how to make sure she was treated gently and kindly and yet not allowed to make a nuisance of herself.

Jonus would welcome having a woman around the lodge who could give him parental advice and help in practical matters. He wished he had someone who would not only take Jennifer shopping for clothes, on paid time, of course, but would enjoy doing it. With luck, Polly might turn out to be that person, he'd reflected early in the interview. Perhaps she even had a little girl near Jennifer's age who could be a playmate.

Remembering that last conjecture, he winced at the cruel irony. In retrospect, he had been unkind, offering her a job opportunity and presenting her with a difficult decision. It would have been more merciful to send her away.

Instead, God help him, even after learning of her personal tragedy, he had still harbored the hope that she might turn out to be the answer to his prayer. Without meaning to be insensitive, he'd mulled over the possibility that Polly might need Jennifer as much as Jennifer needed her. Not that any other child could ever take the place of the one Polly had lost, but her maternal instincts were so obviously a part of her nature.

When he'd walked into the dining room that evening and taken in the scene of his daughter standing next to Polly and radiating a sense of belonging, Jonus had made up his mind again that he would definitely hire Polly. If the waitress job didn't work out, he'd find something else for her to do even if he had to create a job.

That wouldn't be necessary, he could see right from the outset. She would make an excellent waitress. Jonus had been disturbed that she seemed to resent his supervision and acted as though she had taken a personal dislike to him, but at the root of her hostility, he'd guessed, was disapproval of him as a father. Once they cleared the air with an open discussion, and he admitted his shortcomings, he expected her to be fair-minded.

Then had come the letdown of walking into the lounge and overhearing Willie's statement that Jonus didn't begrudge employees an occasional free drink and her correction that she wasn't an employee. The conversation that followed had revealed just how futile all his hopes had been that she was the solution to any of his problems.

Jonus wasn't looking for her to show up tomorrow night. He was back to square one, exactly where he'd been that afternoon prior to his interview with her, with a pressing need for good dining-room help and an even more urgent need for a woman's influence in rearing Jennifer.

It wasn't Polly's fault that, without knowing it, she had raised hopes in Jonus and then dashed them. She probably regretted coming to Logan Valley Ski Lodge as much as he regretted that she had come, seeming the answer to a prayer.

Jonus turned onto his side. He was so damned tired. He needed to clear his mind and get some sleep. But in addition to being disheartened, he was tense tonight and physically dissatisfied.

Polly Dearing was responsible for that, too, again without having any inkling, he was sure. Her womanliness was innate and unconscious, as much a part of her generous nature as her mothering instinct.

Physically she was as unlike Trish as it was possible to be, a tall brunette built on a voluptuous scale, while his wife had been blond and slender and dainty. Jonus hadn't even realized at first that he was taking notice of Polly's figure during the evening with something more than objectivity.

The fact that she appealed to him sexually had come as a surprise, but hadn't been a complicating factor for him. Jonus knew himself well, and he had faith in his iron self-control. After all, it was what had kept him functioning like an automaton when he had lost Trish and his world had turned black with despair.

Eventually the black had dulled to gray. Grief had turned into an acceptance that joy and happiness were something in the past. Now he was left with duty and responsibility as a father, as an employer, as a businessman in the community.

Jonus had gotten through his ordeal alone. He had never wept in front of anyone, never articulated the pain or the hopelessness or the outrage that warred inside him, threatening to tear him apart. His loss had been and still was utterly private. It wasn't anything that he even disclosed voluntarily. He discouraged the prying questions of strangers with reserve and formality. The most he said on the subject of Trish's death was, "My wife is deceased."

Today when he was interviewing Polly, and again tonight in the bar, he'd been struck by the urge to tell her about his own tragedy. But he had repressed the urge both times and been left feeling stirred up.

His brief association with her had been unsatisfactory in every way, but he would forget all about her in a day or two, he reflected.

No, he wouldn't.

Once again, Jonus was too honest to lie to himself. He knew where she lived, just a few miles down the mountain. Whenever he drove past the side road to the small chalet she was renting, his memory would be triggered for quite a while.

Chapter Four

Jennifer was stationed at the dining-room entrance, waiting for Polly the next afternoon.

"I've got my homework all done," she announced when Polly arrived. "My daddy said I could watch TV and make popcorn in the microwave, but I told him that I had to keep my promise to help out. He doesn't like me to watch too much TV, and usually he doesn't let me have a snack this late," she explained to emphasize her virtuousness.

Jonus had apparently tried to keep his daughter away from the dining room, even resorting to bribery. Polly was glad he hadn't been successful. She would have felt cheated. All day she had looked forward to seeing the little girl again.

It was only an hour till six o'clock, when the dining room opened. Polly could safely allow herself to enjoy being in the little girl's company for that amount of time during the few days that she would be working at Logan Valley Ski Lodge.

Jonus couldn't know that she'd come to that conclusion last night after arriving home in an overwrought condition. Once she'd regained her perspective, she'd thought matters through. He had been acting out of consideration for Polly. Still, she didn't approve of his bending his rules as a parent for her, when his first priority was doing what was best for Jennifer. He was lodge owner and then father, rather than vice versa.

"You wore a black skirt today instead of your red pants," Jennifer observed with a disappointed note, looking down at herself. She was wearing bright red jeans this afternoon and a white knit top.

Polly was touched to realize that the little girl had deliberately chosen her clothes to match the outfit she had worn the previous evening.

"Diane and Carol both wore black skirts last night, and I felt like I stuck out like a sore thumb," she explained lightly, but honestly.

"A bloody thumb," Jennifer suggested, giving a literal interpretation. She giggled when Polly screwed her face into a grimace, nodding.

"Now we'd both better get busy," Polly prompted, feeling richly rewarded by the ripple of childish merriment.

This afternoon Jennifer was more relaxed, not requiring as much assurance that she was being a big help, not a bother. She followed directions more unquestioningly, too, mainly because she was absorbed in carrying on a conversation and plying Polly with questions.

Did Polly have any children? she eventually wanted to know. Polly replied that she didn't and then immediately went on to mention that she did have a dog and a cat. The diversion worked, and Jennifer was easily sidetracked into a discussion of Polly's pets.

"I'd like to have a puppy and a kitten," the little girl confided wistfully.

"Maybe if you ask your daddy, he might let you have one or the other," Polly suggested.

The little girl sighed. "No, he won't, because lots of people don't like dogs and cats. Some of them are deathly afraid of them," she explained. "They might go somewhere else to ski instead of here."

Polly pressed her lips hard together to keep from speaking her thoughts. She should have guessed that Jonus's objection to his daughter's having a pet would have something to do with good hotel management.

The hour passed unbelievably fast, and at six o'clock the first diners arrived, unaccompanied by Jonus. Polly had been braced for him to walk in at any moment.

Diane went to greet the party and seat them. Jennifer said her goodbyes and skipped out after promising to report for work again the next afternoon. Several more parties drifted in, and Polly was assigned her first table of the evening. Coming out of the kitchen with a tray of appetizers, she saw that Jonus had finally put in his appearance, and she quickly averted her eyes, before he could look her way.

In addition to whatever else he might read on her face, there would be female admiration. He was somber and handsome in a dark turtleneck and the same dark tweed jacket, his short, neatly trimmed hair the color of old gold in the soft light of the dining room. Polly's low opinion of him as a father couldn't keep her pulses from quickening at the sight of him.

Before she hazarded another glance in his direction some minutes later, she had her expression carefully under control, but his gaze didn't swing to connect with hers. Apparently wearing a black skirt had done the trick, Polly thought as the dining room filled up and she didn't catch Jonus's eyes on her a single time.

Tonight he didn't track her down to give her instructions or stop her to see whether she was having a problem. He used Diane and Carol as go-betweens, instead of seeking her out himself, to make a table assignment or to ask whether she thought she could handle another party.

Admittedly Polly zigged and zagged to avoid coming anywhere close to him, and she didn't make eye contact, so that signaling her wouldn't have been an easy thing for him to do. Still, he was in charge. Apparently it just didn't matter to him whether he established any direct communication with her, now that he knew that she wasn't going to be a permanent employee.

Since she was only filling in temporarily, he was leaving her on her own, not wasting his time with grooming her as a waitress. Polly couldn't help feeling slighted, even though she much preferred having him ignore her to having him breathing down her neck, as he had seemed to be doing the night before.

If he had been paying her some attention, he couldn't have helped noticing that she was doing better her second night on the job. Familiar with the menu now and with the layout of the kitchen, she was better organized and not in a state of frenzy. By the end of the week she'd agreed to work, she wouldn't be surprised if she hadn't turned into a good waitress.

Polly wouldn't have minded a pat on the back from the lodge owner, figuratively speaking. But he left without thanking her for helping out or consulting with her on whether she would return the following afternoon. When the dining room had begun to empty, she had come out of the kitchen and found him gone.

The praise of the other two waitresses made up, to some extent, for his failure to say a few complimentary words. She was able to surmise, though, that he hadn't bothered to tell them about her temporary status, thereby putting her in a very uncomfortable position. It was obvious that both Carol and Diane were operating under the pleased assumption that she would be their coworker during the upcoming ski season.

Polly wanted to tell them the truth, but she would owe them some explanation because they had been so supportive. What would she give as her reason? She liked them, didn't find the work too hard or the schedule objectionable. In fact, it was good to have somewhere to go and something to do in the evenings, her loneliest time. And the money far exceeded what she could earn at some other job. Tonight Polly had made even more in tips, having waited on a few more parties.

She ended up saying nothing and feeling even more resentful toward Jonus. It was really his place to keep his regular employees informed about matters that concerned them.

The cocktail lounge wasn't doing much more business than the night before. Once again, Joan Whitter and Willie Travers invited Polly to stay and have a drink, if she wasn't in a hurry. Polly didn't need any urging.

So what if Jonus came into the bar? She was off duty and her money was as good as anyone else's. If he asked for a conference with her, he would get more than he bargained for, because Polly had a few things to get off her chest.

But he didn't appear, and neither Joan nor Willie brought up the subject of their boss. Polly went home with a strong sense of anticlimax.

There was none of the turmoil that had caused her to bolt from the lodge twenty-four hours earlier. She might have been any employee, knocking off after an uneventful shift.

All her fears and reservations about taking the waitress job seemed groundless. The contact with Jennifer had been more pleasant than painful this afternoon. Hiding how much Polly was attracted to Jonus surely hadn't been a problem. He hadn't given any indication that he was even aware she was alive.

The empathy that had seemed such a threat was gone. She disapproved of him too much to be drawn to him, now that she was getting a clearer picture of what his values were. He put his role of owner-manager before that of father or caring human being.

Tomorrow night was going to mark a change in her behavior toward him, Polly resolved. Even if she was just temporarily in Jonus's employ, he was going to treat her the same as his other two waitresses.

Jennifer wasn't lying in wait for Polly the following afternoon. Had the little girl's father made another misguided attempt to bribe his child, successfully this time? Polly wondered, both disappointed and indignant.

She was tempted to go straight to Jonus's office and inquire about Jennifer's whereabouts. If her suspicion proved true, she would set him straight on the fact that he wasn't doing Polly or his daughter a favor by interfering. Then Polly would tell him her general low opinion of him as a father.

Once she'd gotten that off her chest, he would no doubt tell her to mind her own business. The confrontation would take any decision out of her hands about whether or not to keep the waitress job. It wouldn't be hers for the asking anymore.

While Polly was stewing, Jonus walked in with a younger man in tow. A waiter he'd hired, she surmised with a glance, noting that the young man was dressed in black slacks and a white shirt. With his dark hair and dark eyes, swarthy skin and whipcord leanness, he could have auditioned for a bit part as waiter in a film.

By contrast Jonus seemed even taller and more ruggedly built. He hadn't changed clothes for the evening yet and wore fawn cords and a bulky off-white fisherman's sweater over a cream turtleneck. By now Polly was prepared for her physical reaction to his masculine good looks. As he approached, she steeled herself against the curl of sensation in the pit of her stomach.

Lifting her chin, she met his gaze directly and held it, even though his wintry blue-gray eyes seemed to probe her very depths. His eyes were gravely questioning.

"Polly, I'd like you to meet Louis Martin." Some undertone in his deep voice matched his expression.

Was it uncertainty? Regret?

Polly responded to the introduction and then stood by, her thoughts churning, as Diane and Carol arrived and also welcomed the newcomer to the dining-room staff. He exuded confidence, and it was fairly obvious that Jonus expected him to carry his weight right from the start. Polly was no longer urgently needed to help out.

This could be her last night on the job. Or maybe Jonus had in mind excusing her from even working tonight. Maybe that intention explained the way he was acting toward her.

Polly knew she had hit upon the right interpretation when he called the get-acquainted session to an end and turned to address her. "Polly, could I talk to you in my office, please."

"Certainly," she replied, squaring her shoulders. "I was just about to come and see you, anyway."

The silence was tense and awkward as she trooped along beside him, but she refused to break it when he didn't. He opened the door to his office and stood back for her to enter. She took several steps inside and stationed herself facing him. She had worn her red slacks again and felt dressed to do battle.

Before he'd barely had time to close the door, she spoke first. "I can guess what you want to say to me. Now that Louis has come along, you're no longer shorthanded and won't be needing me. I don't suppose it occurred to you that you could have picked up the telephone and saved me the trouble of coming up here for nothing."

"Yes, it did occur to me," he contradicted. "But I decided that I would rather speak to you in person." He paused as though reflecting on his reasons. From his tone, he was probably having second thoughts about whether or not a telephone conversation wouldn't have been preferable. "I wanted to express my appreciation and wish you well. If there's ever anything that I can do to return the favor and help you out, I hope you will call on me. Feel free to use me as a reference."

"Thank you," Polly said stiffly. "It's just as well. This way I'll have a chance to say goodbye to everyone. I'd like to see Jennifer, too, if that's all right with you."

He nodded after a slight hesitation. "Of course it's all right. But I should warn you. That may not be the best thing for you. She's very upset that you're leaving."

"The question is whether it's the best thing for her," Polly retorted, instantly dismayed to hear about the little girl's distress and irate at his logic. "Where is she? Up in her room alone? I suppose you wouldn't let her come down this afternoon to spare my feelings. What kind of a father are you, Jonus?" she demanded, reading an affirmative answer in his face. "You should be looking out for your little girl before everyone and everything else in the world! Instead all you think about is running your damned ski lodge!"

Polly had hit a raw nerve. He tensed, clenching his big hands, and for a split second was on the verge of losing his restraint and lashing back at her. She was ashamed of the thrill that chased up her spine and then the pang of letdown as he visibly controlled himself, loosening his hands and drawing in a breath. Subconsciously Polly had wanted to break through his reserve, she realized, deeply disturbed by the insight.

"I give a great deal of thought to my daughter's welfare," he defended himself quietly. "I'm constantly aware of how she's going to be affected by the day-to-day management decisions that I make, including hiring employees. Jennifer deserves a better father than I'm capable of being. I can't argue that. But part of my responsibility to her is to provide financial security and safeguard her heritage. Logan Valley will be hers someday.''

''Jennifer needs a real home. She needs love and attention. She needs...'' Polly faltered.

''She needs a mother. Don't you think I realize that?'' he asked. His voice held reproof and was edged with bitter frustration. ''It's not exactly a position I can fill by placing an ad. You, of all people, should know that life doesn't always work out according to plan, Polly. We do the best we can.''

''I know that I would give *anything*, Jonus, if I had been as fortunate as you. Can't you see how selfish you're being? You owe it to Jennifer to stop grieving over her mother and start living again. She's such a bright child and sweet and eager to please. An absolute delight. She should be a joy to you, not just a responsibility.'' Polly had to stop to blink hard against a glaze of hot tears and to get control of her voice. It was still husky with emotion as she admitted to herself, as well as to him, ''I've gotten so attached to her in such a short time. I'm going to miss not seeing her.''

''You've done wonders for her,'' he said. ''For the past two days, she's shown her first enthusiasm for going to school because she had something important to share at show-and-tell, about how she'd helped you out in the dining room. Nothing would have kept her from reporting for work yesterday afternoon. I didn't have the heart to order her to stay in her room, though my judgment told me it would be better not to let her get too attached to you.'' He sighed, his expression bleakly discouraged. ''It's a bad feeling to know you haven't acted in your child's best interest, however good your intentions.''

Polly had misjudged his motive for trying to bribe Jennifer and keep her away from the dining room.

''I'm the one at fault, not you. Is she terribly upset?''

"When she got home from school today, I broke the news that I didn't expect you to be working tonight or coming back. I felt I had to prepare her. She started crying."

"Poor little darling," Polly murmured, wanting to comfort him, too. "I'll go up and talk to her." She bit her lip, giving herself a moment before she continued. "Just because I'm not working here doesn't mean I couldn't still spend some time with her. It would cheer her up if she had something to look forward to. I could invite her for a visit tomorrow afternoon and let her play with my dog and cat."

Her mental picture of Jennifer with her pets made Polly wistful. Jonus was looking at her so oddly that she was afraid he was going to refuse. Before he could answer, she went on urgently, "You said I was good for her, and it would give me a great deal of pleasure to take her on outings and see that she had some fun. The child needs to get away from this lodge and learn that there's a world out there. You can trust me to take good care of her."

Polly could arrange to pick Jennifer up and drop her off, without having any more than minimal contact with her father.

"I agree with you," he said. "She spends too much time here. And I would trust her completely to your care. But if being around Jennifer isn't a problem, why not stay on and work for me? The waitress job is still yours if you want it."

"But you've hired Louis already," she blurted out. Everything had seemed safely settled. "It wouldn't be fair to him."

"I didn't hire Louis as a replacement for you," he corrected her. "It takes four people on the evening shift to give good service when the dining room is full. Plus, I have to schedule nights off and allow for sickness and emergencies. I do have another qualified applicant, whom I haven't hired. You don't have to give me a definite answer this minute. If you're at all open to the idea, I'm perfectly willing to stick by our original agreement.''

"By then the person you've interviewed may have found another job," Polly protested.

"She may have," he agreed. "But you shouldn't feel pressured by that fact. Someone else equally qualified will come along."

"I would feel pressured, though." His whole tone and manner put her into a strange panic. He seemed to be trying to *persuade* her. "With ski season right around the corner, you need to fill the positions you have open with the best-qualified people. As for our original agreement, you're not bound by it. After our conversation in the bar night before last, we both knew I was just working temporarily to help out."

His behavior toward her the previous evening came back, awakening a welcome smart of resentment.

"Last night you appeared to be so much more relaxed," he remarked. "You weren't nearly so rushed, in spite of waiting on more parties. I thought perhaps you might be liking the work more and feeling more capable."

"I was," Polly had to admit in all honesty. To have noticed all that, he must have looked her way occasionally. "I think you're right. I could be a good waitress. The job is perfect for me, in so many ways. I live just minutes away and like working evenings and having my days free. My coworkers are all nice people. The pay is very good." She listed the advantages, with no mention of the only problem. Him.

"As an employee, you would have a pass to ride the ski lifts on your off time and a discount in the ski shop on the rental of equipment, and purchases. Have I mentioned that?" Jonus asked. "When the beginner classes aren't crowded, you could get in on them free of charge and learn the fundamentals. Living so near and working nights, you could get in a lot of skiing."

No, he hadn't mentioned any of those benefits before.

"If I don't turn out to be a total klutz on skis."

"You won't," he assured her. "You look athletic."

It was an objective observation and not especially flattering. There was no reason for Polly to feel flustered as though he'd paid her a compliment.

"I am," she stated. "I was a tomboy growing up and played sports in high school. Like Jennifer, I was usually the biggest girl in my class."

He frowned. "Is she? She's never said anything about that to me."

Polly found it hard to believe that Jennifer hadn't mentioned to her father something that assumed such importance in her mind. He either didn't remember or hadn't paid attention.

"She's quite self-conscious about being a large child. It bothers her a great deal that she isn't petite and pretty, like her mother apparently was as a little girl." The latter information came as disturbing news to him, too.

"Jennifer doesn't resemble her mother." He spoke in the same formal tone he'd used before in expressing sympathy. But then he went on, getting the words out with some difficulty. "My wife was only five foot two and fine boned. She was a very beautiful woman."

Polly's heart went out to him, but at the same time, she had never felt more empathy for Jennifer. She understood completely how his daughter felt—oversize and gawky and plain.

"I'm sure if Trish had lived, Jonus, like any mother she would have wanted her little girl to feel pretty," she told him gently. "You need to let Jennifer know you love her just as much even though she doesn't look like her mother." *We can't all be beautiful,* Polly managed not to add.

"For God's sake, of course I don't love Jennifer any less because she doesn't resemble Trish." Jonus shook his head, looking as appalled and deeply offended as he'd sounded.

"You really do have a low opinion of me as a father, if you think that."

"I don't think you would deliberately give Jennifer an inferiority complex, but she's such a perceptive child. She knows that you idolized her mother and put her up on a pedestal. Just pay Jennifer little compliments on her appearance. Tell her she looks cute."

"I will," he promised gravely. "If you don't want the waitress job, Polly, I can use you in some other capacity. I hate to lose you. You have a lot to offer. We can sit down and discuss your options. Set up something long range where you could work yourself up to a supervisory position. There are several areas, food and beverage, front desk, housekeeping."

Polly opened her mouth and closed it, completely at a loss. Two days ago in her interview with him, she had described the same open-ended employment opportunity that, with no forethought, he had extended to her just now. She could tell he had been outlining it in his mind as he went along.

"After the things I've just said to you..." she murmured.

"Your outspokenness is one of your traits I admire," he replied. "Especially since it's coupled with sincerity. I *would* expect you to come to me in private, not air any criticisms of me, either job related or personal, in front of other employees or guests. But then I doubt it's necessary for me to tell you that. You don't strike me as the type who would gossip, either," he added.

"Not maliciously, but I'm human." Polly was unwilling to have him build her up into some kind of paragon. "And sometimes I'm not nearly as patient with people as I should be. My husband, Brad, was always having to remind me of that shortcoming. He had the patience of Job, along with so many other good qualities."

"Was he a big, strong, even-tempered man?"

"Yes, a wonderful, gentle man." The thought of Brad was accompanied as always by a rush of love and sadness. Polly's equilibrium was restored, and she was able to think clearly and sensibly. "I don't need any extra time to decide what to do, Jonus. I'll take the waitress job." It entailed obligation enough to stay through the winter during his busiest season. Beyond that, she wasn't locking herself in. "Now I'd better get back to the dining room. Will you tell Jennifer for me that I'll be counting on her tomorrow afternoon?"

"I'm going up to our apartment to change. Why don't you come with me and say a few words to her yourself?"

Polly looked down at her watch to hide her reaction. Accompanying him to his living quarters seemed far too intimate, even though there was nothing of a male invitation in the suggestion. But she would like to see Jennifer.

"I should be helping Diane and Carol."

"They have Louis and can manage without you." He brushed aside her conscientious reminder and led the way out of his office.

It apparently caused him no awkwardness that they received curious glances from the employees they encountered in the reception area, all of whom seemed to need to consult with Jonus while she had to stand by and wait for him. Several guests recognized her and spoke politely to her, as well as to him. Polly knew there was no reason for her to be uncomfortable, either, but she hadn't dated at all since Brad's death and instinctively rejected the notion of being paired off publicly with a man, however mistakenly.

There was an elevator to the second floor, but Jonus didn't suggest taking it. He escorted her to the main stairway, where they met more guests who were coming down while they were going up. Once again she could read the curiosity and interested speculation. Mounting the stairs, side by side with him, Polly was desperate to give off signals to anyone within earshot or sight of them that their relationship was purely that of employer and employee.

"Where is Louis from?" she asked, seizing upon the new waiter as a topic of conversation.

"He grew up in New York City," Jonus replied, and then went on to tell her that Louis was a part-time student at the University of Vermont in Burlington. He came highly recommended as a waiter, having worked at a couple of Burlington's best restaurants.

Not surprisingly, Polly wasn't familiar with either restaurant. Still just making conversation, she repeated the names, as though filing them away for future reference, and remarked, "When I go into Burlington to shop, I'll have to try them, if they're open for lunch."

When he was silent, she thought she would die of embarrassment, realizing she might have sounded as though she was angling for a date. Nothing could have been further from her mind.

"The French onion soup at the Citadel is excellent," he said in the telltale remote tone of voice that told Polly he wasn't thinking about her at all. His memory had been triggered, and he was thinking about his wife.

As relieved as she was that her words hadn't been misconstrued, Polly also felt foolish and excluded. "I'll remember that."

"Trish was very fond of it. She always ordered it. The Citadel was her choice any time we were dining out on a special occasion."

"Brad was crazy about French onion soup," Polly recalled. All her nervous tension was gone, leaving her strangely deflated.

They had reached the top of the stairs. "To the left," Jonus said, gesturing with one hand and placing the other on the small of her back to guide her. His touch was strictly courteous, but it set off shivers of pleasurable sensation.

Polly stiffened in resistance to her body's response, and immediately he removed his hand.

"How many guest rooms are there?" she inquired, not daring to look at him as they walked along the carpeted corridor. She was so intensely conscious of him that he couldn't possibly not be aware of it.

"There are fifty rooms and ten suites, five with one bedroom and the other five with two. Jennifer and I occupy one of the latter."

"Oh. I thought perhaps you'd had the architect design an apartment." In her surprise, Polly glanced up at him and saw from his expression that there was no worry that he might be seeing right through her defenses. His thoughts were on his wife again.

"No, Trish and I didn't intend to live on the premises indefinitely. It was just a temporary economy measure. I inherited the land, but we borrowed heavily, using it as collateral to build the lodge and make all the necessary improvements to turn Logan Valley into a skiing facility."

Trish's name came from his lips more easily than it had before, and the explanation didn't seem to cost him enormous effort.

"It's uncanny the parallels," Polly observed sadly. "Brad inherited our farm, but it was run-down, and he mortgaged it to the hilt to improve it and buy up-to-date farm machinery."

"You sold it?"

"I tried to operate it alone, with hired help, for two years." There didn't seem any need to explain to him that she had held out from selling the farm because it had been more than just a source of livelihood. When she'd married Brad, she'd made his dream of making the farm prosperous her own, and had worked and sacrificed and shared the satisfaction of good harvests.

Jonus could read between the lines, because his marriage to Trish had been a partnership, too, and the development of Logan Valley a joint venture. Polly knew without being told that the lodge interior bore the evidence of his beautiful wife's taste.

"Here." Jonus grasped Polly's arm and stopped her before a numbered door. But then he didn't open it or release her arm. His clasp was gentle and yet strong. Polly gazed up at him, helpless to pull free. "I've never been a superstitious man, Polly. Nor devoutly religious. During the past two years, I've even questioned the existence of a merciful God. Life has seemed senseless and utterly without meaning." He paused. "There have even been moments when I questioned the whole point of going on. Moments when..."

Polly nodded, making it unnecessary for him to put into words that, like her, he had contemplated suicide. "I know. It will get better, Jonus. I promise. You won't ever be happy again the same way. Neither of us will. But we have our memories. And you have Jennifer. Let her be a joy to you."

He squeezed her arm gently. "Yes, I do have Jennifer. Compared with you, I've been fortunate. But let me finish. Those parallels you mentioned. They're more than uncanny. When I think of the odds against your having moved a few miles down the mountain from me and applied for a job at my ski lodge, it seems more than blind chance. You appeared out of nowhere, when I was at the end of my rope with Jennifer. For the first time, I'm able to open up and talk about Trish to another human being."

A door opened, and voices floated out into the corridor. "I really should go in and see Jennifer a few minutes and then get back down to the dining room," she said, glad of the interruption, glad not to have to answer him.

It did seem as if more than blind chance had caused their paths to cross. But Polly wasn't at all sure that the forces in motion were leading her in a safe direction.

Chapter Five

As he got out his key, Jonus had to suppress his frustration. There wouldn't be any privacy inside his suite, either, since Jennifer was there.

Immediately he was ashamed of the thought. His main concern at that moment should be his daughter.

It was just such a relief to open up to Polly. He could tell her the feelings he'd kept locked up. Her understanding went beyond words, because she had been through the same hell he had.

Jonus and Polly were on the same wavelength, sadly enough. They could help each other. Somehow it was *meant* that they would. Jonus had never been more convinced of anything.

She could be the surrogate mother Jennifer needed. In return, Jonus could look after Polly, give her the masculine support a woman needed, even a strong woman like her.

Probably it was just as well that he had been cut off, Jonus reflected, opening the door. He had been on the verge of blurting all that out. He might even have added that he was willing to be not only employer and friend and protector, but also lover.

Once again, he saw it as meant to be that they would become intimate once the barriers were down. Jonus had never felt so close to a woman on such short acquaintance, not even Trish, a fact that caused him no guilt. The two sets of circumstances were so entirely different, the emotions different.

Jonus and Polly were like a couple of war victims, carrying on the best they could with lives that would never be the same. They could minister to one another's needs, including sexual needs.

But Polly might not share that view.

She was visibly ill at ease, as she had been since leaving his office with him, bothered that there might be even the appearance of impropriety. Her behavior indicated what he would have guessed, that she hadn't been with a man since her husband had died three years ago.

"You'll get to meet Mrs. Allen, Jennifer's sitter," Jonus stated, gesturing for Polly to enter. He not only wanted to ease her awkwardness but to focus his thoughts on his daughter and nullify any male reactions to inviting Polly into his living quarters. "She'll be along any minute to serve Jennifer her supper. Then she'll stay with her until bedtime."

Polly preceded him through the small hallway and stopped just inside the combination living room and dining area. As Jonus came up beside her, she moved away several steps, putting distance between them. He followed her quick glance around, which took in the fireplace, the contemporary decor and location of the two bedrooms. The door to Jennifer's room stood ajar, while his door was wide open, affording a glimpse of his bed.

"There's an intercom in Jennifer's room," he explained, forcing his mind back on track. He was stimulated in spite of himself. "The girls at the front desk are on the alert for any sound after Mrs. Allen has left at night. I have a monitor in my office that I keep tuned in when I'm working late. Plus, I come up and check on her."

"Don't you ever have supper with her?" Polly didn't look at him as she asked the question, a note of accusation in her voice.

"Very seldom," Jonus admitted. "I'm not hungry that early. I have most of my meals in my office, sitting at my desk." For the past two years, he'd had little interest in food and ate just to keep up his strength.

His loss of appetite wouldn't elicit much sympathy, he suspected, even if he'd mentioned it. Polly's gaze was fixed on the glass dining-room table, surrounded by six chairs. From her expression, she was visualizing Jennifer seated there alone.

"You don't have breakfast with Jennifer in the morning, either?" she asked grimly.

"I'm up a couple of hours before she gets up. I see that she has a well-balanced breakfast."

Jonus wished she would look at him, so that he wasn't free to let his eyes roam over her figure. Her erect posture thrust her full breasts against the material of her blouse. He caught himself searching for the imprint of her nipples and sounded even more humble as he continued in his own defense.

"On school days, Louise, one of the cleaning women, brings a tray up from the kitchen. She gets Jennifer up and helps her get dressed. Louise has been with me since the lodge opened. She's a very kind, motherly type who has five or six school-age children of her own."

Polly's lips were pressed together, and she gave her head a slight disapproving shake.

"Do you see Jennifer at all before she goes off to school?"

"I drive her. The school bus would come up here to the lodge and pick her up, but she doesn't want to ride it," Jonus explained. "I don't know exactly why, although I've questioned her."

"She may value the opportunity to have you all to herself," she pointed out. "Do you pick her up in the afternoons, too?"

"No, I'm usually tied up about that time with phone calls, interviews, a dozen and one problems that have cropped up during the day."

"You send one of your employees, I suppose."

"A *trusted* employee," he said with emphasis. "And I never forget to make arrangements. There's always a person Jennifer knows waiting for her when she comes out of school."

Jonus had lost Polly's attention. He glanced over and saw that his daughter had come to the door of her bedroom. With puffy, tear-stained face and tousled hair, she was a woebegone little figure, touching off familiar emotions in his breast, fierce protectiveness, love... and inadequacy.

He didn't have to guard his expression or put up a front, because her attention was all for Polly, just as Polly's was all for her.

"Polly..." The child spoke the name in a tremulous voice.

"Hi, sweetie," Polly greeted softly. Her face and her whole demeanor had changed. She had dropped her disapproving attitude and radiated warmth and sympathy.

"My daddy said you were quitting."

"That's because I had told him that I was. But I've changed my mind. I plan to work here at his ski lodge all winter. And I'm depending on a lot of help from you."

Jonus might have been down in his office from the way they both referred to him.

"I can wash my face and go help you now," Jennifer offered, swiping her cheeks with her hands.

"The dining room will be opening up in a few minutes, sweetie." Polly went over to Jennifer and dropped down on her knees to tuck the little girl's blouse in. "But why don't we wash your face, anyway? It'll make you feel better."

Jonus was beginning to feel like an intruder, standing back and observing the tender scene.

"Okay," his daughter agreed.

"And no more tears. Promise?"

"Promise."

Polly hugged her, and Jennifer hugged back, slipping her small arms around Polly's neck. Watching, Jonus was taken unaware by a twist of yearning deep in his gut.

He was glad for his child, but he couldn't help envying her. He could use some of that same kind, warm affection that Polly was lavishing on her. The thought of how Polly's arms would feel, wrapped around him, made him ache with a need that wasn't sexual.

At least not all sexual.

Her strong embrace would press her full breasts against his chest . . .

A tapping at the door brought Jonus to his senses. Mrs. Allen was here. He went to admit her, thoroughly ashamed of himself for lusting after Polly in his little girl's presence.

When Jonus ushered Mrs. Allen into the living room, he saw that Polly had risen to her feet and was standing, holding Jennifer's hand and waiting for him to return. He performed the introductions and excused himself.

In his bedroom he stripped, conscious of his body. A shower at this stage in his day was as much for therapy as for hygiene. Ordinarily he tried to clear his mind of everything and stand under the hot spray, letting it pelt away tension and fatigue. Tonight he deliberately reviewed several troublesome management matters while he got in and out of the shower quickly, toweled off roughly and got dressed.

As he pulled on his briefs, though, he wasn't oblivious to the snug fit. Jerking his turtleneck down over his head and tugging it onto his broad shoulders and down his chest and back, he felt the give of the tight knit. The soft wool of his dark slacks was gently abrasive against his legs as he stepped into them.

Jonus was aware that he was muscle and sinew covered by sensitive skin, his manhood ready to burgeon. All he had to do was allow himself to think about making love with Polly, and he became aroused.

Sitting on the edge of his bed, Jonus took himself to task. It was true that he had gone without sex for over six months now, but he was reacting like a horny high-school boy, obsessed with getting into the pants of a teenage girl.

Polly might not be open to an intimate relationship with him any time in the near future. He needed to exercise some of the iron self-control he prided himself on having.

She had already left when he went out into the living room. In the meantime Jennifer's supper tray had been delivered. Jennifer was sitting at the table while Mrs. Allen uncovered the dishes and placed them in front of her charge.

"The salad goes on the *left* side, Mrs. Allen," Jennifer was telling her patiently.

The elderly woman clucked good-naturedly. "I keep forgetting, don't I?"

"Is Jennifer trying to train you as a waitress, Mrs. Allen?" he asked, hiding a smile that was part amusement and part paternal pride. His daughter was such a bossy little thing, but nine times out of ten when issuing orders, she was right on the money. Her memory was faultless, and she missed nothing that went on around her.

His employees didn't appreciate being supervised by his child, though. And they naturally expected to be treated respectfully as adults. Jonus wanted Jennifer to have good manners, to be liked by the lodge workers and to make a favorable impression on guests with whom she came in contact, for her sake, not his.

"Aren't I right, Daddy?" she demanded righteously.

"You sure are." He chucked her gently under the chin and sniffed appreciatively. "Your supper smells good." The aroma was tantalizing.

"You can have some of it, Daddy," she offered eagerly. "Kurt always sends me a grown-up's meal, even though I tell him I can't eat that much."

Jonus opened his mouth to refuse and then said instead, "I don't think you'll manage to get around all that food. Maybe I will have a little of your supper." Mainly he wanted to keep her company while she ate, but he was hungry all of a sudden. Lunch had been a sandwich.

Jennifer was up out of her chair, pulling another chair out for him. "You just sit down right here, Daddy, and I'll set you a place."

She got a place mat and napkin and silverware, while Mrs. Allen did her bidding and brought a plate and a glass of ice water from the small kitchenette. Then she took her chair again, so obviously delighted at having him join her that Jonus felt a stab of guilty conscience.

"Don't give me too much," he cautioned as Jennifer heaped his plate generously.

"Asparagus salad, Daddy. Your favorite."

She had a refined palate for a child. At least that was one advantage of her upbringing.

"I wonder how many little girls your age eat asparagus salad," he remarked with a fond, proud note.

Jennifer squirmed with pleasure. Jonus felt another pang of conscience, realizing he probably didn't convey nearly enough approval. In his concern for her well-being, he had been free to scold, but not to praise.

The conversation with Polly earlier in his office came back. *Pay her little compliments, Jonus,* he could hear Polly urging him.

"Don't you have a new hairdo?" he asked.

She nodded her head and reached up with both hands to touch a pair of pink barrettes, being very careful not to muss her short, silky cap of hair, which was fine and straight like his and the same sandy color. The barrettes served no function as far as he could see. Polly had evidently combed her hair and fastened them for her.

"Do you think I'd be prettier if I grew my hair long?"

"Not to me," Jonus answered promptly. "I think you're cute as a bug the way you wear your hair now."

"Cute as a *bug*!" she repeated, giggling. "I never heard of a *bug* being cute."

She was satisfied, nonetheless.

Jonus noticed as they both started to eat that she seemed very hungry.

"What did you have for lunch today?" he inquired.

Jennifer chewed more slowly. After she'd swallowed her mouthful of food, she sipped her milk. "Meat loaf and mashed potatoes and green beans and a cookie," she said, wrinkling her nose with faint disgust. "Meat loaf is hamburger meat in a slice with catsup on the top. It's gray."

Jonus couldn't have come up with a more accurate description of the typical institutional version of meat loaf. Since it wasn't on the menu at the lodge, it wasn't a food that she would have been familiar with.

"You don't like the taste?"

"It doesn't have much taste. None of the food at school does. And it doesn't look 'appetizing.'" She enunciated the four-syllable word clearly, which was quite a mouthful for a six-year-old. "You wouldn't think it did, either, Daddy. You would fire those cooks if they worked for you."

Unless Jonus missed his guess, she was passing along the gist of what she'd announced to the cafeteria workers in the hearing of both children and adults who happened to be present.

"Did you tell the cooks that?" He kept the tone of his voice merely interested.

Her expression gave him his answer even before she confirmed miserably, "Yes. That's why they don't like me. They all look at me funny. I wish I didn't even have to go into the cafeteria. My teacher doesn't like me, either, Daddy." She had laid down her fork to pour out a full confession. "I heard her talking about me to a second-grade teacher the first week of school. She said that I was a handful because I was 'precocious.'"

Jonus put down his fork, too. He had never felt more of a failure as a parent. In a roundabout way she was answering the question she'd evaded until now: "Why don't you like school?"

If he had been a good father, he wouldn't have had to ask. She would have trusted him and confided in him. It hurt like hell to think of her carrying her burdens on her own small shoulders.

"'Precocious' doesn't mean anything bad, baby," he explained gently. "Your teacher was just saying that you are a very bright child and catch on fast. She made the same comment to me when I spoke with her on the telephone. You have to understand her problem. She has a whole class to teach, and not all children learn at the same rate."

"You talked to Mrs. Jameson on the telephone?"

"Yes. I was concerned because you weren't enjoying first grade." Tomorrow, when he took her to school, he was going to pay a visit to the cafeteria and have a talk with the cafeteria workers. "Now I want you to make me a promise, and then we'll finish our supper. Whenever something's bothering you, I want you to tell me about it."

"Okay, Daddy. You can tell me when something's bothering you, too," she offered. "I might know what to do."

Jonus smiled, his gravity lifting. "It wouldn't surprise me."

She smiled back at him almost shyly. Then she picked up her fork and resumed eating. Talk of school obviously hadn't dulled her appetite.

Nor his. Jonus savored his food. His taste buds seemed to have come alive again.

"Polly's coming a whole hour early tomorrow." Jennifer shared her thoughts with him. "She didn't have time tonight to see all my toys and books." She started to say something else and then didn't, shooting him a worried look.

Whatever it was, she wasn't certain whether it would meet with his approval. "That will be nice for you and Polly to have some time together," Jonus said. "I'm glad."

He was learning that he couldn't just interrogate her. He had to gain her confidence, win her trust, and then she would confide in him.

"Polly likes me," she declared with absolute confidence, then nibbled her bottom lip before going on tentatively, "She said that Mommy would be very proud that I was her little girl."

Jonus's fingers tightened on his fork. He tried to control his expression, but he knew from hers that the flash of pain showed on his face.

Her reference to Trish had caught him unaware because she never mentioned her mother, or at least not to him. It disturbed Jonus, but he couldn't bring himself to encourage her to talk about Trish.

"Polly is right. Your mother would have been very proud of you." The bleakness he heard in his own voice robbed his words of the reassurance he'd meant to impart, but he went on anyway. "She wanted a little girl so badly, and so did I."

The whole truth was that Jonus hadn't had any preference for a girl or a boy. He'd have been happy with either, but he'd wanted Trish to have her heart's desire. He'd wanted to lay the world at her feet and make her every dream come true.

Someday, when Jennifer was older, Jonus might explain all that, but not now. Now she needed to know only that she'd been welcomed into the world by her mother and her father.

"You did, Daddy?" she asked, not with skepticism but with wonder.

"When the nurse brought you in, that was one of the happiest moments of my life and your mommy's," he told her huskily. "We counted all your fingers and toes."

She was thrilled and intrigued with her own vision of the scene he's conjured up for her. "Did I cry?"

"No, but you waved your arms and kicked your feet and made fussing sounds."

"Maybe you and Mommy were tickling me." She sighed and then came back to the present. Reaching over, she laid her small hand on his. "I'm sorry, Daddy. I didn't mean to make you sad."

Jonus covered her hand and squeezed it. "It's not your fault I'm sad. I just miss your mommy an awful lot. But I know that you do, too."

She nodded. "I tell mommy good night every night when I look at my picture album. Polly thinks she was very pretty."

Jonus was able to make his own transition. Evidently Jennifer had shown her album to Polly tonight. He had forgotten about the child's picture album that Trish had been assembling for her, with photos and snapshots of all three of them. The reminder jolted his memory painfully, but he was more disturbed by the information that Jennifer kept her album put away. Was she deliberately keeping it out of his sight?

Still another emotion was the odd sensation he got at the thought of Polly looking at Trish's picture. Somehow it didn't surprise him that he didn't feel any violation of his privacy.

"Your mommy was very pretty," he said.

"I don't guess you need to look at her picture to remember what she looked like, do you, Daddy?"

Jonus didn't have any photographs of Trish displayed in his bedroom, a fact that hadn't escaped his observant little daughter. From the anxious note in her voice, he gathered that she worried about not keeping her mother's image in her mind.

"Every now and then I take out your mother's picture and look at it," he told her. "There's one of you and her in a frame. If you'd like, you can have it to put on your dresser."

"I would like that," she said uncertainly.

With his new insight into the workings of his child's mind, Jonus thought he knew what was troubling her. He spoke gently to give her the only honest reassurance he could.

"It wouldn't make me sadder than I already am when I go into your room."

A few minutes later as he left her in Mrs. Allen's care and went downstairs, Jonus reflected upon what amounted to a breakthrough in communicating with his daughter. All because he had acted on the impulse to keep her company for a few minutes.

Polly had spurred the impulse, of course. She had made him feel guilty about not having his meals with Jennifer. He was grateful. If Polly walked out of the lodge tonight, and he never saw her again, she would still have done him an invaluable service because she'd pushed him into making the discovery that he *could* be a better father.

She had pinpointed his problem. He had been too bound up in his own grief to be responsive to Jennifer's deeper needs. But that was going to change. Jonus was going to start allotting more time to his daughter. He was going to schedule her into his day, beginning with breakfast tomorrow morning. From now on, he would make it his habit to sit down with her at supper, whether he had his dinner that early or not, and take the opportunity to talk to her. More importantly, to *listen* to her.

Everything was going smoothly in the dining room, he saw when he entered, his glance automatically searching for Polly. She was at a table near the fireplace, where her party of four had been perusing menus and were ready to order. The firelight flickered over her as she replied to their questions, occasionally nodding and smiling, and wrote on her pad.

She seemed to embody womanly graciousness and hospitality. There was nothing in her manner to indicate that she found her waitressing duties demeaning in any way. Nor was there any effort on her part to ingratiate herself with the strangers she was serving.

In a different age and less modern setting, she might have been an innkeeper's wife attending to the needs of travelers who had stopped in. Not a local wench who worked for the innkeeper, but his helpmate and the mother of his children, a strong, capable woman who could run his business in his absence.

Who warmed his bed.

Jonus was embarrassed to realize that he was standing and staring at Polly admiringly while he played Walter Mitty. Before he could look away, she lifted her head and saw him.

He smiled at her sheepishly, and her eyes widened with surprise. Now she stared at him, as though mesmerized, holding his gaze across the room for long seconds that felt like minutes. Jonus's heart beat faster, the increased circulation sending warmth through his long body.

One of the members of her party spoke to her, thank heaven, and broke the spell. But he still watched her long enough to note that she was flustered.

It gave him male pleasure to suspect that her heart was beating faster, too, and her body temperature several degrees warmer.

Jonus wasn't at all pleased by the way Polly acted toward him from that point on, though. She avoided any further eye contact and didn't pass anywhere near him if she could help it, causing herself extra steps, as she had done the previous night.

Last night he'd gone along. He had thought he understood her behavior. She disapproved of him too much as a father to want to relate to him in any other way, as employer or man, he'd reasoned. Since she was doing him a favor by working and was noticeably more relaxed when left on her own, Jonus had cooperated and kept his distance.

Admittedly, he'd had his own motives, too. Last night he had been fighting his physical attraction to her, trying to resign himself to the disappointing reality that she was temporary help in the dining room and that was all.

Tonight was a different situation entirely.

Polly had taken the waitressing job. Jonus was her employer now. He refused to pass along messages via the other two waitresses and the new waiter.

Each time he stopped her and spoke to her, he was more certain of what he'd learned in that single unguarded look between them. She was attracted to him, too. On some level, he'd known that all along.

She obviously didn't want to be attracted to him. Why? Did his deficiencies as a father loom so large in her eyes that she couldn't give him the benefit of the doubt as a man?

If so, Jonus didn't think that she was being very fairminded. He had admitted that he was a less-than-perfect parent, but also tried to impress upon her that he was conscientious and did care about his daughter. In time he would raise himself in her estimation as he improved his father-daughter relationship with Jennifer.

Still he couldn't help feeling both rejected and frustrated by the way she acted toward him.

With the addition of Louis, things were going like clockwork in the dining room. Ironically, Jonus would almost have welcomed a small crisis or two, which he would have to deal with. His main function was that of host. Even the realization that he was able to be sociable tonight with relatively little effort didn't bring satisfaction.

He felt restless and out of sorts. It was a mood that he hadn't experienced in so long that he didn't know how to cope with it. All of a sudden he wasn't bearing down and gritting his teeth, straining every muscle, figuratively speaking, to carry on. The going was unexpectedly easy.

Instead of being flooded with relief, his shoulders felt too light without the usual weight of heavy responsibility. He had a surplus of energy.

For the first time since his wife had died, Jonus was lonely, rather than alone.

He didn't want to shut himself up in his office or go up to his suite by himself and close the door against the whole human race. He felt the need for company. For companionship.

Polly had sparked that need, and she was the person who could satisfy it. But she wouldn't, not tonight. Maybe not ever.

No, Jonus couldn't accept the latter possibility. Polly was resisting the natural order of things.

He kept checking his watch. Time seemed to drag. At ten o'clock he decided to go upstairs and look in on Jennifer. Then he'd come back down and have a drink at the bar. The dining room would soon start to empty out.

Perhaps Polly would consent to join him and let him buy her a drink after she got off work. He would prefer to have some conversation with her in private, without Willy or Joan present, but he knew that he could pretty well rule that out.

"Jonus."

The sound of Polly's voice behind him brought him up short as, absorbed in his thoughts, he made his exit from the dining room. He registered her reluctant note as he turned around. Then he saw that she had stopped at least five or six yards away from him.

"If you have a minute, I want to ask you something before you leave," she said.

"I'm just going up to look in on Jennifer. I'm coming back down."

"Oh. You seemed to be keeping track of time. I thought you probably had somewhere to go."

To have made that observation, she had to have been watching him surreptitiously.

"For the first time in a very long while, I was wishing I did have somewhere to go tonight," Jonus said quietly. "And someone to be with."

Polly glanced over her shoulder, calling his attention to the fact that this was hardly the time or place for a personal conversation. Dinner guests could walk up behind any minute.

Jonus frankly didn't care. He waited for her answer, which came in the form of a grudging compliment.

"You shouldn't have any problems in that area. All you have to do is look in the mirror to see that you're a better-than-average-looking man."

"But have very little else to recommend me?"

"I wasn't implying that," she denied. "Don't read something into my words that isn't there. I'm sure you have a lot to offer a woman."

"Some other woman besides you."

"For heaven's sake, Jonus, we can't stand here and discuss this in public!" she protested, pitching her voice low.

"I have to go and wait on my tables. All I wanted was to get your permission to pick Jennifer up at school tomorrow afternoon."

Jonus didn't believe for a second that had been her only reason for coming after him. It might have been her ostensible reason, the only one she could admit to herself.

"I'm a safe driver," Polly went on, as though she were interpreting his silence as indecision. "And my station wagon is only a couple of years old. I have it serviced regularly."

"You have my permission," he told her quietly. "In our conversation in my office earlier I told you I would trust Jennifer to your care."

"I'll need directions to her school. Of course, I suppose I could get them by phoning the school tomorrow."

"I'll give you the directions tonight," he said. "We need to talk, anyway, and clear the air."

"Yes," she agreed, avoiding meeting his gaze.

"After you've finished in the dining room, we can go up to my apartment and have a cup of coffee or a drink."

"No. I'd rather see you in your office."

"We're more likely to be interrupted in my office," Jonus pointed out with a touch of impatience. "And certainly there wouldn't be anything improper about the two of us sitting in my living room, with my daughter in the next room. For God's sake, Polly, you're not actually afraid I'd make a pass at you?"

"I would prefer not to go up to your apartment," she replied stubbornly. "What we have to say to each other won't take long, anyway."

He gave up the argument.

"In my office, it is. I'll be waiting for you."

Chapter Six

Polly took a deep breath, summoning her courage, and then tapped briskly on Jonus's office door. Quickly she opened it, stepped inside and closed it behind her.

He was rising from his chair behind his desk. He'd taken off his jacket, she noted, and his charcoal-gray turtleneck molded his broad shoulders and long, lean upper torso. He was deeper chested than she'd realized. His midriff was flat and tautly muscled.

"Don't get up," she said, panicky at the very notion of his coming close to her. "I'll just have a seat."

He ignored her words, walking around his desk, anyway. Polly couldn't seem to move and just stood there. In the few seconds it took for him to reach her, she tried desperately to marshal her defenses and organize her thoughts, but her mind wasn't under her control, either.

It reviewed irrelevant facts. The room wasn't dimly lit, but the indirect lighting was soft. The blinds on the windows were closed. His office didn't have a sofa.

"I wrote down the directions to Jennifer's school," Jonus told her, breaking the charged silence as he stopped in front of her, then reached out and locked the door.

Polly jumped at the quiet clicking sound. Her heart was pounding so hard she was afraid he might hear it.

"Why did you do that?" she demanded, her breathless note betraying her shamefully. She could feel embarrassed color flooding her cheeks. The heat traveled down through her body, melting every joint, as he searched her face and then glanced lower, at her breasts rising and falling with her breathing.

"Write down the instructions or lock the door?" he asked, his voice telling her he wasn't any calmer than she was.

Polly tried to shut out the knowledge that if she placed her palm on his chest she would feel it reverberating with his own rapid heartbeat. On weak legs she took a step away from him, turning her back to him.

"Lock the door, of course. I hardly think that's necessary."

"It just ensures we won't be interrupted." Jonus spoke from right behind her. His hands captured her shoulders gently as he went on in a low, earnest tone, "I'm not going to force myself on you, Polly. Not tonight or any other time. When and if I make love to you, it'll be with your full cooperation."

"That's not ever going to happen, Jonus," Polly said with desperate bravado. "Let go of me." Her body had turned traitor and refused to stiffen at his touch. She was utterly powerless to jerk her shoulders free.

"Why?" he asked, sliding his hands down her arms. Then he clasped her waist as lightly as he'd held her by the shoulders. "What could possibly be wrong with it happening, Polly?"

"Don't do that," she ordered weakly as his arms came around her waist. But instead of struggling, she leaned back against him and moaned as he hugged her tight.

"We're so right for each other. Surely you can see that, too." Jonus held her in the strong embrace as he continued, an urgent note in his deep, quiet voice, "Nature never meant for either of us to go without sex. I need to touch a woman like this..." His arms loosened, and his hands lifted to cup her breasts gently. "Don't you need to have a man touch you here, Polly?"

"No," she whispered, almost unable to speak because the pleasure was too delicately excruciating. "I get along fine without sex— Jonus, *don't*..." she begged as he squeezed her aching fullness. His fingers went lax as she placed her hands over his, but rather than lifting them free, she pressed them harder. "Touch some other woman, not me."

"I don't think your body agrees with you," he replied softly, and moved his palms ever so slightly, rubbing her hardened peaks through the layers of fabric covering them.

Polly gasped with the shooting spasms of pleasure and tightened her hands on his as she arched her back, stopping the abrasion but also thrusting out her breasts and re-cupping his fingers around them.

"Don't be so gentle," she murmured as he squeezed and kneaded. He obeyed her, taking a rougher possession, and she moaned helplessly and murmured the shameful truth, "That feels so good! It's been such a long time!"

"My hands are just barely big enough." Jonus's observation was low and intimate.

"I'm too big chested, I know."

"Your breasts are the perfect size for you." He was unbuttoning her blouse.

Polly didn't stop him. "You shouldn't do that."

"I know I shouldn't, not tonight." His fingers moved down to the next button. "We can't go to your place. I don't have a sitter for Jennifer. All the rooms are occupied."

"I wouldn't invite you to my place—" Polly broke off as he slipped his hand inside her blouse and caressed a breast through the lacy fabric of her bra. Gently he pinched her hard nipple, causing her to arch her back again and sag against him with the weak tide of pleasure.

While he was removing that hand and slipping his free one beneath the opposite side of her blouse, she picked up her train of thought. "I'm not going to have an affair with you, Jonus. It goes against my morals, and besides that—"

Speech was interrupted again, along with all rational thinking, as he found a hard, sensitive peak.

"I don't want an affair, either, Polly. I want a relationship. I want us to spend time together, to get to know each other." While he talked, he was trying to undo the front clasp of her bra.

"But I *don't* want that, Jonus. I don't want to get closely involved with you or any other man. I don't ever intend to remarry."

"Help me," he requested. "I don't want to break it."

Polly brushed his fingers aside, knowing she should button her blouse and put an end to what she'd let him start. Instead she undid the clasp with a single practiced movement and freed her breasts for him.

Disappointment welled up in her when he didn't immediately thrust a hand inside the gaping front of her blouse and bra and caress bare skin. Instead he was undoing more buttons. He meant to remove her blouse, she realized, as he tugged it free of the waistband of her slacks.

"You can't undress me here in your office," she protested, making no effort to stop him.

"That's the only way I can touch you with both hands at once," he pointed out, then warned unsteadily, "After I do that, I still won't be satisfied. I'll turn you around so that I can see your breasts and kiss them. The next step will be stripping myself to the waist and feeling your chest against mine. There won't be any stopping after that, Polly."

There wasn't any stopping now.

"It will only be this once," she said, helping him to take off the blouse. Her bra came off with it, and she shivered, not from cold but from the stimulation of being partially naked and desirable.

"Cold?" he asked solicitously, still behind her and enveloping her in a warm embrace.

"No. I'm just excited," she admitted with shamed honesty. "Don't hold me, Jonus, touch me."

He responded to her urging, cupping her bared breasts in his big, strong hands. Polly moaned her pleasure as he squeezed and kneaded with less gentleness than before. "Yes, like that," she murmured.

"I'm not being too rough?" he inquired.

"No. Your hands feel wonderful..."

"Your skin is so soft and your nipples are hard, like rocks. You're firm and full. Turn around so that I can see you, Polly."

Her only reluctance was that she didn't want him to stop what he was doing, not even for a second. When his hands dropped to her waist, she let him turn her to face him. Any sense of modesty and shyness melted in the heat of erotic pleasure as he looked first into her eyes and then dropped his gaze to her body. Polly sucked in her breath as his hands left her waist and lifted to her breasts. She could feel the tremor of passion in his fingers as he stroked the dark circles around each jutting peak.

"Jonus..." She whispered his name, squeezing her eyes closed as he lowered his head to her chest. The anticipation of his mouth on her sensitized flesh was almost more than she could bear. When he nuzzled a hard peak with his lips and then opened his mouth and suckled with hot, hungry pressure, the pleasure was unendurable.

Polly gripped his shoulders and cried out, "Jonus, please stop! It's been too long for me." She was trembling and weak, physically incapable of standing.

"Did I hurt you?" He was instantly concerned. He planted a tender kiss. "I'm sorry. I'll be more careful."

"You weren't too rough. That's not the problem. No, *don't*," she implored as he moved to her other breast.

Jonus straightened. His struggle for control was visible in his expression. "What is the problem?" he asked quietly. Despite the strain in his voice, there was no rebuke. "Would you like to put your clothes back on and talk?"

Polly blurted out the truth. "My problem is that I haven't had sex for three years. Could we just turn off the light, finish taking off our clothes and lie down on the floor?"

"I shouldn't have started this tonight. I honestly didn't mean to." Jonus squeezed her shoulders apologetically.

The strength and warmth of his big hands sent fresh shivers of desire through Polly. She wanted to end the discussion.

"It's as much my fault as yours. I let you start it."

"These are not the conditions I would choose for our first time together." He stroked his palms down her back.

Polly closed her eyes, weak with anticipation for the feel of his hands on the part of her body that was still clothed.

"Our first and *last* time," she reminded him. "I'm still not going to have an affair with you, Jonus. After tonight I won't ever put myself in this same situation again."

"You think the attraction between us is going to go away after we've made love?" he chided. "It's going to be stronger."

"I'll be stronger. Now, turn out the lights. Please."

He obeyed. In pitch darkness Polly quickly finished undressing to the sound of his stripping off his clothing. Then there was only silence and the awareness that they were both naked in the darkness.

"Are you there?" Jonus asked from several feet away.

"I'm right here," she replied.

His arms came around her, and he gathered her close against him, crushing her breasts against his bare chest and bringing her hips and thighs into intimate contact with his.

"I want you," he said, verbalizing what she could feel for herself. "Put your arms around me, Polly. Hold me tight." When she did as he requested, he groaned and hugged her with all his strength.

His embrace was more than sexual. It touched off a yearning deep inside her. Polly slackened her arms, fighting the urge to hug him back harder.

"Jonus, you're squeezing the breath out of me," she protested.

"Forgive me." He immediately loosened his hold and held her gently. Then he caressed her back and slid his hands down to shape her hips and buttocks. "You're such a lot of woman. I got carried away."

Polly welcomed the tide of physical desire that made her press her hips against his. It was sexual need, pure and simple. She desperately wanted the actual physical coupling and explosive release, unaccompanied by any tenderness or emotion.

"Jonus, there's no necessity for foreplay," she told him, stroking his back roughly. "We're both ready."

His muscles quivered at her touch. "Touch me," he urged. "Get to know my body with your hands, Polly, while I get to know yours."

As he talked, he was easing her away from him so that he could rub his palm along her abdomen. Polly clutched his shoulders as he slid lower. She whispered his name as he slipped his hand between her thighs.

His hand was trembling, she realized, and she raked her fingers down his chest, stopping to feel the thud of his heartbeat. He sucked in his breath as she rasped her short nails over his taut stomach on her way down to his groin. Now he was clutching her hips.

"Go easy," he cautioned as Polly made an intimate capture. Temporarily she had lost sight of her original intention, which was to arouse him beyond his control, and was awash in her woman's enjoyment of touching him.

He was breathing audibly. Her eyes were accustomed enough to the dark to make out the shadowy silhouette of his tall frame, but not distinguish his features. Still, she knew he had his eyes closed as she fondled him.

Polly felt a stir of tender emotion that frightened her. She released him and took his hands. "Jonus, lie down on the floor with me. I can't wait any longer."

"Neither can I."

There was a brief delay while he found his trousers and located what he needed for birth control.

"You haven't asked if I was prepared," he commented.

"It's a safe time of the month for me. Are you always prepared?" she asked.

"No, I went to the drugstore on Tuesday. I had trouble falling asleep Monday night." He had hired her on Monday. "I haven't needed to do that kind of shopping for a long time."

"I came along just as your sex urge was coming to life."

"You came along and brought it to life," he corrected her. Then before she could answer, he ended the conversation, requesting softly, "Could you help me?"

The intimate preparation erased any thought except the act of making love. Polly had never felt such deep, all-consuming sexual need as she sank onto the carpet with Jonus and lay on her back. Now that the moment was finally here, she was desperate to have him join his body to hers and fill the empty, aching void of her sexuality.

"Hurry, Jonus," she urged, shamelessly pulling him down on top of her.

"I'll have to go slow, Polly," he warned, poising himself for entry.

His penetration seemed to take a lifetime as he eased into her carefully, going deeper and deeper. Polly bit down hard on her bottom lip to keep back a scream of joy and frustration. She wanted him to drive into her with force, with even more depth.

"Not like that, Jonus," she protested. "I don't want you to be gentle."

He withdrew and entered again, thrusting harder and deeper. Polly arched her back, lifting her hips and increasing the impact.

"Yes, more like that," she encouraged. "Just let go, Jonus."

"If I let go, Polly, I won't last long. It feels too good to be inside you."

"It doesn't matter how long it lasts." She writhed under him, taking him deeper.

He gave her more force and depth, but he still tried to pace himself and prolong his rise to climax despite her efforts to get him to join her in a state of utter abandon. Polly didn't understand herself why she wanted so badly to snap his control.

Then suddenly all his restraint was gone, and he drove his body into her with all his strength and passion, speaking her name with a kind of pained wonder. She gripped his shoulders with her hands and clamped her legs around his hips, wild euphoria swelling up inside her as she rode with him upward and outward to a realm where joy exploded and obliterated any remaining sense of time and place and identity.

Polly cried out with her physical release. Freed from both body and mind, she floated in a state of peaceful satisfaction where neither past nor future existed and the present had no significance.

Jonus's spent weight on top of her wasn't heavy. She hugged him, happy that he was with her, happy for him to be experiencing the same warm complacency.

"Don't move..." she murmured in protest when he sighed and she could feel him summoning strength into his body. "Let's just stay right here and feel like this forever."

But with her words, reality was already setting in.

Jonus raised himself on his elbows. "You're a lot of woman, Polly. You bring out caveman tendencies I wasn't aware I had."

Along with his male satisfaction was a hint of embarrassment.

"I needed for you to be a caveman, Jonus, because I guess I needed to be a cavewoman tonight."

"Then maybe I shouldn't apologize for the primitive conditions. It's like a cave in here with the lights turned off."

"Especially with the blinds closed. If you opened them, we could probably see well enough to get dressed, couldn't we?"

He lifted free of her and sat beside her on the floor as he answered, "Yes. I sit in here lots of times late at night with the lights turned off, after I'm too tired to work any longer."

But still didn't want to go upstairs to bed alone.

"Ordinarily you don't close the blinds."

"No, ordinarily it never occurs to me to close them. But I only closed them tonight for the same reason I locked the door—to ensure privacy."

Polly sat up, too, and began feeling around for her clothes. The discussion had completely dissipated for her the blissful aftermath of lovemaking.

"Thank heaven no one has knocked on your door. I only wish there was some other way out of here." She had found her bra and was putting it on.

Jonus stood. "You'll get over feeling embarrassed before you leave," he said, walking over to open the blinds. "I'll go and get us drinks from the bar and something to snack on from the kitchen. My appetite seems to have come back, too."

Dim light filtered in. Polly got to her feet, able to see her garments strewn about on the floor. She picked up her panties and stepped into them as she answered.

"I don't want anything to drink or eat. Just give me the directions to Jennifer's school you wrote down, and I'm going straight home."

He was silent as he detoured around his desk to make use of the wastebasket and then crossed to where he'd discarded his clothes, a few yards from her. Polly couldn't help herself. She paused and watched as he drew on dark briefs.

"In other words, you're not interested in talking and getting to know me as a civilized man," he said.

"I already know you better than is good for me, Jonus. I swore to myself after Brad died that I would never care for another man like that." And she could so easily care for him. Polly didn't think it was necessary to add what he surely could figure out for himself.

"It's bad enough that I've let your daughter work her way into my heart," she went on, resuming her dressing. "But she's a child, and she needs me."

"I need you, too, and not just for what happened here tonight."

"You won't have any trouble finding female companionship, as well as sex, now that you're getting over your wife."

"I'll never get over Trish. She'll always be the only woman I've ever loved. That's why I can understand, the way most men couldn't, that you could never love another man the way you loved your husband. We're coming from exactly the same place, Polly. Can't you see we have a lot to offer each other in a relationship?"

He had finished dressing and took a step toward her. When Polly backed away, he stopped.

"What you're suggesting is that we have an affair. I know it's old-fashioned by today's standards, but according to mine, sex was meant to be an expression of love between two married people. I'm not proud of what I did tonight, Jonus," she stated in a shamed voice.

"Sex between us wouldn't be like this was tonight." He made another movement and checked himself when Polly raised one hand as though to ward him off. "We didn't even kiss. There was no tenderness."

Polly closed her ears to his note of pleading. "I don't want an intimate relationship with you. It's that simple. There's nothing personal. I like you a great deal and think that you're a fine, honest person with many good qualities. Now, could we please turn on the lights?"

He sighed in frustration, walked over and flipped a switch, flooding the room with soft light again.

Polly had hoped that awkwardness would dispel all the intimacy, but it didn't. Jonus didn't try to hide his bafflement and rejection as he looked at her, but there was possessiveness in his eyes. He apparently felt no restraint now about letting his gaze roam appreciatively over her figure.

In sheer desperation, she want over to sit in a chair facing his desk. "Is it going to be a problem for me to continue working for you?" she asked. "If it is, just say so, and I'll quit."

A clicking sound told her he'd unlocked the door.

"If your real question is, will I take advantage of being your employer and make it uncomfortable for you, then the answer is no," he replied quietly, coming over and perching on the edge of his desk rather than going behind it, as she had intended for him to do.

"I wasn't in the least worried that you would harass me," she hastened to assure him. "It's just that we would both need to put tonight out of our minds and treat each other with friendliness and respect. In other words establish the same kind of employer-employee relationship you have with Diane and Carol.''

''That's asking for the impossible, but I give you my word that I won't mention tonight or make any conscious attempt to prevent you from erasing it from your mind,'' he answered sincerely.

''Is there anything I can do?''

''You can act natural, not avoid looking at me, speak to me in a kind voice and not freeze up every time I come near you or touch you casually. That might ease some of the tension.''

''I'll work on it,'' Polly promised doubtfully. He was asking her to let down her guard.

''Are you open to having friendships with men?'' he inquired. ''Or are you afraid of even platonic relationships?''

''No, of course I haven't ruled out being friends with men,'' she denied. ''I like men in general. I just don't want to get involved with any one man in particular.''

''You would be open, say, to going out to dinner or to a movie or that sort of thing.'' He smiled wryly. ''I'm trying to think of a word besides 'dating.' It seems so juvenile.''

It was only the second time Polly had seen him smile, and the very first time she had ever heard amusement in his voice. As attractive as she found him when he was somber and reserved, she didn't have a prayer of resisting him when he was low-key and relaxed.

Her lips twitched into an answering smile. ''Yes, it does sound ridiculously young, doesn't it? At my age after having been a wife and mother, I can't quite think of myself as going on a 'date.' But to answer your question, working nights, I won't have much opportunity for social life. That brings up a matter I wanted to clarify. Is there any rule against employees having a drink in the lounge on their off time, as long as they pay for their drinks?''

"No, none at all. Business will pick up in the lounge, though, and it won't be quiet in there in the evenings the way it is now. I'll have live music playing. This year several of the slopes will be lit for night skiing. The view from the lounge is going to make it even more popular."

"I can't wait to see that!" Polly exclaimed, visualizing the scene he evoked. "I can just imagine how beautiful it's going to be. Are you going to wait until it's fully dark and then turn the lights on?"

"Make a dramatic moment out of it?" He tried out the picture in his mind. "I hadn't really given that angle any thought, but it's a great idea. I'll use it."

"You'd have thought of it, anyway," Polly demurred, flushing with pleasure.

"This is going to be my best fiscal year since the lodge opened," he stated, a shadow crossing his face. "It's been an uphill battle, but everything is falling into place, according to plan."

Except for the fact that Trish wasn't there to share his sense of achievement, which robbed it of all meaning. Polly could read his thoughts.

"I came very close to putting Logan Valley Ski Lodge up for sale after Trish died," he reflected. "The only reason I didn't was that I had inherited the land and felt I was obligated to pass it on to Jennifer."

"Someday you'll be glad you didn't sell out." He wasn't through, but Polly didn't want to to hear any more, not tonight. She went on, "And eventually you'll take satisfaction in what you've accomplished. Plus, you'll leave Jennifer a very valuable inheritance. By the way, what time should I be at her school tomorrow afternoon to pick her up?"

"Three-thirty," he said quietly, and reached behind him to pick up a sheet of paper. "Here are the directions." He handed the paper to her.

Polly took it and read the directions aloud. Even hearing her voice say them, she had difficulty concentrating under his steady scrutiny. "This is easy enough. I shouldn't have any trouble finding her school."

"I'll notify the principal that you're picking her up. Will you bring her straight back here to the lodge?"

"I thought I would take her to my chalet and spend a hour or so there, if that's okay with you."

"It's fine. I just need to know so that I won't worry. You said that you have a dog and a cat," he recalled. "Jennifer loves animals, so I know she'll enjoy meeting them."

"I was thinking of them, as well as her," Polly confessed, a lump suddenly coming into her throat. "They'll be in heaven with a child to play with."

"You brought them with you from the farm?"

She nodded. "My dog, Sandy, is a collie. He's as gentle as a lamb. My cat is more temperamental, but she won't scratch Jennifer."

"What's your cat's name?"

"She answers to almost any name as long as you speak to her in a certain tone of voice," Polly said evasively. She really didn't trust herself to go into details without breaking down and getting emotional.

"They must be a lot of company." Jonus stood up.

"They are," she concurred, rising to her feet, too.

There had been no intention on her part to throw up a wall and discourage any further questions, but that apparently was the message he had gotten.

"Drive carefully going home," he told her, accompanying her to the door. "And if those directions aren't clear when you read them tomorrow, don't hesitate to call me. For that matter, if anything comes up that you'd like a male opinion on, feel free to pick up the phone. I'm not that busy."

"I wouldn't bother you unless it was something important," Polly assured him, "but it's good to know I do have someone to turn to in case of emergency."

He opened the door wide and walked out with her in full sight of the reception desk as he bade her good night. Polly felt no embarrassment making her exit from his office. Her female pride was smarting at being ushered out, as though she had been just any employee conferring with him on a matter concerning her job.

"Good night, Jonus," she told him briskly, and marched off toward the dining room to retrieve her handbag and coat.

She knew she wasn't acting rationally, but she thought he might at least have given her some indication that he hadn't already totally forgotten their impassioned lovemaking, as she'd stressed that he should. But he didn't so much as squeeze her arm or touch her on the shoulder.

For all his insistence that they were so right for each other, he had given up very easily and didn't even show a sign of bruised male ego. Evidently she'd convinced him that he would do better to look elsewhere for a more willing companion and sex partner.

Jonus watched her for a few seconds before he went back inside his office. Closing the door, he flipped off the lights and went over to stand at the window. If Polly didn't emerge from the lodge in a few minutes, it would mean that she had stopped in the lounge instead of going straight home.

Would she have any desire to socialize tonight? He would place money on it that she wouldn't. She would be too filled with regrets over what had happened to spend an extra minute at his lodge.

"Someday you'll be glad you didn't sell out," she had declared, cutting him off before he could tell her that he saw now he would have been doing the wrong thing. While he still couldn't use a word like "glad" to describe his state of mind, for the first time he thought it possible that he might be "glad" in the future.

She hadn't wanted to talk and share thoughts and feelings any more than she'd initially wanted to make love with him. Jonus had never experienced a frustration like that. He had never had sex with a woman and not been allowed to display any affection or express any emotion, either before or after.

He had never had sex like that, period. The memory brought back embarrassment, but also brought his body to life. He smiled a pained smile, remembering Polly's admonition that he should forget the whole episode. She was only asking him to forget feeling more virile than he'd ever felt before in his life. He'd exercised more restraint in the back seat of a car when he was in his late teens.

Maybe when he went upstairs, the guilt would strike him, but the wonder of it was that he had no sense of betrayal. Somehow Trish's memory wasn't tarnished. As he'd stated openly and honestly, no other woman could ever take Trish's place in his heart.

That was no obstacle in Polly's case. She didn't want a man to fall deeply in love with her and covet the place her husband had held in her heart.

Jonus's train of thought was interrupted as Polly entered his field of vision, headed for the employee's parking lot. He noted her long, hurried stride, noted her quick, reluctant glance over her shoulder toward his darkened office.

Just as he'd expected, she was making a hasty departure, going home to her chalet where she would shore up her defenses and return tomorrow night armed to resist him. The important thing was that she would return.

By now she should be familiar with the stretch of mountain road between the lodge and her chalet. The hairpin curves were especially treacherous at night. Jonus hoped that she wasn't too upset to concentrate on her driving and would take them slow. He would feel terrible if she had an accident tonight.

Disturbed by his own anxiousness, he turned away from the window, left his office and went upstairs. Looking in on Jennifer, he remembered his promise to give her a photograph of her mother for her room.

The one he had in mind, of Trish and Jennifer at the age of two, had been put away in a drawer in his bedroom, along with several others in frames, including a wedding picture of him and Trish. It had been too painful for Jonus the past two years to have Trish's pictured likeness in view.

Occasionally he had taken the photographs out and looked at them, always at times of blackest despair. Tonight he gazed at each one, memory bringing the sting of tears to his eyes. For the first time, though, remembrance was bearable.

Jonus's favorite picture of Trish was a studio portrait taken at the time of their engagement. It was the picture that had been published in the newspapers, along with the announcement. She had insisted that the photograph flattered her, but it hadn't. She had been every bit that lovely, and the photographer had captured a mood of radiant happiness.

"He told me to think about opening a wedding gift from you and finding something fabulous, a full-length mink or a diamond necklace," she had confided to Jonus after the photography session. "Instead I just thought about walking down the aisle three months from now and seeing you standing there, waiting for me, big and tall and handsome."

"Not to mention nervous," he had quipped, enchanted with his own vision of her, his bride-to-be, floating to meet him in a white wedding gown.

It was that conversation, actually, that had always made the picture so special.

Instead of putting the photograph away, Jonus placed it on his bureau and took the other one he'd kept out for Jennifer to her room, so that she would see it in the morning when she awoke.

As he got ready for bed, he still didn't feel guilty about having sex with Polly or pursuing a steady, intimate relationship with her. If anything, he was even more convinced that he and Polly were perfectly suited for each other.

It was going to take patience. He was reconciled to earning her trust, step by step, over a period of weeks or even months. But Jonus was encouraged by the fact that Polly wasn't only going to be holding out on him. She was going to be holding out on herself, as well.

The greatest thing working in his favor was that she was trying to deny her own woman's nature, and considering how much woman she was, that was like Jonus trying to hold back an avalanche with his bare hands.

Chapter Seven

"What did you have for lunch today?" Polly asked Jennifer, making another attempt at conversation. The little girl thought a moment before she answered, reciting the day's menu and then lapsing into silence again.

They were riding in Polly's car. Jennifer had seemed thrilled to see her, but was behaving strangely. First, she'd made a production of putting on her seat belt and now sat docile and still, showing no inclination to talk.

Was the child nervous in an automobile as a result of the terrible accident that she had been in with her mother? Surely Jonus would have said something to Polly if he suspected that his daughter had a deep-seated fear. But then, as buried as he was in his own thoughts and business matters, he might not have noticed anything amiss.

"Are you this quiet in the mornings on your way to school?" Polly managed to keep her voice light and interested, not wanting to show concern.

"When my daddy asks me questions, I answer him, but I don't cut up and misbehave like I did when I was little. I never unfasten my seat belt or climb into the back seat."

Jennifer's answer set off a cold chill down Polly's spine. Dear God, the poor child didn't blame herself for her mother's death, did she? Polly shoved aside the glimmer of insight as simply too horrible to be true. To have gone through such an experience was trauma enough.

"You're an excellent passenger," she praised. "But I'm a little worried. I think I might have picked up the wrong little girl, and any minute now a policeman is going to stop me and arrest me for kidnapping. Did you notice how I keep glancing in my rearview mirror?"

Jennifer giggled at Polly's feigned anxiety. "I'll tell him who I am, and then he'll let you go. My daddy thinks you're a very nice person." She volunteered her first bit of conversation.

"I have a lot of respect for your daddy," Polly said, carefully choosing her words with the knowledge that they might very well be quoted with accuracy. Then, even though she didn't want to probe further, she asked, "When did he tell you I was nice?"

"This morning when we were eating breakfast. We both had mushroom omelets and Canadian bacon. My daddy says I'm quite a little gourmet." She gave the word the proper French pronunciation—goor-may. "That means I eat things that lots of children don't."

Jonus had had his breakfast with Jennifer this morning. That was the disclosure Polly was digesting.

"When Louise woke me up this morning, there was a picture of me and Mommy in my room that my daddy put there last night when I was sleeping."

"What a lovely surprise," Polly said.

"It wasn't really a surprise, except that it was already there," the little girl explained. "When I was having my supper last night, Daddy sat down with me. I set him a

place, and he ate part of my food. We talked about
Mommy, and he told me I could have a picture of her in my
room if I wanted one. It wouldn't make him too sad, he
said, so I told him yes, I would like a picture of Mommy."

"That's why you keep your photo album put away, so
your father won't see it and feel sad." It had struck Polly
as odd that the child had immediately put the photo album
away after showing it to Polly last night. A glance around
Jennifer's room was evidence that she wasn't any more
fastidious than most children her age.

Jennifer nodded. "After Mommy died, Daddy came into
my room one night when I was looking at it. He left, and I
could tell that he was almost crying. The picture that my
daddy gave me was in his and Mommy's room before. I remember it. There was a picture of him and Mommy, too,
and one of Mommy by herself."

Jonus's perceptive little daughter had connected the dis-
appearance of the photographs and his reaction to seeing
her album. She'd sensed that it was painful for him to look
at her mother's pictures and therefore had kept her album
hidden. If only he were half as sensitive to his daughter's
feelings, he would be a far better father, Polly reflected,
taking her hand from the wheel long enough to reach over
and squeeze both of Jennifer's, clasped in her lap.

"Maybe it would be a good idea for you to leave your
album out now," she suggested. "Your daddy has had
some time to get over feeling so sad about your mommy.
He might like to look at the album with you sometime. Did
your daddy mention that I was taking you to my house this
afternoon?" There had been enough gloomy talk. Polly
was more determined than ever that the afternoon would be
fun for the little girl.

Jennifer's face lit up. "No, he must have forgotten! Or
maybe he just wanted it to be a big surprise," she amended.
"Because he said that if you did want to take me some-
place, it was all right with him. I'm not supposed to ever go

anywhere with anybody unless my daddy says it's okay. He always wants to know where I am.''

"That's because he loves you.''

"I know. My daddy said that this morning, too.''

The shy satisfaction in the little girl's voice carried its own message for Polly, confirming what she would have guessed, based on her own observation. Jonus wasn't nearly vocal enough in expressing his affection. That was just one more matter to add to the list Polly was compiling of things she had to talk to him about concerning Jennifer.

He had indicated that he welcomed parenting advice from Polly. Well, he was going to get some, along with some positive reinforcement. Obviously he was trying harder to be a good father. He had sat down with Jennifer at supper last night and had had breakfast with her this morning.

It was important that he realize he shouldn't just salve his conscience and then lapse into his old habits. Jennifer needed her father's attention on a consistent basis. She needed to be able to take his love for granted, whether she was good or bad.

Polly meant to tell him all that, but what weighed heavily on her mind was the fear that Jennifer might have been holding herself responsible for her mother's death for two whole years, carrying a burden of guilt on her small shoulders. Considering how attuned the child was to her father's emotional state, Polly was forced to consider a possibility that she dreaded broaching with Jonus.

He didn't subconsciously blame his daughter himself, did he?

To get at the truth, for his sake and Jennifer's, it was going to be necessary to question him about Trish's accident. The prospect made Polly feel physically ill. Who knew better than she the cruelty of asking him to recreate those tragic seconds?

She couldn't afford to think ahead to that discussion now, though. Arriving at her chalet, Polly had all she could handle emotionally. She had known in advance it wouldn't be easy to bring home another little girl named Jennifer, close to the age her own daughter would have been if she were still alive. Fortunately, the two family pets made a welcoming fuss, allowing her to get through the first difficult moments without Jennifer's noticing that the scene roused inevitable poignancy.

Polly's pleasure soon eased her sadness. She was glad she hadn't put away the photographs on the mantel, as she'd considered doing. She was ready with her answer when Jennifer noticed them and asked curiously, "Who is that little girl?"

"She was my little girl. Her name was Jennifer, too, and you remind me of her a whole lot."

Polly's use of past tense and fondly reminiscent tone hadn't escaped the bright, perceptive child.

"Is she up in heaven, where my mommy is?"

"Yes. I miss her and so do Sandy and Precious. That's why all three of us are so happy to have you visit us. One of the things she used to like to do was help me in the kitchen, especially when I was baking cookies. I have a batch all mixed up and ready to drop on the cookie sheet and pop into the oven. Do you think you could give me a hand?"

"I never have 'dropped' cookies, but you could show me what to do." Jennifer was uncertain about the whole procedure, but eager to try.

"I have no doubt that you'll catch on immediately," Polly declared with conviction, leading the way into the kitchen.

The subject of her daughter's death wasn't closed, just postponed. Jennifer would bring it up again at some later time and want to know details, Polly knew. She would inquire eventually about the other Jennifer's missing daddy.

Polly would give only honest answers, but also do what she could to soften the harsh realities of life. The child knew far too much about those already. She needed lessons in the simple joys of human existence. She needed to learn the language of carefree communication.

In order for Polly to teach her those lessons, she had to put aside her own cares. At first she was consciously making an effort to be cheerful and lighthearted. But at some point, she wasn't providing a good experience for Jennifer. As she and the little girl peeked through the glass door of the oven and watched the cookies rise and turn golden brown, with the mouth-watering aroma filling the small kitchen, Polly was happy and content in a way she had never expected to be again.

"This wasn't a long-enough visit," Jennifer complained wistfully when it was time to leave. She carried a packet of cookies.

"No, it wasn't, was it?" Polly agreed, and then spoke the words of consolation that Jennifer wanted to hear and she wanted to say. "But there'll be plenty of other times."

In the car, the little girl was quiet. Polly was reminded of the discussion she had to have with Jonus and felt her nerves tighten. Once again, she put it out of her mind and concentrated on the present.

"You know, it doesn't bother me in the least for you to talk to me while I'm driving," she commented. "My little girl used to talk a blue streak. Sometimes she would even throw temper tantrums. Of course, she was younger than you are now."

"Did she ever undo her seat belt and climb in the back seat?"

"As a matter of fact, she did, more than once. Another of her tricks was to turn the radio up full blast."

"She must have been a bad little girl," Jennifer ventured.

"She was a real handful, like most small children are,"
Polly replied. "When I took her somewhere in the car, I
was expecting her to misbehave, but I liked taking her
places with me, anyway. I just drove slower and was more
careful. Don't forget to tell your daddy that you helped to
bake those cookies." She redirected the conversation with
the totally unnecessary reminder, having given Jennifer
some food for thought.

"I won't. Will you come and pick me up at school every
day, Polly?" she asked, changing subjects herself without
pause.

"I don't know about every day, sweetie, but I'll pick you
up at least a couple of times a week. I promise."

Jennifer sighed. "I wish tomorrow was a school day."

"Then I wouldn't be able to take you shopping and to a
movie," Polly said, smiling over at her. "Providing your
father says it's okay, of course."

"I'm going to ask him as soon as we get there!" The little girl forgot herself and bounced up and down in her seat.
For the rest of the ride, she chattered away in eager anticipation of the next day's outing.

The idea was a spur-of-the-moment inspiration. Polly
knew she really should have asked Jonus first, before getting Jennifer's hopes up, but he was almost certain to give
his permission. And he wouldn't go back on his word, no
matter how offended he was by anything Polly said later
that night. She meant to have the dreaded conference with
him and get it over with.

The employees' parking lot was a beehive of activity, as
it usually was at that hour. The men on the outside crew
were knocking off work, while other employees on the
night shift, like Polly, were arriving. Diane was just getting out of her car. She smiled and waved and waited for
Polly.

When Polly and Jennifer joined her, she was engaged in
conversation with a couple of men, and she introduced

Polly. The taller of the two was Glenn Busby, the foreman. Polly had heard his name mentioned. He was about Jonus's age, mid-thirties, and a rawboned, quiet-talking man she liked immediately.

Polly ignored Diane's coy wink, which along with the frank interest in Glenn's keen blue eyes, indicated that he was single and a dating prospect. She smiled and offered her hand for a friendly shake.

The other man, Mark Owens, was heavyset and wore glasses. His shy, but cordial manner told her he was married and faithful to his wife, in thought as well as deed. If Polly had a breakdown on the mountain road late at night, she would be glad for either man to come along, and she would feel perfectly safe.

Jennifer was fidgeting, trying to restrain her impatience over the delay. "Why don't you run ahead and say hello to your daddy," Polly suggested, on the one hand sympathetic, but on the other not wanting to rush off. She welcomed any opportunity to make the acquaintance of her fellow employees.

The little girl didn't need any urging. All four adults watched her as she ran full speed toward the lodge.

"I picked her up after school, and we made cookies at my house. She can't wait to tell Jonus," Polly explained indulgently.

"The boss was up on the mountain today," Glenn remarked, sounding pleased. "He was acting almost like himself again. I think he's finally coming out of the woods."

Mark nodded solemnly in agreement. "First time I've seen a smile on his face since his wife passed on. Sure was good to see. Climbed up on a bulldozer and wasn't in any hurry to get off it. Seemed to be enjoying himself."

"I've been noticing a difference here lately, too," Diane put in. "Just when I was about to give up hope."

Polly said nothing, grateful that no comment from her was expected.

"Karen tells me that lady doctor from Boston is coming back this year," the foreman said musingly. He was apparently referring to Karen O'Neill, who worked on the front desk and would be privy to information about reservations.

"The week of Thanksgiving, same as last year." Diane was more specific. "When she called to book her room, she asked to speak to Jonus."

"She sure was a nice lady." Mark spoke up. "I picked her up at the airport and drove her here last year. She's a children's doctor, you know. When I mentioned that our youngest was always breaking out in a rash, she asked me all kinds of questions, like she was diagnosing the problem, then wrote down the name of a salve for my wife to get the doctor to prescribe. It cleared the rash up, and that was the end of it."

"In the dining room, we all appreciated the way she treated Jennifer, who acted like a real little brat at the table. Several times Jennifer had meals with Jonus and Dr. Carver," Diane recalled for their benefit. "Dr. Sandra Carver. That's her name."

"She's one of the best women skiers I've seen. She can hold her own skiing with Jonus, and that's saying something." The male admiration in Glenn's tone was for more than athletic prowess. It suggested that the woman doctor also looked fetching in her ski outfit.

Polly had had quite enough of standing there and listening to what amounted to gossip, however harmless. "It was nice meeting you, Glenn and Mark," she said pleasantly. "Diane, we'd better go in, hadn't we?"

The other waitress responded good-naturedly to the prompting. She evidently was still mulling over the conversation, thought, as she bustled alongside Polly, having to take two steps to Polly's one. She spoke her thoughts aloud.

"It could just be coincidence that Jonus has started to take an interest in life again. Having a romance might be the furthest thing from his mind, but I'd sure take it as a healthy sign."

"He didn't have a romance with her last year when she was here?" Polly despised herself for wanting to verify exactly what had taken place between Jonus and the woman doctor.

"In a manner of speaking, he very well may have," Diane answered noncommittally. "Whatever happened was strictly her doing, though. Jonus didn't make any advances. He never does. But being such a fine specimen of a man, he all but has to fight the women off with a stick, anyway. Come Thanksgiving week, we'll see what happens. Jennifer could sure use a mother."

Polly let her silence serve as agreement with the last. But then, instead of allowing the subject to be dropped, she asked, "When did Dr. Carver call and make her reservation? I gather it was recent."

"Monday of this week. The same day Jonus hired you," the other waitress recalled cheerfully. "Things are looking up, Polly. If Jonus could only pick up the pieces now and get on with his life, the whole atmosphere around here will improve. We could all be one big happy family again." She sighed and seemed content to walk along and think her own thoughts while Polly pursued hers.

Jonus's loyal employees apparently gave her no credit for boosting his morale. Her visit to his suite to see Jennifer the previous evening, followed later by the session in his office, seemingly had not attracted notice or started rumors circulating on the lodge grapevine.

After seeing Trish's picture, Polly could understand why no one was quick to make Jonus and her an item. His wife had been beautiful and looked chic, even in jeans. Polly didn't fit into the same female category, but she bet the woman doctor did.

Had his phone conversation with Dr. Sandra Carver on Monday been the primary factor behind the sudden awakening of Jonus's interest in a sexual relationship? All too likely that was the case, whether or not he realized it himself. Polly had just happened to turn up the same day, unattached and sex starved.

With her new hindsight, she was even more ashamed of herself, not just for how she'd behaved in his office the night before, but for how she'd reacted to him from the first moment she'd seen him. It was humiliating to realize that when he opened the door of his office on Monday and she'd gotten all flustered at the sight of him, he might have just hung up the phone from talking long-distance to Boston.

"Polly, where's the fire?" Diane gasped. "I'm about out of breath."

"Sorry, Diane." Polly immediately slowed her pace. She had been striding along, going faster as she grew more mortified and indignant.

In her present state of mind, the last person she wanted to encounter upon entering the lodge was Jonus. En route to the dining room, she had to pass his office. That was bad enough in itself.

But as luck would have it, he was standing by the reception desk, surrounded by a small group of people. Polly spotted him immediately, since he was a head taller than anyone else. She also saw that he'd hoisted a flushed, beaming Jennifer up in his arms. The little girl looked in seventh heaven, one small arm circling her father's neck possessively while her free hand clutched her packet of cookies to her chest. She was basking in the attention focused on her, but especially his.

Unexpectedly Jonus turned his head. His smile of paternal pride changed fleetingly to one of private welcome, and then it faded when Polly nodded, but didn't smile back at him. Among her other emotions, she was sorry to have shown up and intruded on a happy moment for father and daughter.

"Polly!" Jennifer had followed her father's gaze and called out her name, drawing everyone's attention to her. "Daddy says you can take me shopping and to a movie tomorrow!"

Polly smiled and waved at the little girl and walked quickly on with Diane.

At the other waitress's suggestion, Polly accompanied her to the kitchen, leaving Louis to supervise Nathan in the dining room. The change of assignments really made no difference to Polly. She simply wanted to go immediately to work and get her mind off Jonus.

She knew generally what had to be done. Among the kitchen tasks were making up individual house salads in advance and storing them in the cooler, separating pats of butter and putting them on small serving plates, pouring cream for coffee into little pitchers.

Jonus's theory, which he had explained to Polly four days ago when he'd hired her, was that it was better for his waitresses and waiters to perform these minor preparations themselves. A kitchen worker who had no contact with diners might not be as particular. Polly had been skeptical at the time, she remembered, but now she had to concede that he probably was right. Anything that a waiter or waitress could do to guarantee a pleasant dining experience paid off in the long run.

But she didn't want to think about that day or about Jonus.

The atmosphere in the kitchen was surprisingly jovial. The usually taciturn couple, Lucille and Raymond Trace, looked downright animated, and Kurt was grinning from ear to ear. Polly did a double take and couldn't help staring. She'd never seen the head cook without a scowl on his face.

Before either Polly or Diane could inquire about his rare good mood, Kurt boomed out the good news that Jonus's appetite had returned, then launched into a full account of the breakfast and lunch that Jonus had consumed that day and the dinner he had ordered for Jennifer and himself that night.

Kurt hadn't presided over the kitchen at breakfast, but information had been passed along to him by kitchen staff members who worked the early shift. Thanks to Jennifer, Polly already knew the basic morning meal Jonus had eaten, mushroom omelet and Canadian bacon. Now she learned that he had had tomato juice and whole wheat toast.

If he had gotten the two of them a snack from the kitchen last night, that would surely be common knowledge by now, too, she reflected as she busied herself and made a futile effort to close her ears to the talk in the kitchen, which centered around Jonus's tastes in food. Diane and Carol had served him meals numerous times and joined in the conversation Kurt carried on with his two assistants.

Her own silence went unremarked, just as it had earlier out in the parking lot. No one expected her to contribute anything, since she was a newcomer. When the subject of Jonus's palate finally seemed to have been exhausted, Carol and Diane began comparing notes with each other on how seldom he had dined with women at the lodge during the two years since his wife's death.

In addition to the woman doctor, there had been a couple of other female guests who stood out in the waitresses' memories. In all three instances, apparently, Jonus hadn't had his heart in pursuing the relationship, but had, Polly gathered, in all probability slept with the three very attractive women.

Listening to Diane's and Carol's admiring descriptions, she was appalled by her own jealous dislike for total strangers, one of whom would be returning.

Polly might have to wait on the woman doctor. It was an uncomfortable thought, but the next one was even worse. If everyone's expectations proved true and Jonus picked up where he had left off last year, he would be dining with Dr. Sandra Carver. Polly would be forced to watch the two of them together from the sidelines. Why, it might even fall her turn to take their table and serve them.

When she had committed herself to working for Jonus, she hadn't known she would be subjected to a microscopic view of his personal life. Knowing his likes and dislikes was one thing, but Polly wasn't at all sure she could handle being kept constantly updated on his intimate involvement with this woman or that one while he searched for a companion other than her.

"Polly, you've hardly said a word," Diane observed when only a few minutes remained before the dining room would open. With three pairs of hands all the work had been done with ease tonight.

"Is anything wrong?" Carol inquired, concern in her voice. "I noticed how quiet you were being, too."

The clatter of pans and noises of food preparation hadn't stopped over on the other side of the kitchen, but Polly sensed that the cooking staff was also awaiting her answer.

"Quite frankly, I don't have as much sympathy for Jonus as the rest of you have," she said bluntly. "He should have pulled himself together long ago for Jennifer's sake. In case you think that I'm hard-hearted, I'm not. I just happen to have been less fortunate than Jonus. Three years ago I lost my husband and my little girl in an automobile accident. Lots of people have terrible tragedies in their lives and still go on, with a lot less moral support than Jonus has had."

Polly concluded her speech, taking a public stance as Jonus's harsh critic. From the very first, magnifying his faults had been her only defense against him. Now it seemed the only way she could divorce herself from the ranks of his doting employees, as much as she regretted having to be an outsider.

"I wondered why you seemed to take such a dislike to Jonus," Carol murmured. She and Diane both were all horrified sympathy.

"I don't dislike Jonus," Polly stated firmly. "I'm sorry if I gave that wrong impression."

"You act very unfriendly toward Jonus," Diane pointed out gently. "I thought it was just nerves over starting a new job that was making you so touchy with him." She nodded to herself, her expression compassionate and comprehending. "I suppose he knows how much you have in common. That's why he hired you, with no experience, and why he's been handling you with kid gloves."

The last thing Polly had intended was to start another discussion about Jonus. "He knows all about my background," she confirmed. "And I know as much about his as I care to know. There are other subjects beside him that I would rather discuss on the job."

Her exasperated voice seemed to echo in the suddenly quiet kitchen after she'd finished speaking. Carol and Diane exchanged a startled look. Polly knew as she accompanied them into the dining room that she had only succeeded in alerting them to a new interpretation of her behavior toward Jonus. They would watch her and Jonus tonight and look for telltale signs that she was attracted to him.

The strange thing was that Polly wouldn't take back a single word she had just said. She felt good about opening up and sharing her own personal tragedy with her kind coworkers. Honest by nature, she was more glad than sorry to have revealed true, conflicting feelings about Jonus when her whole purpose had been to throw up a protective screen to hide behind.

Hiding the fact that she found him attractive suddenly wasn't of paramount importance. He knew it himself, so what did it matter if others knew, too?

What was crucial was resisting his deeper appeal and safeguarding her heart. Polly was desperate for any help she could get, including the self-conscious awareness that curious eyes were trained on her and Jonus. The less privacy where he was concerned, the better.

Only two parties had been seated when he came in shortly after seven o'clock. Tonight he wore a camel-hair jacket and a white turtleneck with dark brown slacks. Polly's heart gave its usual leap of pleasure. Instead of averting her head the way she normally did, she assumed a welcoming expression as he headed over to where she stood with Carol and Nathan.

Her greeting mingled with theirs. Then she spoke up first, inquiring whether he had enjoyed his dinner.

Jonus replied that he had. "For dessert I had several of the cookies that you and Jennifer baked this afternoon. They were delicious," he complimented her. "I hope she behaved herself."

"She was an angel," Polly assured him. "We had a ball." She explained for Carol's and Nathan's benefit, "Jennifer and I made cookies at my house after she got out of school. My dog and cat were in seventh heaven, having a visitor. Jonus, if you're not too busy tomorrow, I'd like a few minutes of your time when I come to pick up Jennifer. There's something important I need to bring to your attention concerning her." Polly had revised her plan to speak to him that evening.

"If it's important, then let's talk about it tonight," he said.

"It is important. After asking to talk to you about another matter last night, I hesitated to suggest another meeting tonight. I wouldn't want to give you or anyone else the wrong impression that I was looking for excuses."

Carol's and Nathan's mouths dropped open.

"I appreciate the interest you're taking in Jennifer," Jonus replied. "In less than a week's time, since you've started working here, she's turned into a whole different child. She had a wonderful time today and is looking forward to tomorrow. If you don't mind, I'd like to tag along myself, act as chauffeur and take you both to lunch."

Polly had to find her voice before she could answer. Without batting an eye, he was using her public approach to put her on the spot.

"That would be nice for Jennifer, but you'd only be bored. We're going to a children's movie."

"The idea is to do something fun with Jennifer. She was very much in favor of my coming along when I suggested the possibility. I told her you would have to okay my butting in without an invitation," he added.

Diane came up and joined the group, eyeing everyone curiously. Carol filled her in.

"Jonus is taking Polly and Jennifer to lunch tomorrow, and they're all going to see a children's movie."

"How nice!" Diane declared. "It's supposed to be a nice day."

"Jennifer and I will come by your place and pick you up at eleven, if that's okay." Jonus waited along with the others for her agreement to his plans.

"I'll be ready," Polly said.

She was glad to see several parties entering the dining room before the next day's itinerary could be outlined in more detail, for the interest of the whole group.

Chapter Eight

Jonus got Polly aside privately to determine where they would have their talk later on that evening—at her chalet or up in his suite. He didn't mention his office as a possible choice.

"If you'd feel more comfortable going to your place, I can arrange for a sitter for Jennifer," he said.

Polly would feel on safer ground being alone with him at her chalet. What had happened last night didn't seem a remote possibility there, what with her pets present and familiar mementos in plain sight reminding her of Brad.

"All I can offer you is coffee or tea."

"Coffee's fine."

"I'd just as soon the whole lodge didn't know. It would only confuse them." Polly could have bitten her tongue for adding the last sharp-edged comment.

Jonus raised his eyebrows in surprise. "What do you mean?"

"Just that everyone thinks you're counting the days until Thanksgiving week."

He still looked blank momentarily, then his confusion cleared, and he stated simply, "Sandra Carver. You've been hearing stories about her and me. I'd like to tell you my version."

"I really don't want to hear it," Polly informed him briskly. "Your personal life is no business of mine. I just thought you might like to know you live in a fishbowl and are a main topic of conversation around here."

"Apparently I don't have to worry about whether my telephone conversations are private," Jonus remarked quietly. "Otherwise there wouldn't be rumors flying around because Sandra has booked a reservation. If any of my employees had been listening in when she called and asked to speak to me, they would have heard her sound me out on whether she should come alone or with a male friend. I urged her to do the latter."

"I don't think any of your employees would go so far as to eavesdrop on your telephone conversations," Polly assured him, her heart suddenly lighter. "They don't even mean to pry. They're just genuinely concerned and interested."

"But on the wrong track entirely. Of course I'll be discreet, if that's what you want. We can leave the lodge separately tonight, and I'll just write down your number for the sitter and not your name."

"That way no one will ever suspect." Polly's tinge of sarcasm betrayed her again. She could feel her face growing warm with embarrassed color as he frowned, not knowing what to make of her comment. Before he could question her, she excused herself with as much dignity as possible to go and tend to her tables.

There wasn't much danger that Polly would have to explain herself later on. They wouldn't pick up the threads of this conversation at her chalet. It wouldn't have any importance for him once she shared her worries about Jennifer and took him back in memory to Trish's fatal accident.

Polly dreaded having to learn still another set of tragic circumstances, which might get branded into her mind. She dreaded the revelations that might come out into the open and wished that someone else besides her had the role of forcing Jonus to examine his deepest part of his soul and determine whether he blamed his daughter for his wife's death.

Yet she didn't dare shove her grim purpose in seeing Jonus tonight to the back of her mind. She had to keep reminding herself of it when she caught herself thinking like a woman who had plans to entertain a man, wondering if she would have time to change clothes when she got home and if she should serve him coffee using her good china.

Polly would keep on her same clothes, she decided, driving to her chalet. She would use her everyday china and make no pretense of being a polished hostess. Nor would she apologize for how she'd furnished and decorated her rented home. It pleased her, and that was all that mattered.

Jonus knew exactly who and what Polly was—the widowed wife of an Illinois farmer. He wouldn't expect her to have sophisticated tastes.

In the end, she did hurriedly shed her black skirt and white blouse and slip on a pair of dark brown slacks with a matching pullover sweater. But she chose the outfit for comfort, not because it was slenderizing.

Polly had just finished putting on the coffee when Sandy's barking alerted her to Jonus's arrival. She went to the door and held it open for him as he mounted the steps to the small front stoop. For the second time that day, she was glad of the welcoming fuss her animals made over a visitor.

In this instance, her emotions were totally different. There was no sweet, painful reminiscence, just extreme awkwardness. Jonus's quick once-over made her regret that she'd changed into different clothes. She hoped that he didn't get the wrong idea. Contradictorily, she also regretted that she wasn't wearing something more alluring.

He seemed perfectly at ease as he bent down to pet Sandy and talk to him, and then squatted and held out a hand to stroke her meowing cat, who promptly stalked off toward the kitchen.

"Did I fail the test?" he asked ruefully, rising and looking inquiringly at Polly, who stood nearby. "She made friends with Jennifer, I understand."

His eyes stayed on her face, but she still couldn't relax her tense posture. "For some reason she has never particularly liked men. Not even Brad, although she would occasionally decide to be friendly to him. Won't you come in and have a seat?"

Polly gestured as she extended the invitation, which came out sounding stilted and old-fashioned.

Jonus took several steps into her living room and glanced around with interest. His eyes rested on the rocking chair and folded afghan, the hooked rug in front of the fireplace, the collection of small photographs on the mantel.

"This is very homey," he said. "Did you bring furniture from Illinois with you?"

"No, I got rid of everything except a few pieces before I moved here. The furniture I had in Illinois was very similar, though. My taste is traditional, as you can see. I'll go and get the coffee while you make yourself comfortable," Polly announced abruptly, furious at herself for the proud, defensive note in her voice.

"Can I do something to help?" Jonus asked.

"The coffee's made. I just have to pour it," she answered over her shoulder.

He followed along behind her and stood in the kitchen doorway, looking around. "You have a real homemaker's touch," he ventured. "No wonder Jennifer is ready to move in with you."

"That's all I ever wanted to be—a homemaker," Polly informed him, getting cups and saucers down from a cupboard. "It's a full-time career and, in my opinion, a very rewarding one for a woman with a husband who wants a wife who is the domestic type. Not every man does." Jonus obviously hadn't.

"If Trish had wanted to be a housewife, that would have been fine with me," Jonus said. "Not that she was a career woman. Being a wife and mother came first with her."

"But she would never have been happy staying home and cooking and cleaning and sewing and doing laundry, the way I was."

"No, I don't think she would have been. Not all women have an aptitude for domestic work," he pointed out. "I doubt Trish would have been good at being a housewife. Her talents ran more toward planning a dinner party than cooking the meal itself."

"Whereas the whole concept of giving a fancy dinner party is foreign to me," Polly stated. "In our social set, we invited groups of friends to our homes for supper, but it was all very informal. Nobody dressed up in their best clothes. The women helped serve and clean up afterward."

"That sounds very enjoyable," he said. "More often than not, our socializing combined business with pleasure and wasn't that relaxed and low-key. But Trish was glad for any excuse to dress up."

"I don't have any cream. Would you prefer milk or powdered creamer?" Polly asked, feeling dowdy and plain in her brown slacks and sweater.

"Neither. I take my coffee black. Don't bother with a tray," Jonus suggested as she got one out. "I can just carry my cup in my hand."

She ignored him, putting both cups on the tray and then picking it up. "We have *some* etiquette in the part of Illinois where I'm from."

"Then here. Let me carry it." He reached for the tray.

"It isn't heavy. I carry heavier trays every night," Polly said.

"I'm aware of that." He took the tray from her.

In the living room he set it on the low table in front of the sofa and waited courteously until she was seated before he himself sat. Polly handed him his cup of coffee, took hers and settled back, putting more distance between them on the sofa. Sandy was lying on the rug in front of the fireplace and had raised his head to watch them come in. He rested it on his paws again, heaved a contented sigh and dozed off.

"I know how he feels," Jonus remarked, stretching out his legs. "That fire feels nice and warm." He took a sip of coffee. "I could have brought in the firewood for you, though."

"I already had a fire laid. I've been carrying my own firewood now for three years."

"How is your supply?" he asked.

"I'll need to buy some."

"In the next few days, I'll have some delivered from the lodge. It'll have to be cut into smaller pieces, but that's no problem."

"You don't provide firewood for your employees?" she queried skeptically.

"Not as a matter of common practice."

"Then I'll pay you whatever the going price is. I can't accept a favor like that."

"Why not? You did me a favor this afternoon by picking up my daughter at school and giving her a rare treat. I'd like to do something in return to show my gratitude. There are no strings attached." He smiled at her. "You don't even have to take pity on me occasionally and invite me here to share this peaceful, cozy atmosphere.''

"I definitely won't be inviting you here," Polly told him, not smiling back.

"Not just to sit on your sofa, like this, and have a cup of coffee and conversation? You said last night that you were willing to be friends with a man," he reminded. "Well, obviously I'd like to be more than your friend, but at least I want to be that. Relax, Polly. I don't intend to let anything sexual happen between us again unless you're willing, mentally as well as physically. I swear it."

"Then nothing will ever happen. I'm not ever going to want to have an affair with you, Jonus."

"Okay. I accept that as your final word." He extended his hand toward her, palm up. "Trust me?"

Polly laid her hand in his reluctantly. He squeezed it gently and then released it.

"I'm looking forward to tomorrow," he said. "I hope you don't mind too much that I've invited myself along. If you do, I'll back out of going."

"That's not fair, to put me in the position of deciding," she hedged. "I know how much it will mean to Jennifer to have you along. She adores you. I can't not encourage you to spend some time with her."

Jonus gazed into the fire as he said thoughtfully, "Thanks to you, I'm finding out all over again what a joy it is to be a father. One reason I haven't spent more time with Jennifer the past two years is that I didn't think it was good for her to be around me too much. It wasn't just that I was too buried in myself to realize I needed to give her more attention. Intellectually I knew I was neglecting her in important ways and missing out on a lot myself, but I was incapable of dealing with the problem. But now I am going to deal with it."

"It was only a matter of time before you began making an effort on your own to be a better father, whether I had come along or not," Polly replied.

"I'd like to think so." He sipped his coffee before asking, "What was it you wanted to bring to my attention about Jennifer?"

She set her cup and saucer down, not feeling at all prepared. "Today when Jennifer rode with me in my car, she seemed to change her personality and became quiet and subdued. I wondered if she was like that when she rode with you."

He frowned. "She doesn't have much to say on the way to school in the mornings, but until just lately she hasn't wanted to go at all. I thought she was sulking."

"What about when you're taking her somewhere besides school?"

Jonus put his cup and saucer on the coffee table, too. "The only other places I've driven her since the accident were the doctor's or the dentist's office and once or twice to a dancing class, before she refused to go. I haven't taken her anywhere for her pleasure or mine," he admitted in a shamed, troubled voice. "What are you telling me, Polly? That Jennifer may have a fear of riding in a car?"

"I'm afraid she may have."

He shook his head slowly from side to side. "My God, how could I not have known something like this about my own child? I thought about taking her to a child psychologist after the accident. But she didn't seem to have any memory of it. She was in the back seat of the car at the time."

"*No...*" Polly murmured in horror, and squeezed her eyes closed. She opened them to find him looking at her searchingly.

"Tell me," he urged in a voice low with dread. "Whatever it is, I have to know."

"Jennifer made a big production about fastening her seat belt and commented about how she never misbehaved in the car, never climbed into the back seat." Polly's throat muscles constricted. "I'm afraid she may be blaming herself, Jonus."

His face was a mask of torment. Polly couldn't bear to look at him. Mercifully, tears welled up, blinding her as she pleaded, "Jennifer was only four years old, the same age my little girl was. Whatever happened, she can't be blamed."

"The accident wasn't Jennifer's fault, Polly." Jonus moved closer and gathered her in his arms, one hand cradling her head against his shoulder. He stroked her hair, comforting her while he continued in the same quiet, despairing tone. "If she hadn't been in the car at all, it would still have happened. Even the other driver can't be blamed. He was a forty-five-year-old man with no history of heart disease, and he had a massive coronary. He broadsided Trish and sent both cars over the interstate rail. There were witnesses."

Polly reached up and touched his face, wordlessly sharing the horror with him.

"Why," he went on, "did she have to be driving along next to him, on that day, at that moment, Polly? Why? I can't tell you how many times I've asked myself that question."

"I know, I know," she murmured, caressing his cheek. "I've wished a million times that Brad hadn't gone into town that day. And that if he had to go himself, he hadn't taken Jennifer with him. But if it had to happen, I couldn't understand why I couldn't have been in the truck, too."

Jonus's arms tightened around her. "How did it happen?"

"A head-on collision with another pickup truck. The driver was a teenager and was speeding on a two-lane highway. He came around a curve and lost control. A woman, who had walked out to her mailbox, saw the whole thing. It had been raining, and the road was slippery. There was nothing Brad could do, no time for him to react. He was such a careful driver. He'd never had an accident," Polly recalled brokenly.

"The other driver?"

"Killed instantly, too. We knew him. He wasn't even a wild, irresponsible boy. He had a part-time job and was late because of some unavoidable circumstances. He was rushing to get there on time. It was just as tragic for his parents as it was for me."

"I'm so sorry, Polly." Jonus's voice held a helpless anger. "You're such a good, kind person. You didn't deserve to lose your husband and child."

"And you're a fine, decent man, Jonus." Polly raised her head from his shoulder and looked into his face. "I'm so glad for you that you still have Jennifer. That you both have each other. It's a weight off my mind that you don't hold her responsible. I was afraid you might," she confessed gently. "It would have explained so much. You always seemed to be holding back from touching her and expressing your affection."

He nodded. "I live with the constant fear that some harm may come to her. I haven't wanted to be overprotective, but it goes deeper than that. For so long I just didn't dare to let my emotions go, or I might fall apart. Plus, I'm a reserved New Englander and not demonstrative by nature."

Polly was aware suddenly that their faces were only inches apart. She sat back, but Jonus kept an arm around her shoulders and didn't move away. He leaned forward and kissed her on one tearstained cheek and then the other. Polly closed her eyes with the sweet sensation, and he kissed her on each eyelid.

"Jonus, please don't . . ." she whispered.

His lips barely touched hers. "Don't worry. I just want to kiss you like this, Polly, and hold you. That's all I'll do. I promise."

He shifted her position and his own so that she leaned against him in the circle of his arms. Then he held her close, his cheek resting against her head. A log settled in the fireplace, sending up sparks, and the collie, lying on the rug, heaved a sigh.

"God, this is peaceful," Jonus said. He drew in an audible breath and nuzzled her hair. "Your hair is soft and smells nice."

Polly's lungs were full of the faint masculine scent of his after-shave lotion. "I shampoo it often and keep it clean, even if I don't fuss with it."

"Your hairstyle is very becoming. You're an attractive woman, as I'm sure you know. My foreman, Glenn Busby, has been trying his best to pump me for information about you."

"I met him today in the parking lot. Diane introduced us. I gathered from her tone of voice that he isn't married."

"People aren't very subtle, are they?"

"Not at all. I also met Mark Owens and liked him. It sticks out that he's a married man," Polly remarked approvingly.

"Mark's a real family man and as dependable as they come. Glenn's a hell of a nice guy, too, but a womanizer. Watch out for him, because he'll definitely make a play for you," Jonus warned. "The meeting in the parking lot probably wasn't accidental."

"I wouldn't have thought I was his type. He sounded as though he would have liked to be in your shoes last year with the woman doctor. The main topic of conversation in the parking lot was Dr. Carver," she added.

"Was that the first you'd heard of Sandra?" He sounded more than idly curious.

"Yes. Why do you ask?"

"No reason," he replied in a pleased voice, and was quiet for several seconds before he said musingly, "If looks could kill, I wouldn't be here."

Polly followed his train of thought all too easily. He was remembering how she'd glared at him as she'd entered the lodge from the parking lot.

"Would you like more coffee?" she asked abruptly.

"Yes, I would." He hugged her tight and then let her sit up. When she stood, he rose to his feet, too, saying, "While you're getting the coffee, I'll put more wood on the fire. Oh, and if you have any of those cookies you and Jennifer baked, how about bringing out a few of them?"

"I have crackers and cheese and sandwich makings. I could fix you a snack, if you're hungry," Polly offered.

"That's too much trouble. The cookies will hold me."

"I could use something to eat myself," she said, surprised to discover that was the truth.

"In that case, then, a sandwich sounds good."

"You can make yourself more comfortable, put your feet up," Polly suggested over her shoulder on the way to the kitchen.

"In other words, don't come out there and get in your way?" he asked teasingly.

"Exactly." Her smile was in her voice.

In a different kind of way, she felt as happy, getting out food and preparing them both a snack, as she had felt that afternoon, baking cookies with Jennifer.

Such a load was off her mind now that she'd had the dreaded discussion with Jonus and knew that her worst fears weren't true. Everything was going to be fine with him and Jennifer. With his new attitude, he could become a model father.

Now that he and Polly had arrived at an understanding, she was even optimistic that they might be friends and spend occasional quiet evenings together. It was so good to have a man's company.

He had taken her at her word and made himself at home, she saw, when she reentered the living room, carrying what amounted to a small repast. His jacket was tossed over the back of an armchair, and he had kicked off his shoes and was sprawled on the sofa with his feet on the coffee table, gazing into the fire, which blazed cheerily.

Her complacent mood was shattered when he got up and came to take the tray, this one larger than the other. She was conscious of his height and the breadth of his shoulders beneath the white turtleneck. Sitting beside him on the sofa, she was tense with the effort of not responding to his masculinity.

He didn't appear to notice. At her invitation he helped himself and ate with evident enjoyment. Polly gradually relaxed and felt her own appetite returning.

"That hit the spot," Jonus declared, sitting back when he had finished. He patted his hard-muscled stomach. "It's a good thing that ski season is coming up soon. I can use the exercise, now that my taste for food has come back."

"Judging from the complimentary things I've heard, you're a very good skier."

"I started skiing when I was Jennifer's age. This year I'm going to enjoy it in a whole new way," he said. "I'm planning to get Jennifer on skis. It will be fun sharing the sport with you, too. I'm hoping you like it. We can ski at Stowe and Sugarbush, as well as up here. Then in the spring, maybe we'll take a trip to Colorado. I've always wanted to ski out west, but never have."

"Colorado! We can't take a trip together, Jonus!" Polly protested. "And skiing with me won't be any fun for you. You're an expert skier, and I'm a novice."

"You'll advance very quickly beyond the novice stage," he predicted. "So will Jennifer."

Disappointingly that was all he had to say by way of argument with either of her statements.

"Was Trish a good skier?" she asked.

"She wasn't a strong skier, because she wasn't particularly athletic. But she had a graceful style," Jonus answered. He smiled, his tone turning reminiscent. "I always accused her of being more enthusiastic about shopping for her ski outfits than she was about skiing itself. Speaking of clothes, Jennifer needs a winter wardrobe. Maybe we can do some shopping for her tomorrow? I would gladly carry packages if you'd take charge."

"I'd love it," Polly said. "I'm not the best shopper when it comes to buying clothes for myself, but I'm in my element in a children's department."

"Don't you like clothes?"

"Well, yes, of course, I like clothes. But I have no flair for dressing and putting together outfits, so I stick to basic fashions." She indicated her brown slacks and sweater. "With my type of figure, I just don't wear clothes well."

He gave her figure a judicious inspection and slid to the edge of the sofa and began putting on his shoes. "I think most men would agree with me that you wear that outfit you have on very well. Maybe the saying that women dress for other women is true. Can I help you clean up before I go?"

"There isn't much to clean up. I can take care of it in no time." Polly refused his offer as she got to her feet, too. She didn't quite know what to think of his sudden haste in leaving. "Was it my conversation? I didn't mean to bore you. Brad always got a glazed expression any time the subject got onto clothes and shopping," she recalled in pure self-defense.

"I wasn't bored," Jonus stated, putting on his jacket. "It's just time for me to go. I don't want to wear out my welcome." He bent down to pet Sandy, who had risen and come over, wagging his tail. Polly couldn't see Jonus's face as he went on, his thoughts back in another time. "Trish was never completely satisfied with her figure, for just the opposite reasons. She wished she had larger breasts. She actually sounded me out on the idea of having them enlarged surgically."

"You didn't encourage her to do that, of course."

Jonus gave Sandy a final pat and stood up. "No, I think the whole idea of changing the body nature gives us is foolish. I wouldn't have loved her any more, just like Brad wouldn't have loved you more if you'd looked like a fashion model in your clothes, would he?"

Polly shook her head. "He was always of the opinion that fashion models would look better if they gained some weight." She led the way to the door, thoroughly dissatisfied with the way the evening was ending.

Jonus put his arms around her, hugged her tight, and then continuing to hold her, said, "Thanks for everything, Polly. For your company and hospitality tonight and for giving me more insight into my daughter. I'll follow up immediately and have a talk with her about the accident. Sleep well, and I'll see you tomorrow."

With an affectionate kiss on her cheek, he was gone.

Polly leaned against the door, her whole body aching for a different kind of good-night kiss.

She had been wrong in thinking that there wouldn't be any chance of repeating the previous night's mistake here at her chalet. Passion could just have easily flared up between them the same way it had in his office.

If Jonus had told her with his eyes that he wanted her, if he had touched her differently, expressed desire for her even in his tone of voice, Polly wouldn't have been able to resist him. He could have made love to her right there on her sofa if he'd wanted to.

Not even the mention of Brad had calmed her responsiveness to Jonus's masculinity. The thought of her beloved husband now didn't dull Polly's female need to couple her body with Jonus's and let him fill her emptiness.

Chapter Nine

Outside, Jonus breathed in deeply and then emptied his lungs, blowing the air through his mouth. Walking to his rugged four-wheel-drive vehicle, parked next to Polly's station wagon, he could hear her asking him, *Was it my conversation?*

"Hell, yes, it was the conversation." As he got behind the wheel and slammed the door, he spoke the answer he'd held back while in her chalet. His voice contained pained humor and male frustration. "Have a heart, Polly. I'm sitting here alone with you, doing my damnedest not to think about taking your clothes off, and you expect me to discuss your figure."

Shaking his head, Jonus started up the engine. She hadn't had an inkling that she was being unintentionally provocative, tempting him to give the conversation an intimate turn and change the whole mood. Her soft brown eyes had been earnest and her expression had held a hint of wistfulness. Visualizing her face did nothing to soothe his half-aroused condition, because he focused upon her full, tender mouth and felt the yearning he'd had to fight all night.

God, how he'd wanted to kiss her, kiss her softly, kiss her hard, have her kiss him back, feel the pressure of her lips, the meeting of their tongues.

Jonus groaned as he shifted into gear and backed out. He had to cut off this train of thought, unless he wanted to test out the cold-shower theory.

Tomorrow he wouldn't be under the same strain, because Jennifer would be present. It would be their first outing with the three of them, man and woman and child, and a preview of what their being a family unit could be like.

On the drive home Jonus thought about the next day and about the future. Polly was the perfect stepmother for Jennifer. He had never been more certain about anything. Nor did he have a problem with the idea of being married to Polly. Marriage was just legalizing the relationship he wanted to have with her, where she would be his companion and he would be her lover. They would share the duties of parenthood and be helpmates.

Making Polly his wife would be entirely different from the way he'd joined himself heart and soul to Trish. Thus, there was no sense of guilt or disloyalty.

The lodge was quiet. As he went upstairs to his suite, Jonus compared it with Polly's chalet. The contrast was like night and day, a fact that pleased him, too.

Jennifer's sitter was Mrs. Allen's granddaughter, a high-school senior. After he'd paid her and she'd left, Jonus looked in on his daughter, who slept with a smile on her face as though she was having a happy dream.

Her photo album lay on her bedside table. Jonus picked it up and sat on the other twin bed, which was never used, since she never had girlfriends staying overnight.

That would change, he decided, as he opened the album. Polly would see to it that Jennifer did all the normal things a little girl was supposed to do.

Jonus looked at each page and traveled back in time. He had to blink at the hot sting of tears in his eyes, but the memories the pictures awakened also brought a smile to his lips. He closed the album and placed it back where it had been, then bent to kiss Jennifer's warm cheek again and eased out of the room, his glance falling on the ballerina lamp.

He would tell Polly about Jennifer's refusal to take dancing lessons. Polly would get to the bottom of the matter and know what was best.

As he got ready for bed, Jonus pondered the best approach to opening a discussion between him and his daughter about the terrible accident she'd survived two years ago. He didn't want to let another day go by without erasing any shadow of doubt from his child's mind that she was in any way responsible.

An opportunity presented itself naturally the next morning when he went up to their suite to see if she had gotten up yet. She was still in bed, but awake and watching cartoons on her TV set, as she was allowed to do on Saturday mornings.

"Ready for some breakfast, lazybones?" he asked, going over to give her a good-morning hug and kiss. When her small arms squeezed him hard around the neck and clung, he scooped her up and sat down on the edge of the bed with her in his lap. "I ordered us some blueberry pancakes, your favorite."

"Your favorite, too, huh, Daddy?" she said, yawning and snuggling further into his arms. "I wonder if Polly likes blueberry pancakes."

"You'll have to ask her," Jonus replied, and went on indulgently, "I visited Polly last night at her house after she got off work, and guess what? Her dog let me pet him, but her cat went off into the kitchen and stayed there. She must not have liked my looks.''

"It's probably because you're so big, and she doesn't know you won't hurt her," Jennifer conjectured. "Since I'm a little girl, I might remind her of Polly's little girl named Jennifer. Precious was her cat. Did you see her pictures on the mantel?''

"Yes." Jonus had looked at the small photographs up close while Polly was out in the kitchen. Since she hadn't mentioned them, he hadn't, either.

"She died and is up in heaven with Mommy. Do you think Mommy knows her up there, Daddy?''

"I can't say that for certain, honey, but it's a beautiful thought, isn't it?''

"Polly said her little girl used to turn the radio up loud in the car and undo her seat belt and climb into the back seat. She must have been bad, huh?''

"She sounds like a normal active child. You used to do those things, too, when you were younger," Jonus recalled gently. "You were in the back seat when you and Mommy had the accident that killed her. I'm glad you climbed into the back, because it might have saved your life. We haven't talked about this before because you've never asked questions, and it is a very sad subject. But I wouldn't want you to think that Mommy wasn't a good driver, honey." He combed her hair with his fingers. She had gone absolutely still, her cheek pressed against his chest. "The accident wasn't her fault. Or anyone's fault. The driver of another car got very sick and passed out. His car hit Mommy's car, and that's what happened.''

"I remember a big noise and falling. When I woke up, I was in the hospital, and Mommy was gone.''

"And Daddy was too upset to explain it all to you. But now it's all right for you to ask about anything that bothers you concerning your accident with Mommy— That must be our breakfast.'' The knock on the door couldn't have come at a more opportune moment. "Can you wash your face and hands and comb your hair by yourself while I go open the door?"

"Yes, Daddy. I'm in first grade, remember."

She scrambled off the bed, and Jonus gave her a loving spank on her bottom as she headed for her adjoining bathroom.

"I don't even need Louise to help me get dressed for school in the mornings," she informed him over her shoulder. "She gets out clothes for me to put on sometimes that don't match. I have to tell her they're wrong."

"Be sure to tell her in a polite way," Jonus scolded, a tender smile tugging at his lips.

When she emerged from her room, she had changed from her nightgown into pink corduroy jeans and a pink striped turtleneck. He complimented her on how nice she looked, and she blushed with pleasure.

Apparently she'd already forgotten their talk. As they sat down to breakfast her thoughts were on the day ahead. And so were Jonus's. He was in complete agreement when Jennifer lamented having to wait until eleven o'clock to pick up Polly.

"Couldn't you call her and ask her if she could be ready sooner?" Jennifer asked.

"She might be sleeping in this morning," Jonus objected mildly. The idea of having a morning phone conversation with Polly was strongly appealing. Jennifer's impatience to start their outing earlier was a perfect excuse.

"Polly wouldn't mind if I woke her up," his daughter stated confidently. "I could call her."

"No, I'll call her."

It wouldn't be a good precedent to set to allow Jennifer to disturb Polly at home.

He used the phone in his bedroom, with the door closed. Polly answered on the first ring, sounding startled and faintly alarmed.

"Hi, this is Jonus." He identified himself immediately. "I hope I didn't rouse you out of a sound sleep."

"No, you didn't," she assured him.

She was either in bed or had been within arm's reach of whichever telephone she had picked up. Jonus wanted to know exactly where she was.

"Are you sure I didn't wake you up?" he asked apologetically. "Just say so, and I'll hang up and let you go back to sleep."

"I wasn't asleep. I had gotten up to let Sandy out and was just lying here in bed being lazy."

The embarrassed note in her voice was more titillating than she could have imagined, causing him to wonder exactly what kind of nightclothes she was wearing.

"Jennifer and I just finished a big breakfast and are ready and raring to go. We discussed the possibility of stepping up our schedule, but obviously that would be rushing you."

"My first thought was that you had probably changed your mind about going," she said honestly. "It would be better to allow more time if you want to do some shopping for Jennifer, as well as take her to a movie. I had originally planned to go earlier, since I'm working tonight and need to be back for five o'clock."

"If you're late, you won't get in trouble with the boss," Jonus pointed out.

"I still would rather report to work on time," she replied firmly. "Give me half an hour, and I'll be ready."

"Half an hour," he repeated with mild amazement. "Can you really get dressed in that short amount of time? That must be some kind of female record."

"Sometimes I do take longer, of course, if I have to wash my hair and dry it. You may not have noticed, but I don't wear much makeup."

Her answer was defensive.

"I have noticed," Jonus hastened to correct her. "The natural look suits you."

"It goes with my hairdo and my style of dress, anyway," she said matter-of-factly. "If I'm going to be ready in thirty minutes, we'd better hang up."

He wasn't going to end the conversation on that note. "You're an attractive woman, Polly. The more I'm around you and the better I know you, the prettier you are." Not to mention sexier.

"Thank you, Jonus. That's nice to hear. To return the compliment, you're a very good-looking man."

"Do I get better looking the more you're around me?" Jonus coaxed, ignoring her proud tone.

"Unfortunately."

"Now that I've fished that out of you, I'll let you get dressed. Before I hang up, though, on a more serious note, I had a talk with Jennifer this morning. I'll tell you about it tonight."

She was silent.

Jonus went on, "There's another matter concerning her I'd like to discuss with you, too. Unless you'd just rather go to your place, I'll play host tonight. It would make things easier for me if Jennifer were in the next room," he explained frankly.

"You didn't seem to have a problem last night."

"I did have one, though. Why do you think I got up and left so suddenly?"

"Well, if it's easier on you at your apartment, I'll come up after I'm finished in the dining room."

"Good. I won't get a sitter then. Could we bring you some breakfast? A cinnamon roll and some coffee and juice?" He tried to clear his mind of the selfish wish that he could deliver her breakfast in bed by himself.

"A cinnamon roll sounds good. I have some orange juice in the refrigerator."

"See you in thirty minutes."

It was an autumn day in Vermont. The air was clean and sharp and tangy with the scent of evergreens. Overhead the sky was blue and cloudless. Shafts of brilliant sunlight from the morning sun illuminated the mountainsides, spotlighting the gaudy reds and golds of the birch and maple trees.

As Jonus walked outside the lodge with his daughter, he inhaled deeply and felt light-headed and exultant. When she let go of his hand and ran ahead, skipping and jumping, he almost envied her child's freedom to vent emotions and act out moods.

In the car she buckled her seat belt without being reminded, but didn't sit quietly. She chattered and twitched with excitement and occasionally bounced up and down to release a spurt of high spirits.

At Polly's chalet, Jonus looked on, once again with wistfulness, while Jennifer greeted Polly, throwing her small arms around Polly's waist and hugging her. If only he, too, could be that spontaneous with Polly when his turn came to say hello.

"Why the hell not?" he thought, swept by a sudden recklessness. Without waiting, he stepped up and put an arm around her shoulders, gave her a hard squeeze and, taking advantage of her wide-eyed surprised, kissed her on the lips.

"Good morning. You look fresh and pretty," he said, smiling at her.

"Daddy! You kissed Polly!" Jennifer giggled, both shocked and delighted.

Polly was blushing. "You two are certainly in good moods."

Her dog was barking a welcome in the background, and her cat was meowing. Their clamor distracted Jennifer and she turned her attention to petting the animals, giving Jonus a private moment with Polly. He still had his arm loosely around her.

"You're going to give Jennifer the wrong idea," she warned in an undertone.

He kept his voice low, too, as he answered with the simple truth, completely unrepentant, "I was glad to see you. It's a great day outside, and I got carried away."

"She's only a child. You can't expect her not to report everything she sees."

"So what if she does? What she saw was perfectly innocent. As long as we know that and our consciences are clear, isn't that all that matters?" He smiled and cautioned only half-teasingly, "Be on your guard, because the way I feel today, I may steal a few more kisses."

The color rose high in her cheeks again, most becomingly. "Be fair, Jonus," she pleaded with a hint of breathlessness in her voice. "This is Jennifer's day."

"You're right." He patted her on the back.

"Look, Daddy, Precious lets me pick her up." Jennifer made a timely interruption.

Polly fled to the kitchen, announcing her intention to pour herself a glass of orange juice in a plastic cup to drink in the car with the cinnamon roll they'd brought for her. Thoroughly pleased with the interlude, Jonus stayed behind with his daughter, who instructed him on how to make friends with Polly's cat.

"Don't make any sudden movements, Daddy, and scare her. Just reach out your hand nice and easy and pet her. Like that," she approved. "Once she gets used to you and knows you won't hurt her, she'll trust you."

It was good advice on how to win the confidence of the skittish feline's owner, too, Jonus reflected. *Be patient. Don't try to rush her into anything.*

When Polly returned, he was careful not to so much as exchange an intimate glance with her. He wanted to put her at ease and not have undercurrents that would interfere with the camaraderie and exclude Jennifer.

His small daughter was in seventh heaven. To be taken on an excursion by both him and Polly was obvious a perfect state of affairs for her. On the drive to Burlington she kept demanding to know if they didn't think this was fun, too, all three of them going somewhere together. Unwittingly she made Jonus feel bad that a simple outing was such a treat for her, yet she couldn't have played his ally any better.

Father and daughter might have been on the same wavelength, for they both seemed bent on convincing Polly she should be a permanent part of their lives. It hadn't occurred to Jonus before now that Jennifer might apply her own pressure once the idea dawned in her head that her daddy and Polly could get married. Especially if he made his position clear—that he thought the idea was a good one.

Polly couldn't hold out against both of them indefinitely. That knowledge buoyed Jonus's spirits. Unfortunately it didn't foster the necessary patient attitude. If anything, holding back and going one careful step at a time until he was on solid ground with her only seemed more of an endurance test.

Jonus wasn't just straining at the leash to get Polly into bed. His hunger was more than sexual. He would like to hold hands with her, casually express his affection and be on the receiving end and have her show affection for him. Just the thought of having her speak to him in a loving tone of voice, the way she spoke to Jennifer, awoke a yearning.

Patience.

The small city of Burlington was a beehive of activity. On a fine Saturday, shoppers of all ages were out in force. Jonus was lucky enough to find a parking spot centrally located, within walking distance of stores with children's clothes, a number of restaurants, as well as the movie theater where the movie was playing that Polly had seen advertised.

Before he had killed the engine, Jennifer had her seat belt undone. She was almost beside herself with excitement, bouncing on her seat and urging, "Hurry up, Daddy! Let's get out of the car!"

"Calm down a little, honey," he remonstrated.

"Why don't we set some ground rules?" Polly suggested pleasantly but firmly. "Either your father or I will hold your hand when we're walking on the street, Jennifer. We don't want to lose you in a crowd, because it would spoil everything for all three of us."

"It certainly would," Jonus concurred.

"I'll walk in the middle and hold both your hands."

Jennifer extended the security measures eagerly and abided by them. After they'd gone several blocks, Jonus relaxed his grip on her hand, and she smiled up at him. "You see, Daddy, I'm not going to jerk away like I used to when I was little and you and Mommy took me with you." She explained cheerfully for Polly's benefit, "Daddy had to pick me up and carry me."

Jonus looked over at Polly and saw her swallow hard and blink. Her own memories had been triggered, he realized. Oddly, his wave of deep compassion soothed his own pain of remembrance. His main concern was for her. To give her a moment to recover, he distracted Jennifer's attention, pointing out an antique car passing on the street.

Two older women were approaching, walking abreast and carrying large shopping bags. Jonus made way for them, dropping to the rear and marshaling Jennifer and Polly over to one side. He slowed them almost to a stop, clasping each of them by the shoulder.

"We don't necessarily have to shop today," he said, and gave Polly's shoulder a squeeze to finish out his thought.

Whatever she preferred to do, so that her tragic past wouldn't be evoked, was fine with him.

"If you have errands to run, Jennifer and I can meet you somewhere," she offered.

"Are you trying to get rid of me?" Jonus wasn't totally successful at keeping his voice light. His feelings were too hurt.

Before he could point out that he hadn't come to town to be sent off by himself, Jennifer piped up, begging, "Please come with us, Daddy! You can run errands some other time."

"I don't have any errands to run," Jonus reassured his daughter. "My whole purpose for taking the day off was to spend some time with you and Polly. You two are stuck with me."

He took his daughter's hand again, and the three of them continued along the sidewalk, with her in the middle. She hauled them to a stop in front of a shop window that had child and adult mannequins dressed in handsome ski outfits.

"This store has little girls' clothes. Karen brought me here before when she took me shopping," she recalled.

"Shall we go in and check it out?" Jonus asked Polly, who looked questioningly at him. "You might find something for yourself to try on, too."

Jennifer seized immediately on that idea. "We can both try on clothes at the same time." She giggled. "You'll have to stand outside the little room, Daddy, because you're a boy and it would be too crowded, anyway. But then we can come out and show you how the clothes fit."

"I'll give my expert masculine opinion," Jonus promised.

"Today we'll concentrate on shopping for you," Polly addressed his daughter firmly, ignoring him. "I'll do my shopping another time. Let's go inside."

Jonus held the door open for them to enter, not knowing what to make of her reaction. He didn't think she could possibly be embarrassed by his daughter's artless remarks or that he could have offended her. Perhaps she had shopped for clothes with her husband and rejected the whole notion of dressing to please another man.

A young saleswoman came to meet them. Her smile for him seemed to contain an element of sympathy. He guessed that she could tell he was feeling extraneous.

"Can I help you find something today?" she inquired.

"We're looking for clothes for my daughter," he replied when Polly didn't speak up.

"That's me," Jennifer clarified, making everyone smile.

"I'm glad you told me, or I wouldn't have known," the saleswoman said laughingly, patting Jennifer's cheek. "Do you know what size you wear?"

Jennifer looked trustingly up at Polly, who readily supplied the information. "She's going to need either a size seven or eight, depending on how the sizes run."

"I have a nice selection. Let me show you."

"Come on, Daddy." Jonus's daughter caught his hand and drew him along when he hung back, uncertain of his role.

Polly was in her element. She exclaimed over the little girl fashions, the warm maternal woman in her taking over. "Isn't this adorable, Jonus!" she would demand of him, holding up a small garment.

"That's cute," he would agree indulgently, most of his admiration for the pink color in her cheeks and the animation in her face. He was deeply relieved that he could detect no sign that shopping for Jennifer was causing her any sadness, relieved also that her coolness toward him had dissipated. She seemed caught up in the present and to be thoroughly enjoying the shopping expedition.

There was no indecision, no doubt of her judgment as she selected outfits for Jennifer to try on and then took the little girl into a dressing cubicle. Jonus stood outside and could hear the conversation and laughing and giggling. He took his cue and made the right fatherly responses when Jennifer came out to model for him.

"Let your father see how cute you look in this," meant that Polly was ready for the rubber stamp of his approval, and he gave it willingly and sincerely.

The saleswoman didn't hover, but she checked with them now and then and took away clothes, either placing them at the cash register if they were to be purchased or returning them to the appropriate bins or racks. She approached just as Jennifer came out wearing a pair of red ski pants and a multicolored sweater.

"That's darling!" she approved. "We have that same sweater in your mommy's size and red ski pants, too. She could get herself a matching outfit."

The young woman's smile faded as she looked from Jonus to Polly. They both were struck mute with a kind of horrified surprise at her very understandable error.

"My mommy was killed in a car accident," Jennifer informed the saleswoman.

"I'm so sorry," she apologized in a mortified tone. "Please forgive my mistake."

"There's no harm done." Jonus found his voice. He could have throttled the woman for giving her sales pitch and wrecking the harmony.

"Let's change back into your own clothes," Polly said to Jennifer.

"Daddy didn't say whether he liked me in this," Jennifer reminded her. She put her hands on her hips and turned around.

"That's one of my favorites out of all the outfits you've tried on," Jonus said. He had been on the verge of saying that, but hadn't gotten the chance.

"It's my favorite, too," his daughter confided.

"When we have a snowball fight, you'll make a good target in those bright colors," he teased, trying to lighten the atmosphere.

"That'll be fun, Daddy! I can't wait! Polly would make a good target, too, if she was dressed just like me."

"Yes, she would," Jonus agreed. "But then she might not want to be a target." A glance at Polly didn't give him a clue about her reaction to lookalike outfits. The red ski pants and boldly patterned sweater would be becoming on her, without a doubt, but he might be putting her on the spot if he said so.

"Why don't you try on the outfit like this that's in your size, Polly?" Jennifer implored. "Please."

"I'm just not in the mood to try on clothes today, sweetie."

"But someone else might buy it before you go shopping again."

"Don't insist, Jennifer," Jonus broke in authoritatively. "Polly has told you her answer. She may not like that outfit on herself."

Jennifer sighed, giving up but not relinquishing all hope. "Maybe we can have another outfit alike," Jonus could overhear her saying wistfully inside the dressing stall.

"I plan to buy some red ski pants. If that sweater is sold, there'll probably be one similar," Polly said soothingly. "We'll have outfits that are almost identical."

"Then you'll still be a target, just like me, when it snows. My daddy will be able to hit us both with snowballs."

"Yes, but there are two of us, and as big as he is, he'll make quite a target, too. We'll give him a taste of his own medicine."

Jennifer giggled delightedly.

"I hear that plotting going on in there," Jonus warned threateningly. His heart felt lighter. Eventually Polly and Jennifer would wear mother-and-daughter outfits. Knowing his daughter, she wouldn't give up on the idea, and eventually it would seem right to Polly, as she grew to love Jennifer like her own child.

The three of them would weather the painful, awkward moments and become a family. Down the road in the future, when Polly was Jonus's wife and Jennifer's stepmother, this scene today would be so different.

Jonus would be able to say what he would have liked to say today, "Try on the outfit. If it looks as good as I think it will, I'll buy it for you."

Or the condition for purchasing the outfit might be silent communication. In time he would be able to exchange glances with Polly and carry on unspoken conversations, not be in the dark about how she was reacting and what she was thinking. Before they could ever arrive at that stage, though, she would have to stop pushing him away and shutting him out.

She would have to learn to trust him and let him into her affections, too. Until then, Jonus had to be patient.

That didn't mean he couldn't give into generous male impulses, as long as he kept them to himself for now. The saleswoman had retreated to the cash register. Jonus walked over to her quickly and instructed her in an undertone, "Ring up that women's sweater, the one like the one my daughter had on, and put it aside for me. I'll have someone pick it up. The name is Jonus Logan."

"Those colors will look wonderful on your wife, with her brunette coloring," she said, keeping her voice low, too.

Jonus didn't bother to correct her.

He would put the sweater away and give it to Polly when he judged the time had come that she'd want to wear it and want to accept a gift from him. Jonus hoped that was only a matter of weeks at the most, not months. He refused even to consider the possibility that it might be never.

After stops at one more clothing store and a shoe store, which went without incident, Jonus was loaded down with purchases, and he humorously referred to himself as their packhorse. After a trip to the car with additions to Jennifer's winter wardrobe that included a new down-filled parka and warm boots with furry lining, the consensus was that they had done enough shopping and were ready for lunch.

The ice was broken, and there was a sense of camaraderie as they trooped along the sidewalk, with Jonus having to fall to the rear to allow room for passersby. Then out of the blue, Jennifer popped out with, "That lady in that first store thought Polly was my mommy. She must have thought you and Polly were married to each other, Daddy."

"It was an honest mistake," Jonus replied cheerfully. "She saw how much of my money Polly was spending on you. That's what wives do—spend their husband's hard-earned money. Right, Polly?"

"Shame on you, Jonus, for filling your daughter's head with such nonsense!" Polly took his lead and pretended to be indignant. "Wives manage their husband's money wisely, Jennifer, and spend hours shopping for bargains. Your father is just teasing us, talking like a male chauvinist."

"What's a male chauvinist?"

"Let me have first crack at the definition," Jonus insisted.

"Ladies first." Polly stood her ground.

Jennifer was thoroughly entertained by their pretended battle of the sexes. She allowed herself to be sidetracked away from her original subject.

It was the first time Jonus and Polly had engaged in light repartee. He thoroughly enjoyed it, and she seemed to, also.

"You aren't really a feminist, are you?" he asked curiously, pursuing the conversation in a more serious vein.

"No. Personally I've never had a problem with the traditional male-female roles. Not that I in any way feel inferior to men. You don't strike me as a male chauvinist, either."

"I'm not when it comes to issues like equal pay for doing the same job and career opportunity. I don't think that women were meant to do heavy labor, though, or go to war. The protective male in me comes out, which is a brand of chauvinism, I suppose."

"It's silly for women not to admit that men are, on average, physically stronger."

Jennifer had been listening long enough and wanted to make her own contribution. "A little boy named Allan in my class at school got sent to the principal's office for hitting a girl at recess. Her name is Louise, and she's in the second grade. She hit him first and made his nose bleed. The teacher who was on duty told him he should be ashamed of himself for being a bully and hitting a girl. Louise is bigger than him. What was Allan supposed to do?"

Polly and Jonus exchanged glances. "Ladies first," he murmured.

The discussion took them to the car, where they unloaded the packages, and then set out for the restaurant Jonus had decided upon in advance. Indirectly he told Polly why he had picked it.

"It's been open about a year and is very popular for lunch. I hear it has good food and a pleasant atmosphere."

He hadn't eaten there himself. The restaurant had no associations, as would one that he and Trish had frequented.

"It sounds perfect," she said. "I'm hungry."

"So am I."

"Me, too," Jennifer chimed in.

The restaurant was crowded. It occurred to Jonus as the hostess was leading them over to the only unoccupied table that he hadn't encountered anyone he knew yet that day. Before the thought was finished, he saw Ellen Craddock seated at an adjacent table with another woman he didn't recognize.

Ellen looked up from her menu and did a double take. "Jonus. That is you." She dropped the menu and got up, demanding, "How on earth are you?"

Jonus took her outstretched hands and squeezed them as he bent and kissed her on the cheek she offered him. "Things are going well with me, Ellen. How have you and Calvin been?"

"Oh, Calvin!" She gestured with a manicured hand. "He's as much a workaholic as ever. Lives at the bank. That's where he is today, if you can believe that. It's been so long, Jonus," she accused softly. "Your friends miss seeing you. We've all been worried about you."

Jonus nodded. "I appreciated your concern, believe me. I'm doing a lot better now, Ellen."

Polly and Jennifer had both sat down, and the hostess had gone, leaving menus.

"And this is your little girl, Jennifer," Ellen said, smiling at Jennifer. "You must be in school now."

"I'm in first grade," Jennifer confirmed.

"Jennifer, you remember Mrs. Craddock."

"A little," his daughter replied honestly.

"Ellen, I'd like you to meet Polly Dearing. Polly has recently come to work for me. She and Jennifer and I have been on a shopping expedition for winter clothes for Jennifer."

"I'm pleased to meet you, Polly." Ellen's blue eyes were full of curiosity as they inspected Polly.

"How do you do," Polly said stiffly.

"It was so good to run into you like this, Jonus. I'm going to be calling you soon with a dinner invitation," Ellen warned. "Now I'll leave you to your lunch. Everything on the menu is good."

She returned to her own table.

"Sit here, Daddy." Jennifer indicated the seat next to her, placing him across the table from Polly. "Then I'll be in the middle."

Aware that her voice carried easily, he did her bidding and opened his menu. Polly was studying hers with grim absorption.

This was another of those inevitable scenes that was rough going, he thought, like the one in the store. Polly would have been able to surmise that he and Trish had seen the Craddocks socially, had known them well. She apparently had found the situation more awkward than he had.

With Ellen sitting nearby, he was inhibited from filling in the gaps for her and explaining who the Craddocks were. All he could do was act as relaxed as possible.

"The Reuben sandwich sounds good to me," he remarked, putting his menu to one side. "Is there anything you can't read, Jennifer?"

Polly looked over at Jennifer, her expression softening with apology. "I'm sorry, sweetie. I didn't even think about offering to read you the menu."

"I was just waiting to hear what you and Daddy were going to order, and then I was going to have the one that sounded the best. A Reuben sandwich has sauerkraut on it, and I don't like sauerkraut much, so I'll just have the same thing as you."

"I was thinking about the quiche or the chicken salad, but I could go for a burger."

"I like quiche."

"Well, then we'll order it."

Polly's tender smile for his daughter lingered on her lips as she finally met his eyes. Jonus sat back, grateful that they'd gotten past another hurdle.

"I see a waitress headed this way," he said complacently.

After the waitress had come and gone, he noticed that Jennifer seemed lost in thought, her small brow furrowed.

"You're awfully quiet, young lady," he observed.

"If you and Polly were married to each other, Polly wouldn't be my stepmother, would she?" she asked in her clear, childish voice.

Jonus cringed. He could sense heads turning slightly and ears straining for his answer. Polly looked as if she would like to sink through the floor.

"Well, actually she would."

"But I thought stepmothers were mean and wicked, like Cinderella's."

"Not all stepmothers are like Cinderella's."

"I wonder why her daddy married somebody mean and ugly? In my storybook, Cinderella's stepmother is ugly like a witch."

"That's a question I really can't answer," Jonus admitted. "Actually I don't recall any mention of Cinderella's father, but then I haven't read the story recently."

"I guess he was in his office working and didn't come out very much."

Jonus winced. Polly met his gaze, and suddenly he didn't mind his predicament, because her embarrassment was losing out to amused sympathy.

"That was long before the days of offices," she pointed out to Jennifer, coming to his rescue. "There were no telephones or computers. No television sets. Can you imagine that?"

"Not even in the palace?" the little girl queried.

"Not even in the palace."

"Cinderella didn't get to watch any cartoons, then, did she? I'd rather live right now and not marry a prince when I grow up," Jennifer decided, the subject of stepmothers forgotten.

Chapter Ten

"The movie's starting, Daddy! The movie's starting, Polly!" Jennifer made the announcement excitedly to the two adults sitting on either side of her in the theater.

Polly wondered if Jonus was as glad as she was to have the lights lowered and the opportunity to sit there in the darkness and recuperate.

It had been one awkward moment after another today for both of them, but she had to give him credit. He had risen to the occasion and handled each one sensitively, trying to spare her feelings and get them back on track.

He so obviously wanted Jennifer to enjoy the outing. Polly was admiring him more all the time as a father. Liking him more as a human being.

And finding him more attractive as a man.

The rest of the female population found him attractive, too. Polly couldn't understand why he didn't have an ego the size of his ski lodge the way women noticed him and smiled at him. Yet he seemed oblivious. He treated women with courtesy, and there wasn't a hint of patronizing male.

His good manners were inbred. Anyone could tell with a glance that he was accustomed to authority, and his speech was further evidence. He didn't have an acquired polish, but carried himself with a quiet assurance. Although she'd never even seen him in a tie, Polly could easily visualize him in formal clothes at a social function with highly successful people in business and politics.

People like the Craddocks. After Ellen Craddock had gotten up and left the restaurant, Jonus had explained that her husband, Calvin, was president of the largest bank in Burlington.

"I do my banking with Calvin," he had added.

Polly's checking account just happened to be with a branch of the same bank. But she didn't do "banking" with any individual. Banks were anonymous financial establishments in her world. She doubted she knew anyone back in Illinois who had ever been in the office of a bank president. People in her and Brad's economic stratum usually dealt with loan officers and had to go through all the red tape.

"Mrs. Craddock dresses very nicely," she had commented.

Ellen Craddock personified the type of fashionably dressed woman that Polly had always secretly envied. She had been wearing a simple tailored dress with a scarf and oversized jewelry, and the whole effect was elegant. Her makeup was perfect, her hairstyle chic. Under her polite scrutiny, Polly couldn't have felt plainer by comparison, in her skirt and blouse and cardigan sweater.

"Ellen always looks like she just came from the beauty salon," Jonus said. "You never see her any other way. That probably wasn't just a lunch with a woman friend, though. She's busy twenty-four hours a day, raising money for worthwhile causes, like building a new children's wing for the hospital. She and Calvin both are very fine people.''

"Is he about her age?"

Polly judged the bank president's wife to be in her early forties and was wondering if she and Jonus's wife had had a lot in common, in spite of the generation gap.

"He's a few years older." Jonus thought br iy. "This year he will be forty-eight. Ellen always has a big surprise birthday party for him, which isn't a surprise, of course. It's a regular event that all their friends can mark on the calender a year ahead of time. The past couple of years I haven't gone.''

Since Trish had died.

"'Cause you've been so sad about Mommy, huh, Daddy?'' Jennifer had spelled out the reason with childish candor. "Will you go to his party this year? Polly could go with you.''

Polly cringed.

"It doesn't sound like my kind of party." She had spoken up quickly, directing her words to Jennifer.

Jonus hadn't said anything.

Of course he wouldn't want to take her, even if he did decide to go to the party this year. If he asked her, Polly wouldn't accept. She would be totally out of place. All of his and Trish's friends would look at her and compare her with Trish. They'd wonder what Jonus saw in her.

Polly sighed and then took herself to task.

It was silly of her to feel miserable and rejected because she didn't have the kind of social background to step out with Jonus and rub elbows with locally prominent people who "entertained." The last thing she was interested in doing was standing around with a cocktail in her hand and making meaningless small talk.

To her, a home wasn't a showplace for impressing people. It was where a family lived and friends and family gathered for good food and fellowship and the commemorating of special events. Being a good hostess didn't mean ordering fancy hors d'oeuvres from a caterer and flower arrangements from a florist. It meant having the house clean and redolent with good cooking smells when guests arrived.

Polly had homespun values. That was the reason she had been totally content as the wife of an Illinois farmer. Now she was his widow, working to support herself as a waitress and asking little of life other than dignity and peace of mind.

That was who Polly was, and she made no apologies, no pretenses of being anything more.

Jonus was her employer and Jennifer's father.

"This is a good movie, huh, Daddy? Huh, Polly?"

Jennifer's stage whisper made Polly realize that she was gazing at the flickering images, but not seeing them. She glanced at Jonus who met her gaze over his daughter's head. He smiled, raising his eyebrows as though to say, "Well? What's your answer?"

"We're glad you're enjoying it," Polly whispered to the little girl, who held a bucket of popcorn on her lap that they were supposed to share. She was poking kernels into her mouth and crunching steadily, her attention fixed on the screen.

Jonus put his arm along the back of Jennifer's chair and squeezed Polly's shoulder. Then he left his hand there.

A warm tingle of pleasure spread through Polly's body. She took a small handful of popcorn and ate it when what she really wanted to do was lift her hand and cover his.

By the time they had walked back to the car after the movie, Jennifer had wound down. She busied herself with a coloring book and crayons on the drive back and seemed to pay little mind to the adult conversation, interrupting only occasionally to show Polly her work.

Polly found herself doing most of the talking, with Jonus asking her questions about herself. He wanted to know how she had happened to relocate to Vermont, and she explained that she had gone hiking in Vermont with college friends the summer between her freshman and sophomore years and fallen in love with the small mountainous New England state, so unlike her native Illinois.

"I always planned to come back on a vacation with Brad, but we never got around to taking vacations other than visiting family in other states. When I came to the decision to move away and settle somewhere in a completely different kind of setting, I suddenly knew where I wanted to go. It's as though the seed had been there all along," she mused.

"Brad wasn't along on the hiking trip?"

"I hadn't even met him then. He wasn't in school. He was twenty-seven and I was nineteen when we met."

"He was already a farmer?"

"Yes, he had inherited the farm the previous year," Polly recalled.

"Your parents are living?"

"Yes, they moved to Tennessee shortly after I was married. My dad works at a General Motors plant down there. I have a married sister who also lives in Tennessee, and a married brother who lives in Michigan."

"But you didn't consider moving to Tennessee or Michigan to be near members of your family?"

"No. They all mean well, but their whole attitude is that I should marry again and live happily ever after." She would have had to contend with matchmaking and unwanted advice, for she would have been a disruptive element, a sad loose end that everyone wanted to tie up.

Jonus nodded with understanding, and Polly didn't need to go into more explanation.

"What about in-laws?" he asked.

"I'm very fond of Brad's parents, who lived about fifty miles away. And also his sister, who is in St. Louis. I'll keep in touch with them and probably visit every couple of years or so.''

''That takes a lot of gumption for a woman to pull up roots and go off her own, like you did,'' Jonus marveled. ''How did you go about it?''

''I wrote to the state of Vermont and got information. After reading it, I decided tentatively on the area between Montpelier and Burlington because I would be within driving distance of both cities and yet wouldn't have to live in a city. I was also interested in learning to ski.''

''You just packed up and came here?''

''I had a moving company pack up the things I intended to bring and hold them in storage. Then I came ahead with the animals to find a place to live. I picked up one of your brochures at a rest stop, and it swayed me to explore the vicinity of Logan Valley Ski Lodge. I rented my chalet, notified the moving company and went out and bought furniture. After I settled in, I started looking for a job.''

''That was your first job interview, the one you had with me?''

''Yes.''

He was silent a moment, thinking his own thoughts. Then he smiled over at her and said, ''Heaven sent you. I was about at my rope's end when you appeared out of nowhere, an answer to my prayer for help.''

''You only hired me because you were desperate,'' she reminded.

''In more ways than one.''

''Look, Polly.'' Jennifer had leaned forward and was thrusting out her coloring book.

Polly took it and spoke words of praise, not commenting on the rather bizarre choice of colors.

''Show it to Daddy,'' Jennifer insisted.

Jonus had already glanced over. ''I like that little girl's purple hair,'' he said solemnly.

After Polly returned the coloring book and Jennifer was once again preoccupied, he didn't pick up the interrupted conversation. She didn't need him to interpret his heartfelt remark that he had been desperate for more than a waitress when he'd interviewed her. It was self-explanatory.

He had been at his rope's end as a father, not knowing how to deal with Jennifer and desperately needing a woman's help. And he had also reached a stage Polly had been through herself, when he had grieved long enough, but couldn't seem to see any light at the end of the tunnel. Opening up to her and verbalizing his loss had helped him.

Now he would go on with his life. He would remarry. Polly didn't have any doubt of that. He wasn't a womanizer, and he would want another permanent relationship with sex and companionship, even though Trish had been his one love. His wife would be someone he could take to the Craddocks' parties, someone who could act as his hostess, dress elegantly, know how to "entertain" guests.

"A penny for your thoughts," Jonus offered gently.

"You wouldn't be getting a very good bargain," Polly evaded, trying to muster a smile. "I haven't heard any mention of grandparents. Are there any in the picture?"

"My mother and her husband live in Palm Springs. She descends upon us about once a year. My father is dead. His wife lives in Miami. My parents divorced when I was in my teens. I went to a prep school in Massachusetts and then to Boston University and spent very little time in either household."

"You were an only child?"

He nodded.

"Your brochure says you're a native Vermonter."

"I was born in Vermont and spent the first few years of my childhood here, but grew up in Massachusetts. I spent a lot of winter holidays in Vermont skiing."

"What was your college major?"

"Architecture. I designed the lodge myself. Trish had a lot of input, of course."

"Are her parents living?"

"No, they were both killed in a plane crash when she was two. She was raised by an aunt and uncle in upper New York state, but was never really close to them. She had a hired nanny. We took Jennifer to visit them when she was a baby, and they haven't seen her since. Neither Trish nor I had the greatest home life growing up," Jonus stated matter-of-factly. "We both spent a lot of time with friends' families and got a notion of what family closeness could be like."

"It sounds as though you both had all the material advantages."

"We did, and we realized that. Don't get the idea we felt sorry for ourselves. It was just important to us that our children would have what we missed out on."

Polly didn't miss the plural, *children*. He and Trish hadn't intended for Jennifer to be an only child. And she wouldn't be. She would have a half brother or half sister, maybe both. Jonus was a virile man, in his prime. He could still have the family he'd wanted.

A big lump had come into Polly's throat, and a wave of misery swept through her. She was appalled at her emotion. The certainty that Jonus's future held happiness for him and for Jennifer should be making Polly glad, not the opposite.

"How much farther is it?" Jennifer inquired plaintively from the back seat. "I'm getting tired of riding."

"Why don't we play a guessing game?" Polly suggested, instantly sympathetic. "I'll start off. My ship came sailing in with something round that bounces."

"A ball!"

"That's right. Now it's your turn."

Jonus joined in, making nonsense guesses that sent Jennifer into peals of laughter and had Polly smiling at his playfulness. Her depression lifted.

"Daddy, you go ahead and take a turn," Jennifer insisted kindly after she and Polly had alternated, taking several turns.

He didn't even stop to think. "My ship came in with something hard and clear that a princess might wear on her feet."

"I know! A glass slipper, like Cinderella wore! *Stepmother* is a funny word," his daughter commented almost with pause. "Did Cinderella's stepsisters have the same daddy she did?"

Polly shot Jonus a look that said he could explain the relationships, since he had been the one to bring on the question.

"No, if he had been the father, her stepsisters would have been half sisters. Cinderella's stepmother must have had another husband before she married Cinderella's father, and that man was the father of the stepsisters."

"If Cinderella's daddy and her stepmother had a little boy baby, he would have been Cinderella's half brother?"

"That's right. It's your turn," Jonus prompted.

But she wasn't ready to proceed with the game. "I think I'd like to have a little half brother." As opposed to a little half sister. Her tone indicated that she was torn when it came to deciding on the gender of her half sibling. "What would you rather me have, Daddy?"

"I believe in letting nature decide those things," Jonus answered noncommittally. "Do you want me to take another turn?"

"No. I have a good one." Her active young mind skipped on.

Jonus participated absently after that, although he wasn't withdrawn. Polly wondered if he wasn't mulling over his daughter's positive reaction toward the idea of a sibling. Whatever his train of thought, he didn't seem troubled by it.

Polly was troubled by her own reaction to the exchange between father and daughter. Jennifer hadn't dealt with the matter of who would be the mother of her half brother or half sister, thus sparing Polly any embarrassment. Instead of being relieved and thankful that her name hadn't come up at all, Polly felt another wave of despondency.

At Polly's chalet Jennifer wanted to get out and go in to visit Sandy and Precious. Jonus spoke up with a firm no.

"We have to get back to the lodge, and Polly has to change clothes," he told his daughter. "You can ride up front with me the rest of the way."

"Not just for a minute?" Jennifer persisted wistfully. "I'll bet they'd be glad to see me. Wouldn't they, Polly?"

"They'd be very glad to see you, but your daddy needs to get up to the lodge and check on things. He's been away all day."

"Couldn't I come in by myself then and you could bring me?"

"You can visit Polly another time," Jonus said firmly again. "Now Polly needs a little privacy. After all, she's spent the whole day with us."

Polly wouldn't have minded at all having the little girl come in without her father. That would have been privacy enough, but she backed him up.

"I have some things to do, and your daddy doesn't want to ride home all by himself." Her chores included feeding her pets, but she wisely didn't go into detail.

"Okay." Jennifer gave in reluctantly. But she pointed out, "You'll have to ride all by yourself."

"Someday there's going to be a husband who will never get in a last word," Jonus remarked to Polly, unclipping his seat belt.

"Don't bother to get out," she urged, but he ignored her words, getting out, anyway, and coming around to help her down out of the passenger seat and lift Jennifer to the ground.

Polly gave the little girl a warm hug and a kiss. "You've been very good all day," she said.

Jennifer hugged Polly hard around the neck and kissed her on the cheek before scrambling up into the passenger's seat. Jonus had been standing by, observing.

"I've been very good today, too, haven't I?" he asked.

Polly looked at him, taken off guard. "Fathers are supposed to be good," she replied, feeling the color flooding her cheeks as she realized what he wanted.

Jennifer giggled. "I think Daddy wants you to kiss him, too, Polly. You're too tall, Daddy. You'll have to bend down so that Polly can reach your face."

"That's easy enough to do." He waited with blatant hopefulness.

Polly's heart was beating ridiculously fast. He was only asking for a friendly kiss on the cheek, for heaven's sake, not a kiss of passion. The best thing to do was play along and not make a big issue, then have a talk with him later about not pulling the same kind of trick again. Jennifer was impressionable.

"You do deserve a kiss, I guess." Her breathless note betrayed her effort to sound grudging.

"And a hug around the neck?" he cajoled as she stepped closer, and he bent down. His smile of encouragement held no element of challenge, and there was no teasing light in his blue-gray eyes. He wasn't being playful, but asking for affection.

"You're pushing your luck," she said as she put her arms around his neck. But it was impossible to feign reluctance. Joy welled up inside her as she hugged him, inhaling his masculine scent into her lungs. As she pressed her lips to his cheek, he murmured her name. His arms closed around her in a hard, brief embrace. Then he kissed her on the cheek and let her go gently.

"I hope you enjoyed today as much as I did," he said earnestly.

"It was a really nice day. I wouldn't have missed it," she answered just as sincerely.

"There were some awkward moments, but that was to be expected."

"You handled them well."

They spoke parting words in the sweet aftermath of the goodbye hugs and kisses. Jennifer had been looking on and made the practical reminder that the two adults would be seeing each other that evening.

"Polly will be working in the dining room tonight, Daddy." Her words carried reassurance rather than impatience or jealousy.

Jonus closed the passenger door, and Polly stepped back. As father and daughter drove off, she smiled and waved back at the little girl, who had rolled down her window and was waving frantically, calling, "'Bye, Polly!"

In the grip of her emotions, she turned to go inside, where her pets eagerly awaited her. She could hear Sandy barking, and Precious would be meowing. But her chalet was no longer a haven, cushioned with precious memories.

Today when she walked through the door, there would be more recent memories, vivid images of the present competing with those from the past. Memories and images she would never blot out because they were dear to her heart, too.

Polly had come to Vermont certain that all the pages in her album of precious memories were filled. Heaven help her, she had been so wrong.

"I wish Polly could have her supper with us at night," Jennifer said when she and Jonus sat down to their evening meal. He had showered and changed.

"That would be nice, but she could hardly do that, working evenings," he replied, when he wanted to say, *I wish she could, too.*

Jennifer munched thoughtfully. "Polly could work at lunchtime, while I'm at school. Then she could eat supper with us and stay and put me to bed, instead of Mrs. Allen."

"You have it all figured out," her father remarked lightly. "But Polly would have some say in the matter."

Actually the idea of having Polly work lunches was a stroke of genius, if she was agreeable. It would mean that Jonus would get to see her during the day, too. He could pay her enough for sitting with Jennifer for a few hours in the evenings to make up the difference in tips.

Her waitressing job was temporary anyway, but of course he couldn't tell her that. As his wife, she wouldn't need to be employed, although she would be a big help to him in running the lodge, he was sure.

When he went downstairs, Jonus had to struggle with himself not to go directly to the dining room. He had time to do some paperwork in his office before he was actually needed. His concentration was poor, though, and he accomplished little because his thoughts kept drifting to Polly.

Self-discipline kept him at his desk until eight o'clock. Entering the dining room, he looked around immediately for her and didn't see her. Then the door from the kitchen opened, and she came out bearing a loaded tray. Jonus was on his way over to her before he realized that his intention was to take the tray from her.

He stopped short. She saw him and smiled a forced smile. Jonus didn't smile back. His surge of disappointment at her lack of welcome was too strong.

Patience.

The dinner crowd seemed to have more than the usual number of large parties. He gave Polly the few tables with only two or three and assigned her none that had more than four, conscious of trying to lighten her work load.

Polly didn't fail to notice what he was doing and she got him aside to inform him, "Jonus, I'm capable of waiting on bigger parties."

"I'll give you the next one," he promised reluctantly.

It happened to be a party of five that included his foreman, Glenn Busby, all dressed up in a suit and tie. He was out for an evening with Mark Owens and his wife and another couple, and was obviously the odd man out, without a date.

Jonus would have gone back on his word if he hadn't seen Polly looking his way.

The Owenses were celebrating their anniversary. Jonus sent them a complimentary bottle of champagne from the bar. As he expected, Glenn took full advantage of being Polly's fellow employee and flirted with her. She didn't seem to mind at all, Jonus noted, even if she didn't flirt back. In fact, she spent far more time at the table than was strictly necessary.

He stopped her on one of her trips to the kitchen and told her as much. "I would be too busy to visit with my co-workers if you gave me my fair share of people to wait on," she retorted.

"Remember, you already have plans for after you get off work tonight," Jonus said, getting around to his real message. "Glenn will ask you to join the party, if he hasn't already." He read her expression. "I see he has."

"They're just going into the lounge afterward. I'm sure they'd be delighted to have you join them, too."

"Is that what you'd rather we did?"

Her eyes widened at his clear implication that they would join the party as a twosome or not at all.

"No, I wouldn't rather—"

"Good. We'll go up to my apartment then, as originally planned. Among other things, I have a proposition to discuss. Here comes a threesome. You can take them."

He could feel her eyes following him as he moved to greet the newly arrived party. A glance at his foreman told him that Glenn had witnessed the conference, which was fine with Jonus. The sooner Busby got the hands-off message where Polly was concerned, the better.

Chapter Eleven

A fire burned in the fireplace in Jonus's living room. The lighting was soft. On the low glass table in front of the sofa was a tray of cold hors d'oeuvres that had been prepared by his kitchen staff. Next to it a bottle of wine stood uncorked, ready to be poured into long-stemmed glasses.

Polly felt as though she'd walked into a romantic scene in a movie. Jonus looked the part of the male lead, tall and broad-shouldered and ruggedly handsome in a slate-blue turtleneck sweater and dark slacks. He'd taken off his jacket.

She was all too conscious of not fitting the role of the glamorous woman he should be entertaining.

"This looks so elegant," she said.

"Sit down and make yourself comfortable," he urged, indicating the long sofa upholstered in muted blues and grays. "I don't even know if you like white wine. This is a California chardonnay. If you'd prefer coffee, I can brew some. Or I can order any kind of drink you want from the bar."

"I'll have a glass of wine. I've never tasted chardonnay, but I'd like to try it."

Polly took a seat, and Jonus sat next to her. He leaned forward to fill the two glasses and handed one to her. She tasted it.

"It's very good. Better than the white wine I'm used to drinking. Brad didn't like wine, so I always just ordered a glass of chablis when we ate out in a restaurant that served wine. That was only on special occasions."

"You're probably a marvelous cook, and he preferred the meals he got at home," Jonus conjectured, sitting back with his glass.

"He did," Polly admitted. "He was a homebody and would have been just as happy never eating out. It was a pleasure cooking for him because he enjoyed his food so much."

"Do you cook for yourself now?"

"Yes, I fix simple meals. It's hard to cook for one. Sometimes I get a hunger for a certain dish I used to make, and I'll make it and then freeze individual portions."

"When you get the urge to cook, you could invite me for a home-cooked meal," Jonus suggested.

"I wouldn't dare cook for you," Polly demurred.

"Why not? I'm not a finicky eater."

"But you're used to gourmet food. I cook dishes like pot roast and macaroni-and-cheese and chicken pot pie."

He smiled at his own thought. "What about meat loaf?"

"That was a favorite at our house. I always made an extra-large meat loaf so that there'd be leftovers for sandwiches. Brad loved meat-loaf sandwiches," she recalled, smothering a sigh. She knew Jonus had to be finding the conversation dull.

"Sometime I wish you'd have Jennifer and me to your place for meat loaf. She had never tasted it until she started school and encountered it in the school cafeteria. You'll appreciate her description: a slice of gray hamburger meat."

Polly shook her head, amused. "I can just imagine the reaction of the cafeteria workers when a child comes through the line and can't identify meat loaf."

"She didn't make herself at all popular with them. As you would expect, she didn't keep her opinion of the food quality any secret and volunteered my services as a kitchen consultant." Jonus chuckled. Then he sobered. "Thanks to you, I found out about it when I started actually carrying on conversations with my daughter instead of questioning her about why she didn't like school. She dreaded going into the cafeteria. I paid a visit and took care of the problem, I think. But maybe you could sound her out, just to be sure."

"I will. What did you say to the workers?" Polly asked curiously.

"I played on their sympathies by telling them the truth," Jonus replied candidly. "That Jennifer isn't familiar with home-cooked food, only restaurant food. Actually she hasn't had a real old-fashioned, home-cooked meal," he added.

"Now you're playing on my sympathies."

Jonus grinned. He shifted his body and stretched a long arm along the back of the couch behind her. "You're too smart for me."

Polly sipped her wine. "Is that what you wanted to talk to me about concerning Jennifer?"

"No. She refuses to take dancing lessons, and I haven't been able to get to the bottom of the reason."

"You sound as though it's important for her to take dancing lessons."

"It isn't important to me, except that her mother had her in dancing class."

"I'll bring up the subject with her. The reason could simply be that she didn't enjoy the classes. Not all little girls like taking dancing any more than all little boys want to go out for Little League teams."

"You're so wise about these things." Jonus's fingers were playing with the ends of Polly's hair. "You have a mother's instincts."

"All it takes is to put yourself in the child's place. Parents sometimes don't take into consideration that children are individuals. My mother insisted that my sister and my brother and I all take piano lessons. I felt so sorry for my poor brother, who hated every minute that he was forced to sit at the piano bench." Polly was chattering.

"Maybe it's better than I haven't taken the time to put Jennifer on skis before this winter," he reflected, touching Polly's barrette. "I'll be careful not to put pressure on her. Although I confess I'll be disappointed if she doesn't show an interest. It should be an incentive for her to learn—so that she can get out on the slopes with us. The great thing about skiing is that it can be a family sport."

Polly looked at him, not quite believing that he'd used exactly those words. He meant, of course, that people of all ages and ability levels could participate in the sport together.

"Jonus, we really do have to talk frankly." She sat up straighter, gathering her courage. "Jennifer is a very intelligent child, whose mind is always working. All that talk today about stepmothers and half brothers and sisters has undoubtedly planted a seed. If we aren't careful, she's going to come up with the idea that I might make her a good stepmother. We need to make it clear to her that you have no intention of marrying me. It's not fair to her to let her build up false hopes, nor is it wise for you, because when you do become serious about a woman, you don't want Jennifer to resent her or compare her with me."

Jonus took a swallow of his wine and put the glass on the table. He seemed in no hurry to answer.

"You're putting me on the spot," he said finally, settling back again. "You see, if Jennifer does come up with the idea that you would make her a good stepmother, I could only agree with her."

Polly stared at him, too stunned to make a sound.

"Here. Let me take that," he said gently, reaching for her glass, which had tilted, spilling wine on her skirt. Polly gave him the glass and used the napkin he handed her to dab at the wet spot.

"In order for me to be Jennifer's stepmother, I would have to be your wife," she blurted out.

"You would be getting a husband in the bargain," he concurred. "And not just in name."

"Jonus, you may not think so now, but you are going to want to remarry eventually for reasons other than to give Jennifer a mother."

He took her hand and clasped it warmly in his. "I need you as much as Jennifer does, Polly. My reasons aren't that unselfish."

"You've only known me for a week," she protested. "You haven't even been around me enough to judge what kind of person I am."

"You're warmhearted and giving and loyal. You're strong and independent and brave. You have high morals, pride in yourself, a sense of dignity. I suspect that you can be very determined, maybe stubborn."

"I can be downright hardheaded, and I have a temper. I'm too outspoken sometimes. Your wife needs to be someone more diplomatic, with a different personality, a different background than mine." Someone more like Trish had been. "I was a good wife for Brad, Jonus, but I'm not the right wife for you." Polly's eyes took in the wine bottle and glasses, the untouched tray of canapés artistically arranged and garnished. "I serve coffee and sandwiches for a midnight snack, and not dainty party sandwiches, either."

"We ate your sandwiches and drank your coffee," he pointed out. "You forced my hand tonight. I didn't mean to say any of this yet. I realize you can't make a snap decision about a matter so important." He squeezed her hand. "There's no rush. We'll be spending a lot of time together and will have a chance to know each other better. There's no question in my mind after today that the three of us, you and I and Jennifer, will get along beautifully."

Jonus's arm was still along the back of the sofa. He draped it around her as he slid closer, so that their hips were touching and Polly's shoulder was against his chest. Still holding her hand, he rested his cheek against her head. Polly squeezed her eyes shut, desperately trying to muster resistance to his nearness.

"I'm not anything at all like Trish, Jonus."

"No, you aren't," he agreed quietly. "I met Trish when I was twenty-four, Polly. That was a whole lifetime ago. The fact that you don't remind me of her is a big plus, not a negative. I'm not anything like Brad, am I?"

"No, not at all, although you have some of his same good character traits. You're honest and hardworking, and I think you care about people. But you're also more serious and reserved. Brad was more outgoing and on the happy-go-lucky side."

"I'll work on being less serious and reserved," Jonus promised.

"That wasn't a criticism of you," Polly protested. "I like you the way you are."

"I like you the way you are." He kissed her hair. "I don't expect to ever mean as much to you as Brad did, Polly. I know he'll always have a special place in your heart, just as Trish will always have a special place in mine. But they're both gone, and we're alive." His voice softened, "We're here, together. And I want to kiss you."

He pulled away a small distance, letting her hand go and bringing his up to lay his palm along her cheek. His thumb stroked her lips as he asked huskily, "Can I kiss you?"

"Yes," she whispered and let him turn her head.

His mouth was warm and tender on hers. Polly braced herself against the jolting sweetness. She stayed with her eyes closed for several seconds when the kiss was over, all too soon. Before she could open them, he kissed her eyelids, one cheek and then the other, and finally found her lips again.

He made a sound in his throat and his arms went around her when Polly put hers up around his neck, but he kept the pressure of his mouth gentle and seeking. Her lips clung, giving him all the response he seemed to require. He ended the kiss, as he had the first one, without deepening it.

Polly stifled a sigh of disappointment and opened her eyes to look at him. His face was only inches away. He smiled with a kind of strained humor.

"The reason I left in such a hurry last night was that I didn't trust myself to stay a minute longer and not kiss you."

"I didn't have any suspicion." Polly caressed the rugged plane of his cheek with her fingertips, taking delight in touching him. He closed his eyes. "If you had kissed me like you just did and stopped, I really couldn't have objected too strongly."

She watched her fingers trail along his jaw, aware she was touching him now with a more deliberate intent. He opened his eyes and waited until she met his gaze before he answered.

"If I kiss you any other way, I'll get more aroused than I already am. And I would forget all about my promise not to make love to you until you want to make love with me."

"I had forgotten it." Her admission sounded like an accusation. "You have a great deal of self-control."

"It's not easy for me to keep my hands off your body or my mind off the fact that there's an empty bed in the next room. You're a very sexy woman, without even trying to be."

"I didn't feel very sexy coming in here tonight dressed like this, in a skirt and blouse."

"No?" He glanced down at the V neck of her long-sleeved white blouse. "Do you have any idea how tempting it is to undo that top button? Then if you're wearing a bra that fastens in the front, like you were two nights ago, I could undo it, too."

"I am," Polly breathed. Her nipples were hardening at his words. "I always wear that style because it's so much easier to put on than the ones that fasten in back."

"You have the kind of figure that men undress with their eyes no matter what you're wearing. Last night when you were talking about not wearing clothes well, all I could think about was how much I wanted to take yours off."

"I didn't have any inkling that you were having any trouble."

"Weren't you at all bothered?"

"Yes..."

"All it would take is your permission," Jonus said, softly tempting her. "Words wouldn't even be necessary. You could kiss me and get the message across."

"What if Jennifer wakes up?"

"She was sleeping soundly when I looked in on her right before you came. It was a big day with a lot of excitement for her. If nothing else, just kiss me the way I kissed you. Please." He pleaded with his eyes, as well as his voice.

Polly drew his head to hers and kissed him on the mouth. Then she kissed him on one cheek and then the other, murmuring, "I don't understand why you aren't vain, the way women look you over and smile at you."

"You could do a lot for my ego if you smiled at me a little more often," he answered. "Don't stop. Kiss me some more. And touch my face with your hands, like you did a moment ago. One of these days, if I wait long enough, I'm hoping to feel you touching me everywhere like that."

Polly stroked his jaw with her palm as she pressed her lips to his again before resuming the intimate conversation. "You're a big, tall man." There was a lot of him to touch. "You're very well built."

"You're a big woman, and you're stacked, if you'll pardon the male expression. Kiss me with your tongue, Polly."

His tongue was there, waiting for hers, warm and ardent and ready for the first meeting. His breathing quickened and his arms tightened around her, but he savored the tentative deepening of the kiss. Now they were kissing each other, neither one the aggressor, their lips moistened by their mating tongues, which were flavored with wine.

The pressure increased and the urgency. Polly clasped his head and kissed him back, as he took over and kissed her with passion, bruised the softness of her lips and used his tongue to express his male need to possess her. She welcomed him into her mouth, as hungry for the union as he was.

Jonus ended the kiss abruptly, kissed her again tenderly and then hugged her so tight that Polly's breasts were crushed against his chest. She could feel his heart pounding in hard rhythm with her own. Over the noise of her blood pulsing in her ears, she could hear his labored breathing.

"Help me not go too fast when we make love tonight, Polly," he requested.

She caressed his shoulders and neck, making no promises. His whole body quivered at her touch.

He sat just far enough from her to unbutton her blouse. Polly helped him pull it free of her skirt and let him slide it off her shoulders, revealing her bra and bare stomach. Then he left her on her own to finish removing the blouse.

All his attention was on her breasts. He stroked her cleavage with his fingertips before he dealt with the front closure. Slipping his hands beneath the loosened cups, he fondled her sensitive flesh, capturing the swelling fullness.

"You're so firm and lush," he said, his tone an added stimulation for her.

Polly tipped her head back and closed her eyes with the rush of weak pleasure as he rubbed his palms across her hardened peaks.

"Your hands feel so good…" Before the words were out, his mouth was taking the place of one of his hands, and his free hand was finding its way beneath her skirt.

Her thighs opened a narrow pathway for him. She gasped his name helplessly as he stroked between her thighs and found her feminine cleft, vulnerable to his touch despite the cloth barriers of underwear and panty hose. Polly regretted the protection, longing for him to probe right to the center of her desire.

Jonus withdrew his hand. He kissed her breasts and straightened to a sitting position, clasped her hand and brought her to her feet with him as he stood up. Polly picked up her blouse and bra and, naked to the waist, accompanied him into his bedroom.

The thought that he had shared the bedroom with his wife passed through her mind, but it didn't cool her heated body or awaken her normal modesty. Her bared breasts ached for more of his attention, not to be covered up. The rest of her urgently needed to be exposed and touched by him until she had no physical privacy remaining.

Polly left judgment and moral strength out in the living room. For the moment, nothing else mattered except the intimacy and pleasure he could give her and she could give him. She wanted to see him naked, touch him, kiss him, couple her body with his.

It was sex without love and devotion. They weren't husband and wife or betrothed couple, committed to a life-

time together, but man and woman satisfying a powerful
and mutual physical hunger. The knowledge brought guilt,
but didn't deter her.

Polly was going to have an affair with Jonus. Her moral
convictions simply weren't strong enough for her not to
take him as her lover while the attraction lasted. She would
just have to live with her conscience.

An affair was temporary, not binding.

Jonus led her over to the side of his bed. Standing a few
feet apart, they undressed. The sight of his long, lean-
muscled body excited her so that Polly wasn't self-
conscious taking off her clothes. He stripped off his dark
low-cut briefs as she stepped out of her panties, and they
were naked together.

They moved closer, reaching to touch each other. Jonus
clasped Polly's shoulders and slid his hands down her back
while she laid her palms on his chest and moved them in
small circles. Tonight she could see, as well as feel, the hard
muscular contours of his chest.

"You have a marvelous physique," she complimented,
her voice soft with feminine appreciation. "There isn't an
ounce of flab anywhere on your body."

"I haven't discovered any yet on yours," he replied, caressing her hips and buttocks. "You're all firm, toned
curves, back and front."

Polly stroked his broad shoulders and biceps for the pure
pleasure of it. His hands stopped and his fingers tightened, taking hold of her hips as she dropped her hands to
his taut midriff and then ventured lower.

"Please," he urged and groaned when Polly fondled
him.

He stayed her hands almost immediately, held them in
the act of capturing him, and kissed her with tender passion. "I go weak as a kitten when you touch me down
there," he explained huskily.

"It has an effect on me, too."

Desire flamed in his eyes as he understood her meaning. He put her hands at his waist. Glancing down, he smoothed his palm across her abdomen, slid his fingers down through her dark curly triangle and found her heat and wetness.

"Do you want me inside you, Polly?" he asked, even though he could feel the evidence for himself.

"Yes, Jonus."

His arms came around her, and he hugged her hard against him. She exulted in his strength and in his male need for her.

"I want to satisfy you," he said with a kind of fierce gentleness. "Make you as happy as I can."

As she got into bed with him, Polly tried to place her actions in a realistic framework of wrongdoing. She was having sex with her employer, a man she'd known only a week. The sole purpose was physical gratification.

Jonus was a considerate, skillful lover, she told herself as he kissed and caressed her, in no hurry to have intercourse. This was foreplay, this wonderful touching, growing more and more urgent, building up sexual tension until she was wild for his penetration.

It was erotic that the bedroom wasn't in darkness, and she could see him as he poised himself to enter her, looking down at her body and then into her face and eyes. The fact that she could feel the tremor in his muscles when she grasped his shoulders was responsible for her tender emotion.

"Go ahead..." Polly raised her hips, urging him to plunge into her.

But he entered slowly, joining their bodies gently. She whispered his name in joy, and he kissed her on the lips lingeringly.

"Help me go slower. Let me be inside you longer tonight," he pleaded, his voice low and resonant with a new possessiveness.

"There'll be other nights," Polly said. She writhed under him, setting off rockets of sensation that were all physical, not unendurably sweet. "I was without sex too long, Jonus."

He still tried to set a slower tempo, but Polly urged him with words, with her body and with her responses, to abandon all restraint. His control slipped and he made love to her roughly with all the driving depth and frenzied speed she demanded, taking them both to explosive climax that almost blotted out consciousness.

Polly lay underneath Jonus's lax weight, her arms around him, awash in mindless satisfaction. She murmured a weak sound of protest when she felt him summoning strength to move.

"God, Polly, you're a lot of woman," he marveled as he raised himself. His voice was weak and dazed. "I hope I'm man enough for you."

Polly kept her eyes closed. "How could you have any doubts?"

The warmth of his breath on her face warned her of his intentions, but she couldn't muster her defenses against his kiss. Sweetness flooded through her at the gentle touch of his lips to her eyelids, the tip of her nose, the corners of her mouth.

"Did the precautions you took hold out?" she asked.

"I think so." He didn't sound at all concerned. "It's hard to believe that any kind of birth control would do its job when you and I make love."

Polly opened her eyes. "Maybe you should make sure."

"Is it a big worry for you?"

"Of course it is," she answered quickly and emphatically.

"Then lie very still." He withdrew with care and got up out of bed. Before he went into the bathroom, he pulled the sheet up over her.

The small considerate act destroyed Polly's willpower. She lay there instead of getting up and putting on her clothes. He was soon back and slid under the sheet with her, announcing as he gathered her close in his arms, "I believe we're safe."

"From now on, I'll take responsibility."

"That's fine with me," he agreed readily. "In fact, I would prefer it that way. There's no danger that I'm not healthy, in case you're wondering. In the few instances I've had intercourse in the past two years, I took preventive measures myself, regardless."

"It hadn't even occurred to me to wonder whether there was any danger," Polly confessed. "I've never even related the modern risks of being sexually active to myself, since I didn't have any intention before now of having an affair."

"We can both put those risks out of our minds, thank heaven," Jonus said confidently, hugging her. "I'll be faithful, Polly. You can count on that. I won't have eyes for any other woman. And I know you won't give me any real cause for jealousy."

"All I ask is that you be honest with me and tell me when the time comes you want to break it off."

"Break it off," he repeated, loosening his arms so that he could pull back and search her face. His expression was reproachful. "Neither one of us is the type to take wedding vows that lightly. The words of the marriage ceremony will be just as binding for me the second time I speak them."

"I know they will be, Jonus. If we were to marry, you'd never divorce me, even after it turned out you had made a mistake. And you would be making a mistake. Don't look so hurt," she pleaded. "One day you'll thank me for not saying yes to your marriage proposal. It will be far better for you, as well as for me, if we have the kind of relationship that can be ended. I'll give you advice and help with Jennifer. The three of us can do things together.''

''I should have waited instead of springing all this on you so soon,'' Jonus said in a totally disheartened tone.

Polly didn't answer because she couldn't trust her voice. She had put all her sad conviction into her words and hadn't given him any hope she might change her mind. Yet, to have him accept they had no future together sent a wave of unbearable misery through her.

''It's late,'' she said after they'd lain there awhile in silence. ''I really must go home. Poor Sandy will be waiting to be let out.''

He raised himself up on one elbow, making no effort to delay her. ''I'll get dressed, too, and walk out to your car with you.''

''That's not necessary. I won't be uneasy.''

''Whether it's necessary or not, I want to,'' he replied quietly.

Polly was self-consciously aware of her nudity as they got out of his bed. She began gathering her clothes. The idea of dressing in front of him made her feel shy and awkward.

''May I use your bathroom?'' she asked.

He was putting on his underwear and glanced at her, noting her garments draped over her arm.

''Certainly. There are clean towels. Feel free to take a shower or a bath.''

''Thank you, but I'll just wait until I get home.''

He looked dumbstruck for a moment as it dawned on him that she intended to use his bathroom as a dressing room.

''There's nothing any less graceful than putting on panty hose,'' she declared, embarrassed and defensive.

''I'll be out of your way in just a minute and give you some privacy.'' He picked up his slacks and stepped into them.

Polly watched him, taking pleasure in the whole masculine procedure as he slid up the zipper and fastened his waistband with practiced movements.

"I wasn't waiting for you to leave," she protested when he swiftly gathered up his sweater and shoes and socks and started for the door into the living room, giving her a view of tautly muscled shoulders and back. "Jonus, I didn't mean to run you out of your own bedroom!"

"Don't worry about it," he said. "Take all the time you need. I'll be out here."

Polly sighed. She was sorry now that she had made a production out of getting dressed and gotten the wrong message across. As much as anything else, she regretted that she'd cheated herself out of watching him dress.

Before she went into the living room, she straightened the sheets on his king-size bed and plumped the pillows. On the way to the door, she noticed that a couple of drawers weren't completely closed, one at the top and another at the bottom. Without even stopping to think she obeyed her housewife's instinct and stopped to close them.

Guided by another impulse, she pulled the top drawer open and saw that it contained his underwear, just as she'd expected. He apparently wore primarily dark-colored briefs like those he had on tonight. The bottom drawer probably contained sweaters. Polly dropped to her haunches and pulled it out, too.

She sat back on her heels, registering the discovery that she'd guessed wrong. A radiantly lovely Trish Logan smiled from a framed photograph. Polly lifted it out and saw the photograph underneath, which was a wedding portrait with a younger, smiling, happy Jonus, as heart-stoppingly handsome in his tuxedo as his young bride was beautiful in her long, white gown.

He must have pulled out the drawer earlier tonight and looked at these photographs. Polly's heart ached for him, but the knifelike pain was for herself as she thought of him, gazing at his wife's likeness while he reconciled himself to a future with a different woman.

With her, Polly.

Out in the living room, Jonus sat at the end of the sofa with his back to the bedroom door. As she came out, Polly saw him raise a glass to his lips.

"I'm sorry to take so long," she apologized to alert him to her presence.

"You weren't very long at all," he assured her. "I poured you a glass of apple juice. Come over and sit down. Before you go, I have a matter pertaining to work I'd like to discuss with you."

He sounded calm and friendly. There was nothing in his voice to indicate that he'd been sitting there brooding. Polly took a seat on the sofa, noticing several empty spots on the hors d'oeuvres tray. Whatever disappointment she'd caused him hadn't kept him from snacking while he waited.

"What is it?" she asked.

"I'm going to need someone to oversee the dining room in the middle of the day, to seat people, assign tables and generally be in charge."

Polly stared at him in surprise. "You mean to act as hostess?"

"Yes. You'd be on salary. It would be only eleven until two."

"But I don't see how you could afford to pay me enough," she protested.

"Hear me out. There's more to it. You would also replace Mrs. Allen—give Jennifer her supper and put her to bed at night."

"But you've started having your supper with her."

"I'll continue to do so, unless something comes up. You could have your evening meal with us. That would be one of the job benefits."

"That's still not enough combined hours of work to justify the kind of money I'm earning waiting tables," Polly objected. "Mrs. Allen is just here from six until eight, isn't she?"

"More like eight-thirty or nine. She leaves after she's made sure that Jennifer is fast asleep. Mrs. Allen is dependable, but she isn't in the same category as you," Jonus said soberly. "I won't have any problem justifying the money I'd be paying you. It's hard to put a price on the kind of care you can give Jennifer."

The kind of care a mother can give. That was what he meant, Polly knew. If she wouldn't marry him and be Jennifer's stepmother, he would do the next best thing and hire her as a mother substitute, whatever the cost.

How could she refuse when he was offering her a chance to do what she would love doing?

"I'll have a problem taking any pay at all," she replied. "If it weren't for needing to earn a living, I'd gladly take care of Jennifer for nothing. I would insist on looking after her in the afternoons after she gets home from school."

"You drive a hard bargain," he said with gentle irony. "I just hope you aren't too conscientious and don't tire yourself out so that you don't have any time or energy left over for Jennifer's father. He could use some care and attention, too."

"I'll be at the disposal of Jennifer's father when he wants company. That was an awkward way of saying I don't expect to be too tired," Polly added when he looked pained at her choice of words. She blushed, realizing what she'd said, and picked up her apple juice to take a sip. "Shall I start the new schedule on Monday?"

"Yes. I'd like you to," he answered.

If he had made the slightest overture, slid closer, held out his hand, done anything whatsoever to encourage her, Polly could and would have responded. But he did nothing, and she lacked the courage and the confidence to move closer to him or reach out her hand to touch him, as she longed to do.

Chapter Twelve

Jonus could hear his daughter's voice as he opened the door to his suite.

"...and Mr. Willis had to stop the bus and fuss at Danny Murphy. He told Danny what he needed was a good thrashing. What's a 'thrashing,' Polly?"

"That's an old-fashioned term for spanking, sweetie."

Polly's reply was fully attentive and warm with affection. Jonus closed the door quietly, feeling a familiar yearning in his breast. What he wouldn't give to have her speak to him in that loving tone of voice.

"There. I'm all finished with my homework. See?"

"Very good," Polly said. "All your letters are turned the right way today."

"Now can we play a game?"

"There's time before supper."

So much for his chances of having any of Polly's attention before the three of them sat down to the evening meal. Then he wouldn't get a fair share.

Certainly Jonus was thankful on his little girl's behalf. After a month of Polly's care, Jennifer was a happy, secure child, who didn't want to miss school now. For the past week she'd been catching the bus to and from school, which was a whole new adventure for her.

Polly had taken a load of the parenting responsibility off his shoulders. She didn't just look after Jennifer in the afternoons and early evenings. She took a mother's interest in his daughter's education and health and general welfare.

Things couldn't be working out any better as far as Jennifer was concerned. But Jonus was far from happy with his relationship with Polly. She held him at arm's length and wouldn't let him get close to her. Sometimes he wondered if she would ever have gotten involved with him at all if he hadn't been Jennifer's father.

The more time he spent with her, the hungrier he was for her company. Yet it didn't seem mutual. She never approached him, never voiced the wish to be with him, never initiated intimacy. She didn't even visit him in his office or seek him out on the premises of the lodge unless she had an express purpose.

Jonus was growing more dissatisfied and more discouraged with every passing day. He was sick and tired of carrying on an affair that wasn't bringing them any nearer to the kind of relationship he wanted, one of mutual give-and-take and commitment.

He was starting to doubt that Polly was ever going to let him be important to her, the way he longed to be. She gave him free access to her body, but refused to admit him into her deepest affections.

True to her word, she'd put herself at his disposal. Jonus wanted so much more. He wanted her to *need* him, the way he needed her.

"Oh, hi, Daddy! What are you doing just standing there?" On the way to her room, his daughter had spotted him in the hallway.

"Hi, honey. I was just eavesdropping, in case you two were talking about me," he replied, trying for a light tone and cheerful expression as he entered the living room.

"Jonus. I didn't hear you come in." Polly didn't get up from where she sat on the floor by the low table in front of the sofa.

"I just finished doing my homework, and I'm going to my room to get a game for Polly and me to play." Jennifer gave him a progress report and then observed sympathetically as she headed out again for her bedroom door, "You look all tired out, Daddy."

"Have you had a hard day?" Polly asked, concern in her face and voice.

"No. Busy, but not hard. I'm not tired physically."

"The forecast is for more snow tonight," she reminded. "You must be glad about that."

"The weather couldn't be more cooperative. The trails already have a good base after the heavy snowfall we had last week." There had been snow on the ground for Thanksgiving.

"This year you aren't even having a lull. Karen says that answering the phone and booking reservations is a full-time job."

"Business couldn't be better." But Jonus didn't want to waste his one or two minutes with her, before his daughter came back, chatting about business. "I missed seeing you today. Or actually I did see you, through my office window when you were leaving after lunch," he added. "Were you in a big hurry to get somewhere?"

"No. I was just going home to do a few things there."

"Why didn't you come in and say hello? Didn't Karen mention I was back from Montpelier?"

Polly nodded. "She said you had just walked in. You'd been gone all morning, and I hated to barge in and interrupt you at whatever you were doing. According to her, you weren't in the best mood," she added hesitantly and gazed down at her hands in her lap. "All your employees can see that you have something on your mind. It puts me in a very awkward position, Jonus, that they think you're upset because Dr. Carver came with someone last week. Of course, they don't say that outright, out of consideration for me."

"You know they're jumping to the wrong conclusion, though," Jonus pointed out. "I told you weeks ago that I encouraged Sandra to bring a man friend with her."

"Yes, you did tell me that." She sighed.

"Do you want to play with us, Daddy?" Jennifer invited as she emerged from her bedroom, carrying a game in a cardboard box.

Jonus had to control a surge of frustration at the interruption. "No, I don't want to play a game right now," he stated. "What I'd like—"

"Your daddy would like some peace and quiet," Polly explained, rising swiftly to her feet. "We'll play in your bedroom, sweetie."

What I'd like, Jennifer, is for you to entertain yourself until supper and give Polly and me a few minutes together. Jonus mentally finished his sentence in the empty living room and walked with slumped shoulders into his own bedroom.

If he'd had the slightest confidence his words would have met with any heartfelt support from Polly, he would have asserted his authority. But he knew she was where she preferred to be.

Given the choice between catering to his daughter's needs and his needs, there was no contest. The reason was very simple. She loved his little girl, and she didn't love him.

She cared about him. He was sure of that, also sure that she was strongly attracted to him physically. But he didn't bring out the wife in her the way Jennifer brought out the mother.

Perhaps he never would. As disheartening as that thought was, Jonus still craved a husband's privileges. He wanted to share a bedroom and bathroom with her. He wanted to sleep with her all night and wake up with her the next morning, not just make love and then get up and go home or send her home. He wanted her to wear his wedding ring on her finger, take his name, become Mrs. Jonus Logan.

Jonus wanted to be a married man again. His patience was gone, and he wasn't going to let male pride stand in his way. Tonight he was going to propose to Polly for the second time and word his proposal in a way she couldn't refuse: *Marry me, and be Jennifer's stepmother.*

He laid the groundwork during supper, by bringing up the subject of Christmas. They were on their dessert. Jennifer couldn't have cooperated better if she'd been coached, commenting on the necessity for putting up two Christmas trees and two sets of decorations, at their suite and at Polly's chalet.

"Otherwise, Sandy and Precious won't get to enjoy Christmas," she pointed out. "We'll have to hang stockings for them with their names on them."

Polly agreed indulgently to hang stockings for her pets. "We'll hang a stocking for you, too," she suggested. "Then Santa will know to leave some presents for you at my house, as well as here."

"What about your stocking and Daddy's?" Jennifer asked, her smooth brow knitting into a frown. "His will be here and yours will be at your house?"

"I probably won't hang a stocking for myself," Polly said evasively. "Santa will be sending me presents through the mail."

"There will be presents under our tree for you from Jennifer and me," Jonus said, giving his daughter more to mull over.

"Will you have a present for Daddy under your tree, Polly?"

"I'm sure I will."

Jennifer sighed, working out the logistics in her mind. "It would be better if we had all the presents under one tree and could wake up on Christmas morning and open them at one time. It's not going to be very much fun, Daddy, with you and me waking up here and Polly waking up at her house."

"No, it won't be nearly as much fun as the three of us waking up in the same place," he agreed, and met Polly's troubled gaze.

"You mean the five of us, counting Sandy and Precious," Jennifer corrected him. "Couldn't we leave a note for Santa here to leave all my presents at Polly's house? Then we could spend the night with her. You could sleep on the couch, Daddy, and I could sleep in her bed with her."

"Polly's couch is not quite long enough for me," Jonus objected mildly to his daughter's sleeping arrangements.

"A better solution would be for me to stay overnight here Christmas Eve," Polly spoke up. "You have an extra bed in your bedroom," she reminded Jennifer, who glanced over at her father.

"Daddy doesn't like that idea, either," the little girl noted.

"Polly and I will work something out before Christmas," Jonus promised.

Jennifer looked to Polly for confirmation.

"Christmas is a whole month away, too long off to worry about," Polly reassured in a hollow tone. Her forced smile faded from her lips as she looked at Jonus.

He directed his quiet reply to her. "It will be here before we know it. Holidays have a way of creeping up on us,

whether we're ready for them or not. This year I'd like for
Jennifer to have a very special Christmas.''

"This year you won't be so sad at Christmas, huh,
Daddy?'' Jennifer suggested, picking up on the serious
undercurrents. "You won't miss Mommy as much because
Polly will be having Christmas with us.''

"No, I won't be so sad,'' Jonus answered, a note of sadness in his voice because he was telling the truth. "But
that's not to say I won't think about your mommy during
the Christmas holidays, just like Polly will think about her
little girl and her little girl's father. None of us wants to
forget our loved ones that we've lost, but life goes on, and
we can't stay sad. We have to try to be happy. I'm sure Polly
agrees with me.''

"What your father says is true.'' Polly's voice had the
same undertone of regret as his.

Jennifer looked from one of them to the other and confessed guiltily, "I feel happy most all the time, even though
I do still miss Mommy. I kiss her picture every night before I get into bed, don't I, Polly?''

"Yes, you do, sweetie.''

"Your mommy would want you to be a happy little girl.''
Jonus reached over and squeezed her shoulder, and she
reached up and patted his hand.

"She would want you to be happy like you used to be,
too, wouldn't she, Daddy? And Polly's little girl and her
little girl's daddy would want her to be happy.''

"That's the way I see it, honey,'' he said.

His reply seemed to satisfy her. She dipped her spoon
into her dish of melting ice cream.

"You haven't told your father that you're going to be in
a Christmas play at school.'' Polly changed the subject,
focusing attention upon his daughter, and they all three
finished eating their dessert.

After supper Jonus went downstairs, following his usual
routine, but tonight his only purpose in leaving his suite was

to kill the hour before Jennifer's bedtime. He didn't want to delay it by staying. Now that he'd made up his mind to propose to Polly again, he couldn't think about anything else.

The dining room and lounge would just have to operate without his supervision this evening. Jonus was going to be delegating more of his management duties to employees in the future as he became more of a family man.

He wished he could propose to Polly in a setting where there were no associations with the past for either of them. At her chalet her dog and cat were living reminders of her husband and child, in addition to the photographs and possessions she had brought with her from Illinois. His suite bore the mark of Trish's personality and taste. Polly was never completely comfortable there, he sensed.

But it was the obvious best choice because Jennifer's presence would be felt strongly. Asleep in her bedroom, Jonus's daughter would apply stronger persuasion for Polly to marry him than Jonus alone could, in the most romantic setting with music and candlelight.

Even if a big snowstorm weren't in the forecast, taking Polly out somewhere neither of them had ever been to make the occasion special and memorable wouldn't have worked in his favor. The knowledge did nothing to boost his masculine confidence, but it didn't weaken his resolve.

At eight o'clock he took the stairs two at a time back up to the suite. The physical exertion wasn't responsible for his rapid heartbeat. He was nervous.

"Come in, Daddy," Jennifer invited when he stuck his head in her bedroom door. He saw that she was snuggled under the covers with Polly seated on the edge of her bed, holding a storybook in her lap. "Polly was just about to read me a story."

"Maybe your father would like to read to you, instead," Polly suggested as Jonus came to stand by her. She made a move to get up. He put a hand on her shoulder to stop her and left it there, after she had submitted instantly to his touch.

"Do you want to read to me, Daddy? It's a real good story. I think you'd like it," his daughter cajoled.

"I can tell by the cover it's my kind of story," he remarked teasingly. "I'll read if Polly will turn the pages for me and tell me all the words I don't know."

"She will, won't you, Polly?"

"Your father doesn't need me to tell him any words," Polly objected, opening up the book to the first page. "He has a college degree."

"Daddy was just being silly," Jennifer explained complacently while Jonus sat down next to Polly and looked over her shoulder. "He said that so you would stay, too, while he reads to me. Go ahead, Daddy."

She sighed so happily and smiled such a sweet, angelic smile at both of them that Jonus vowed to be around at bedtime more often from then on.

He pretended to falter over words on the first couple of pages. His daughter prompted him in each instance. She knew the story by heart.

Her eyelids were drooping by the time he read the concluding sentence, but she requested drowsily, "Now would you read it, Polly?"

"No, it's time for little girls to go to sleep," Polly told her tenderly and leaned over to kiss her on the cheek. "Sweet dreams."

Jennifer's small arms wrapped around her neck. "Good night, Polly. I love you." The words of love came with a sweet childlike confidence that they would be spoken in return.

"I love you, too, sweetie. Have a good day at school tomorrow."

Polly would have left the room, but Jonus reached for her hand and held it to detain her while he bent over and kissed his daughter good night, saying huskily, "I love you, baby."

"I love you, Daddy."

As he made his exit hand in hand with Polly, Jonus's glance fell on the framed picture of Jennifer and her mother. He hadn't even noticed it upon entering nor once thought about Trish during the whole bedtime scene.

The realization gave an added poignancy to the emotion that already overflowed his heart.

Before drawing the door closed, he turned off the lights, darkening the room except for the faint illumination from the ballerina lamp. Tonight the sight of the graceful little figurine didn't touch off despair, but rather a deep, humble gratitude that life could be full and rich with meaning, in spite of tragedy.

"Has it started snowing yet?" Polly asked when they were in the living room.

"It hadn't when I came up." Jonus's tone was low and distracted because he didn't want to carry on mundane conversation. He wanted to share with her his sense of being a fortunate man. He put his arm around her shoulders and steered her toward the sofa.

Her steps lagged, but she didn't resist. "I thought perhaps it had started coming down heavily and you came up to suggest I go home early to be on the safe side."

"I came up because I wanted to talk to you about something too important to put off another minute." It disappointed him that her thoughts weren't in harmony with his. "I was hoping you'd already read to Jennifer and tucked her in," he confessed.

"You didn't mention earlier that you wanted to have a talk as soon as she'd gone to bed. As a matter of fact, you didn't give me any hint about wanting to see me later tonight."

"I guess I took it for granted that you knew I'd want to see you. It's what I want every night. The question is whether you want to spend time alone with me."

"When have I ever refused?"

"When have you ever shown any enthusiasm? You're like a wife doing her duty, only that's not a very good comparison. For God's sake, Polly, I didn't come up here to fight with you!" Jonus broke off. The necessity for keeping his voice low only added to his exasperation.

She sighed. "I think I know what you came up to talk about, Jonus, but I wasn't under the impression that it was an urgent matter."

"It is for me," he replied. "I want things settled between us."

"Then let's sit down and settle them," Polly suggested unhappily.

She let him seat her on the sofa. Jonus sat next to her and took her hand. He drew a deep breath, struggling to cope with his sense of rejection.

"If I wasn't so certain that what I want is good for you, too, I wouldn't persist," he told her. "Goodness knows you haven't given me any encouragement."

"That's only because I'm not certain you're ready to make important decisions. You may regret them."

"What I regret more than anything else at the moment is that this is going so damned badly. Here's what I've been rehearsing for the past hour to say to you: Jennifer needs a stable home with two parents who love her and care about each other. I know you love my daughter, Polly, and I think you care about me." It took all of Jonus's courage to pause and let her answer.

"Yes, I do." She spoke the words unhesitatingly and gave his hand a little squeeze.

He went on, still giving his prepared speech because he was so deeply disheartened by her gentle note. "I care a great deal about you, Polly. I want you to be my wife and

Jennifer's stepmother. I want the three of us to be a family."

She nodded and mustered a wan, understanding smile. "Yes, I know."

Jonus pleaded, ad lib, gripping her hand, "Jennifer and I both need you, and you need us. I'm not asking you to forget your little girl or her father or give up any of your memories. All I'm asking is for you to be a permanent part of our lives. Please marry me."

She swallowed hard. "I would be very proud to be your wife, Jonus. And I'd like nothing more in the world than to be Jennifer's stepmother."

Elation welled up in him, crowding out the regret that her words of acceptance were spoken with a kind of resignation.

"We'll be married right away," he declared, taking her into his arms and hugging her. "Try to be a little happy," he urged. "We're both making the right decision."

"I hope we are," she said in a strangled voice.

Jonus touched his hand to her cheek and was dismayed to find it wet with tears. "You're crying," he accused softly.

"I'm terribly sorry, Jonus. Please don't feel bad."

He held her tight. His only source of hope seemed to lie in the strength of her arms around him, hugging him back. "Everything's going to work out. You'll see."

"I'll try to be a good wife for you, within my limitations," she choked out.

"I'll be the best husband I possibly can," Jonus promised heavily. "Jennifer is going to be thrilled when we tell her." He'd brought up his daughter as a way of offering what consolation he could.

"Yes, I think she will be."

"Aside from having you as her stepmother, she's going to love having a couple of pets. We can furnish your loft bedroom for her." He waited a moment for some reaction. When there was none, he went on, "It seems like the best temporary solution—for Jennifer and me to move in with you. We'll have this apartment for our use, too. We can kind of live between both places. I'll keep the majority of my clothes and personal things here. I realize you don't have a lot of extra space.''

''I could make room, but you'd want to keep this apartment, anyway. You'd never be able to rent it to strangers.''

To his relief, the flow of tears had been staunched. Jonus could tell by her voice that she had her emotions under control.

''It would be difficult,'' he admitted honestly. ''But I figure that I can justify keeping it. We'll want private quarters on the lodge premises, for convenience. There may be times when we find it easier to entertain here rather than in our home.''

Polly took a ragged breath and was silent. Jonus didn't elaborate. At the moment he didn't dare bring up the possibility that they might decide to have children, in which case their home was likely to be strewn with toys and evidence that a family lived there. She might not always feel like having the house presentable for company and might welcome just relaxing and playing hostess without doing any of the work and preparation involved in serving guests food and drink.

''Let's discuss wedding plans,'' he suggested, sitting back and nestling her in the circle of his arm with his cheek resting on her head. ''Would you like to have a simple church wedding?''

''You mean invite people to attend?'' she asked.

''I assumed you would want to invite at least a few people. Not send out engraved invitations or anything like that. What do you have in mind?''

''All that's necessary is a private ceremony with the two of us and Jennifer present. She and I will have to go shopping and buy her a cute little dress.''

It was the first glimmer of any anticipation.

"You and I will have to make a shopping trip to a jewelry store," he ventured.

"Just a plain gold band is fine. I can tell you my ring size."

"And I could tell you mine," he agreed, trying not to sound offended. "But I thought it might be nice if we went together and picked out matching wedding rings."

She was quiet a moment before she said hesitantly, "Not all men like to wear wedding rings. I hope you don't feel obligated."

"Doesn't it matter to you if I wear one?" Jonus was wounded to the core that she apparently didn't care if other women knew he wasn't free and available.

"Of course, it matters. I'm sorry if I said that wrong and hurt your feelings." Polly reached up and touched his cheek in apology. "I just wanted you to know that I'd understand if the idea was too painful. I'd trust you just as much."

"What kind of man would I be if I expected you to do something I wasn't willing to do myself?"

"I wasn't questioning whether you're willing." Polly sighed. "We'll go together and pick out rings."

"We'll choose rings that are entirely different from what we had before. I've seen yours." She had stopped wearing her wide yellow gold band a month ago.

"I've seen yours, in your wedding picture. I looked at it once," she confessed. "The drawer was partially open. You and Trish must have had a big, beautiful wedding."

"We did. What about you and Brad?" Jonus's vision of Polly in a white gown, looking radiantly happy, made him tender and wistful.

"We had a lovely church wedding. Probably nothing as fancy as yours."

"More than half the guests at my wedding were total strangers to me," he recalled and stifled a sigh. This was the last conversation he wanted to be having right now. "You do want to have a minister perform our marriage ceremony?''

"Yes, I don't think I would feel right, not having a minister.''

"I feel the same way. I prefer the straight Biblical version, too."

"So do I."

"Good. We have that settled. Now we just need to arrange time and place with the pastor of a local church. I'm thinking along the lines of having a wedding party here and inviting employees and their spouses. That way you'd get to meet all the people who work for me."

"It's going to come as a big surprise to everyone that you're marrying me," was her only response to that. "But they'll be able to figure out the reason pretty easily—that you need a mother for Jennifer."

"They would have to be blind to think that was the only reason," Jonus replied, pressing his lips to her hair. He went on, "We don't have to have a wedding cake or follow all the traditional rituals. But we can make it a festive occasion, with champagne and live music for dancing."

"It doesn't sound as though you're planning to include children."

"I had in mind more of an adult celebration," Jonus admitted. "Jennifer could come for a little while. She wouldn't be totally excluded, if you're worried about that."

"I'm afraid she would feel left out. Wouldn't it be better for the three of us to have our own quiet celebration? We might give the impression we were trying too hard. And you're into the busy season. The lodge is full of guests. You can't close down operation."

"It could have been worked out," he said quietly. "But there's no point, if you'd rather just skip the whole thing. I don't suppose you'd be in favor of a honeymoon, either, unless we take Jennifer along."

"Jonus, we don't have to go through the motions and put up a front for the outside world."

"If we don't both have our hearts in whatever plans we make, it'll all be pretty empty," he agreed, giving up.

They sat awhile in silence.

"We have so little control over what happens to us in life," Polly reflected. "I never intended to marry again, never intended to become deeply attached to anyone who didn't already have a place in my heart. I put distance between myself and the people I cared about and came here to Vermont to start over again. Then I walked through the front door of this lodge, and Jennifer was coming down the stairs. She walked right into my heart. Then you opened your office door, and there was no chance I could not get involved with you, if you wanted and needed me."

"And I did want you and need you, Polly," Jonus said softly. "In my bed, in my life. Why didn't you have a chance of not getting involved with me?"

"It must have been obvious the kind of effect you had on me right from the start."

"No, tell me exactly how you reacted that first day," he coaxed.

"My knees actually went weak," Polly recalled. "I was aware of my body."

"Your breasts, you mean?" Jonus caressed a firm, full breast through the bulk of her sweater.

"Yes. And my hips and thighs. I felt like I did when I was a teenager and suddenly filled out. When you looked at me, I wished I had taken more pains with my appearance."

"I didn't guess any of that was going on," Jonus said in a pleased tone. "You wore a brown plaid skirt and a brown blazer, I remember. I could see that you had a full figure, but I didn't realize you were as shapely as you are until that first evening, when you wore red slacks to work and didn't have on a jacket."

"You made me terribly self-conscious."

"Did I? I tried not to stare, but I couldn't keep my eyes off you. I still have that problem when you're anywhere near. Haven't you noticed?"

"All you have to do is look at me, even when there are people around, and I'm ready to go straight to the nearest bedroom with you," she confessed ruefully.

"Does that work at close range when nobody's around?"

"You know very well it does."

She let him turn her in his arms so that their faces were just inches apart.

"I must look a mess," she said. "Are my eyes red?"

"Your eyes are soft and brown and pretty." Jonus kissed one tearstained cheek and then the other, and pulled away a little to see that her eyes had closed. She tipped her head back slightly, and her arms went up around his neck. They tightened when he kissed her tenderly on the mouth. "I want to make love with you," he murmured against her lips. "Are you interested?"

"Yes, of course I am."

"But I'd like to hear it."

Her lashes lifted slowly. "I want you, Jonus."

"I'm all yours." He kissed her with tender passion before he urged, "Feel free to tell me that often and also to seduce me any time the need arises. You won't have to go to much effort."

"I'm never sure whether you're in the mood."

"That goes two ways. I can use a hint myself."

"All you have to do is kiss me and touch me. Sometimes just speak to me in a certain tone of voice that says you're thinking about making love."

"Those techniques would work for you, too," he assured her. "Just for the sake of practice, why don't you try them out now, when there isn't any doubt I'm in the mood."

"Where shall I touch you?" she asked, stroking his cheek with her fingertips and delicately arousing pleasure.

"Anywhere. From the top of my head right down to my toes."

"That's a lot of territory."

"We have all night. I don't intend to send you home." Jonus meant for her to sleep with him.

"You don't intend to go back downstairs later?"

"No. It would take a major emergency to rate any attention from me tonight. So take your time."

She combed her fingers through his hair as she commented, "You hair is a sandy color in the daylight, but in artificial light, it's almost blond. It always looks so clean."

"I shampoo it every day in the shower," he explained, inordinately pleased at the feminine approval in her voice.

"Then you comb it and let it dry. You don't use a hair dryer."

"How did you know that?"

"I can tell. I have a prejudice against men looking like they just came from an appointment with the hairstylist," she confessed.

"I go to a barber."

"You shave with a hand razor, too, don't you?" She caressed his jaw and chin. "Every now and then you nick yourself."

"My mind is usually on something else, and I get in too big a hurry," Jonus admitted. "When we're married and sharing a bathroom, I'll have a whole different problem paying attention to what I'm doing."

"You're so handsome in your clothes. They fit like they were made especially for you."

Jonus's shoulders felt too broad for his jacket as she smoothed her hands over the tweed material. His chest swelled and became rock-hard sensitive muscle beneath his knit turtleneck shirt as she moved down to rub the whole expanse with her palms and fingertips.

"I buy the majority of them mail order from catalogs that have sizes for tall men," he disclosed, shrugging out of the jacket and tossing it away. "Even shoes and boots. Right now my male ego is so big from all these compliments that I may need a larger size. Especially slacks."

Her downward glance was a powerful stimulation in itself. Jonus groaned softly as she moved her hand down and made an intimate, thorough exploration. He swelled and hardened more under her touch.

"You see what you can do to me with just your hands and your voice. Imagine how you could arouse me if you kissed your way down my body," he said. "If you aren't disgusted by the idea."

"You must know that nothing about having sex with you disgusts me," Polly chided. "If I don't do something, it's out of shyness or selfishness. I enjoy everything that you do to me."

"Don't ever be shy," Jonus urged. "And don't assume that I know what you're thinking and feeling. *Tell* me with words. It'll make our lovemaking even better than it already is."

"At this moment I'm wondering how to get you into your bedroom and undressed."

"That's easy. Take me by the hand and lead me in there. Then undress me with my help. And it's soon going to be *our* bedroom, not *my* bedroom," he reminded her.

She stood up, holding out her hand. He clasped it and got to his feet.

"I hope you're looking forward to being married again just half as much I am," he said, accompanying her.

"It's going to take some getting used to," she replied.

"Not for me. I'm one of those men who was meant to be a family man, not a bachelor."

"And I was meant to be an ordinary homemaker and a mother."

"There's nothing ordinary about you, Polly. You're a very special woman." Jonus squeezed her hand as he spoke from the heart.

"A very lucky woman, for sure," she said fervently, but with no joy.

"I'm the one who's lucky," he insisted in a hollow voice.

They reached the side of his bed and went into one another's arms. Jonus hugged her tight and clung to blind faith that the time would come when she would feel glad as well as fortunate, being his wife.

Chapter Thirteen

Polly dawdled over every stage of getting dressed for her wedding, but she was ready with time to spare—time for her stomach to twist into tighter knots. Her reflection in the full-length mirror on her closet door told her she hadn't accomplished any miracle.

Jonus wasn't going to be bowled over when he came with Jennifer to pick her up. He'd never guess that she'd agonized over putting together her outfit, tried on dozens of dresses and suits before settling on her powder-blue suit and visited every shoe store in Burlington and Montpelier in search of just the right shoes before buying a pair of simple navy pumps with medium heels.

Her pearl earrings were pretty, but not unique or eye-catching. After hours of bending over showcases with the latest in good costume jewelry, she'd chosen them because she simply lacked the courage to gamble on more stylish, dramatic accessories.

There was too much risk in trying to be elegant and missing the mark. She was better off being safe and simply looking nice. Nothing wouldn't really change if she did succeed in transforming herself, anyway.

Jonus was marrying her because Jennifer needed a mother and he needed a companion. No woman could ever mean as much to him as his first wife had. No woman could ever compare to Trish in his eyes, certainly not Polly, even at her most attractive.

He was making a valiant effort to put his heart into remarrying and forming a new family unit, but he couldn't always hide his feelings. Polly knew that he had his low moments and attacks of uncertainty. A shadow would cross his face, and he would stifle a sigh.

But he was convinced he was doing the right thing for the three of them—Jennifer and Polly and himself. Polly's doubts were as strong as they had been when she'd managed to refuse him the first time he'd asked her to be his wife. Refusing a second time hadn't been in her power.

After a month of being intimate with him and being a daily part of his life and Jennifer's, she couldn't bear the thought of ever breaking off with him or of giving up her role of mothering his little girl.

Polly loved them both, father and daughter.

With a last glance in the mirror, she went into the living room to wait with her pets.

"Everything's going to be fine, Precious," she crooned to the cat who got up from her favorite spot and came over to sit on Polly's lap. "Just don't pick the threads on my skirt." As she stroked the cat she looked at Sandy. "You sense something's happening, don't you, old guy?" she said in the tone of voice she reserved for the collie, as she patted his head with her other hand. "Don't either one of you worry. Nobody's going to forget about you two, despite all these changes going on."

Polly blinked away a glaze of tears, glad suddenly for the opportunity to sit there with her two animals and be comforted by their presence. In another hour she would be giving up her identity of the past three years, which had been forced upon her.

She would no longer be Polly Dearing, widow and bereaved mother, but Polly Logan, wife and stepmother.

In the transition she would be gaining so much, but stepping into a future without a safety net. Everything that made life worth living could be snatched away from her again in an instant.

Polly was going against all the wisdom of sad experience. But there was no going back to being the same woman who had moved to Vermont.

Her memories weren't enough now to absorb all the loneliness. Despite the fear of tragedy and her insecurities, she couldn't deny herself a measure of happiness.

Jonus would be a faithful, conscientious husband. He cared about her and adored Jennifer. He and Polly were compatible. They would both work hard at their marriage and come to depend on each other. With time they would have a comfortable relationship, each giving what they could and not expecting more.

Polly relaxed, feeling her nerves unwind as she took an optimistic view. By the time she heard Jonus's car outside, she had reached a state of serenity. With his arrival, though, she was seized by fresh anxiety about her appearance.

He was wearing a handsome topcoat, not a bulky down-filled parka or a rugged three-quarter-length jacket, as she was used to seeing him wear.

"You look so distinguished I hardly recognize you," she said, glad for the confusion of her pets milling around and Jennifer trying to greet them and command Polly's attention simultaneously.

"You look very pretty."

"You're even wearing a tie."

He opened up his coat to reveal a dark suit. "And a brand-new suit."

"It's very good-looking." *He* was incredibly good-looking.

"I couldn't let you two gals outdo me."

"You have to put a ribbon in my hair to match my dress," Jennifer reminded her.

"That's right, I do. Let's slip off your coat."

Polly tried to cover up her reluctance to shift her attention from him. As she marshaled the child into the bathroom to fix her hair, she was having serious mixed feelings about making her and Jonus's wedding such a plain, totally private affair, with just the minister and his wife. The only concession to traditional pomp and ceremony was having Jennifer hold a little satin pillow with both their rings.

Was it possible Jonus would have liked a church wedding with invited guests? Polly had assumed he'd raised the idea purely out of consideration for her feelings.

"Daddy has corsages for you and me and the other lady, and a flower for himself," Jennifer disclosed as she stood in front of the bathroom vanity, holding her head very still.

"He does? How sweet of him," Polly murmured, touched and yet dismayed that he had gone to the trouble. He had known that the only flowers she'd ordered was a bouquet arrangement for the church, which would be left there for Sunday services the following day. Was it just a considerate gesture on his part to provide a more festive touch? Or was he trying to remedy her failure?

Jonus had slipped off his topcoat and leather gloves while he waited. He brought a blush to his daughter's cheeks when he declared his fatherly admiration for her hairstyle.

"She does look adorable, doesn't she? I'm almost sorry now that there won't be a churchful of people to see her," Polly lamented. "I probably should have gone to more trouble and planned something a little more elaborate."

"There will be lots of other times when we can show her off," he pointed out.

"We should at least take her picture. I didn't even give photos a thought." Polly put all of her growing distress into the admission. "There's a roll of film in my Instamatic camera, but the flash battery may not be strong enough for indoor shots."

"I brought my camera. We'll take pictures at the church."

"I'm so glad you thought to bring it." Polly couldn't keep her bottom lip from quivering.

"Photography used to be a hobby of mine. And it's not every day that I get married."

"Those nature photographs at the lodge—are they yours?"

"Most of them are," he admitted.

"They're so professional," she marveled in a hollow voice. "I just assumed they came from a gallery. You're a man of many talents."

"Daddy was always taking pictures of Mommy and me," Jennifer chimed in. She had been following the conversation.

Jonus winced. His swift glance at Polly was eloquent with apology. "I kept a camera handy and loaded. You were such a little ham, Jennifer. Always ready to pose," he recalled. "Well, are we ready to go? We don't want to keep the minister waiting."

"Will you take lots of pictures of all of us today, Daddy?" his daughter requested as she put on her coat with Polly's help. "Because I'd like to have some."

Polly's heart sank. She could guess why Jennifer wanted her own snapshots—to put in her photo album. "I'll be very careful putting the hood of your coat up so as not to muss your hair," she promised brightly in an attempt to sidetrack the little girl.

"And I'll hold my head real straight. Will you, Daddy, so I can have some?"

"Sure, honey. I have several rolls of film." Jonus was holding Polly's coat to help her on with it. "The only problem is, I can't operate the camera and be in some of the pictures, too. Reverend Wilkerson has assured me, though, that he's a competent photographer." He buttoned up her coat for her solicitously as he added, his voice gentling, "I'll just have to take him at his word. Hopefully we'll get the kind of pictures I want, where we all look happy at becoming a family."

"We have to smile, huh? Like this."

Jennifer fixed a wide, phony smile on her face and held it. Polly welcomed the rush of tender amusement.

"More like the way Polly is smiling at you right now," Jonus said. His tone was almost wistful.

"I'm not at all photogenic," Polly warned as he escorted them out the door.

"That's hard to believe," he replied skeptically. "You're so natural and expressive. I'll bet I can take some great candid shots of you, especially if you're not aware there's a camera trained on you."

"Just the thought makes me self-conscious."

"It shouldn't. I will be admiring what I see through the camera's eye."

"I guess everybody hopes they'll look better in pictures than they look in the mirror."

"We're going to have to check your reflection together later on tonight," Jonus commented. "Either you're getting a distorted view in your mirror or you're overly humble."

Polly's heartbeat quickened at his intimate implication. Before she could answer, Jennifer inquired, "What does 'distorted' mean?"

Jonus patiently defined the word.

After they were in the car, Jennifer resumed the subject of taking pictures to commemorate the day. "When we get back and before we change out of our good clothes, we'll have to take some pictures of us with Sandy and Precious. Then Polly can get some little frames and put them on her mantel, too. There's lots of room."

"She might like to have a picture of you up there," her father said, shooting a compassionate glance at Polly. "Or she may just prefer putting all the pictures in an album."

"I'm going to put mine in my album," Jennifer announced. "I have empty pages."

It was Polly's turn to look at him with compassion.

"That's a good idea, honey," he encouraged quietly.

Polly searched her mind for a safe topic of conversation. "Precious was up in your bedroom today, looking around. You may wake up tomorrow morning and find her sleeping on the foot of your bed," she warned the little girl, knowing that the prediction would delight her.

The diversion worked, and Jennifer chattered excitedly about spending the night in her new bedroom.

"Can I stay up later tonight, since it's Saturday?" she asked. "We can all watch TV and eat popcorn. I can sit in the middle on the sofa and hold the bowl. Doesn't that sound like fun?"

Polly decided to let Jonus answer, but he apparently had decided to let *her* answer. She blushed as the silence hung there awkwardly.

"It'll be late," they said together and then both deferred to each other again.

"You'll be getting to bed later than usual, as it is," Jonus spoke up. "By the time we drive to Burlington, have dinner and drive home again to Polly's, we'll all be ready to call it a night."

Polly remembered his comment the evening he had proposed. *I don't suppose you'd be in favor of a honeymoon, either, unless we take Jennifer along.* As much as she loved the little girl, the thought of a different kind of wedding night filled her with longing, especially when she considered that he might have wanted them to get away together.

"You get to sleep with Polly." Jennifer's observation was half-complaining.

"Yes, I do," he confirmed. "That's the way it works. Husbands get to sleep with their wives."

"And with their stepwives?"

"Polly isn't going to be my stepwife, honey. There's no such word," Jonus explained.

"Why isn't there? If she's going to be my stepmother, and I'm going to be her stepdaughter, it seems like she would be your stepwife."

He glanced helplessly at Polly. "It may seem that way, but the fact is that I'll be her husband and she'll be my wife."

"You mean, the same as Mommy was?"

While he was searching for an answer that was both truthful and spared Polly's feelings, Polly answered for him. "Your mommy was your daddy's first wife, and I'm his second wife."

"And he's your second husband." The little girl persisted in establishing labels for all the relationships.

"That's correct."

"You know what's really nice?"

Jonus and Polly both tensed for still worse to come.

"That I get to go to my daddy's wedding this time. I wasn't even born when he and Mommy got married."

"You get to *be* in his wedding. You're the ring bearer, remember." Polly could hear her own bleakness beneath the thin veneer of enthusiasm.

"I certainly hope you don't drop the rings," Jonus told his daughter heavily, drawing a deep breath and releasing it in an audible sigh.

"I won't, Daddy. Don't worry," Jennifer assured him.

At the church the Reverend Wilkerson met them with an apology. He had been called to the home of an invalid member of his congregation who had passed away during the day. In carrying out his ministerial duties and comforting the family, he had neglected to turn on the heat in the sanctuary well enough in advance. It was icy cold. He suggested that he perform the marriage ceremony either in his office at the church, which warmed up more quickly, or repair to the parsonage next door.

It wasn't Polly's fault, but she had never felt like more of a failure. Jonus had left planning their wedding up to her. She had done a poor-enough job of it without this happening.

"What would you rather do?" he asked her.

Both alternatives were so unsatisfactory that she shook her head and said miserably, "You decide."

He hesitated only a second before turning to the minister. "We still prefer having the ceremony in the church. If it's too cold to take our coats off, then we'll just have to keep them on."

Polly had all she could do to keep from bursting into tears when he pinned her corsage on her coat lapel, kissed her gently on the cheek and murmured for her ears only, "Come on, sweetheart, it's not that tragic. Think of the good story this will make twenty years from now."

"I feel so terrible," she murmured back, blinking furiously. Her emotion was suddenly much more complicated. He had never used any endearment before with her.

"You aren't to blame. Let's see a smile on that pretty face."

Polly smiled at him tremulously. "You're a wonderful man, Jonus."

"Now that's the picture I'd like to snap," he said.

The church was one of those small New England churches common to villages and towns in Vermont. Painted white, it had a steeple. The interior was severely plain with old-fashioned pews, which generations of worshipers had sat on.

Polly had attended services there, and even filled with people, the church had a reverent atmosphere. The sense that it was God's house, a place for people to gather and put aside worldly concerns and nurture the spiritual side of themselves, pervaded. It was a setting where a man and a woman saying wedding vows could feel they were truly sealing an eternal contract.

As she stood next to Jonus, facing the minister, and holding Jonus's gloved hand, nothing mattered except the words of the marriage ceremony and the meaning behind them. Her voice and Jonus's resonated with awareness of the binding commitment of the promises they were making. It was totally irrelevant whether there were three witnesses or three thousand.

When the time came for Jonus to put his ring on her finger, the moment was no less solemn and significant because of the necessity for removing her leather glove. If anything, quite the opposite was true, because he removed it himself and then drew it back on her hand solicitously. Polly did the same, baring his hand, sliding on the ring, and then replacing his glove. The symbolism was all the sweeter because it was imbued with mutual protectiveness.

Only afterward did any comparison surface between today and her first wedding. She remembered how impatient she had been to be alone with Brad and relive the whole experience, share every thought and feeling she'd had with him, and hear every thought and feeling he'd had. There had been the reception to get through. Of the same mind, they'd escaped as soon as decently possible, but it had seemed like hours.

Polly had the same yearning now to be alone with Jonus. She felt guilty to wish so strongly that they could leave Jennifer with a sitter and go out to dinner, just the two of them. Anxious not to convey her feelings to the little girl, she was careful to pay her extra attention.

If Jonus was on the same wavelength, she was unable to tell. He was quiet in the car, but Polly had no way of knowing whether he was regretting his daughter's presence, too, or coping with other regrets.

She did her best to allow him his introspection by carrying on more than her share of the conversation with Jennifer, who sought praise for her role in the wedding.

"You were quiet as a little mouse and didn't move a muscle," Polly declared. Actually she had been aware of the little girl only vaguely.

"It took so long before the minister got to the part with the rings. Where was Polly's other ring, Daddy?"

"What oth—" He broke off the puzzled inquiry and gave Polly a stricken look, his hands tightening on the wheel.

"Mommy had two wedding rings," Jennifer went on to remind her father.

"One of them was an engagement ring, sweetie," Polly explained. "Your daddy and I weren't engaged long enough for me to need to wear one of those." She slipped off her glove. The light from the dashboard illuminated her hand so that she could see the narrow circle of diamonds. "I like the ring your daddy gave me very much. I think it's beautiful."

Jonus reached over his gloved hand. Polly laid her bare hand in it, and he squeezed it and brought it to his lips.

"Not nearly beautiful enough," he said huskily, and then included his daughter as he suggested, "Now why don't we get our minds on something else besides weddings?"

Polly didn't miss the plural. Her tone was hollow as she concurred, "Yes, why don't we? Tell us about your Christmas play you're going to be in at school, Jennifer."

The child allowed herself to be diverted. Jonus and Polly took turns prompting her to keep up the stream of chatter.

"What's the date of the play, by the way?" he asked Polly.

She told him and regarded him questioningly when he grimaced and shook his head.

"Wouldn't you know it?" he said resignedly. "I have to go to New York on business. I'm afraid I'm going to have to miss it."

"That's too bad!" Polly exclaimed in sympathy, and Jennifer voiced her disappointment from the back seat. "Surely someone will be making a videotape, and we can get a copy. I'll call the school and offer to rent a video camera, if necessary." Polly sought to console them both. "One way or another, Jennifer, your father will get to see you in your play."

The girl was so intrigued by the idea of seeing herself on the television screen that she was immediately reconciled to her father's absence from the actual performance. He wasn't so easily cheered up.

"It can't be helped. If your business is that important, then you have to go and take care of it," Polly reasoned with him.

"It is that important, or I would postpone my trip until you could come with me. I had thought we might take in some big-city life, go to the theater, do some Christmas shopping."

"I've never been to New York City." The admission carried Polly's mixed emotions. As thrilled as she was that he had meant to ask her to accompany him, she was also intimidated. She would be so out of her element in such an ultrasophisticated urban environment. "I wouldn't have the right kind of clothes."

"That would be an easy problem to solve," he pointed out. "New York's certainly the place to buy clothes. Maybe the next time it will work out."

He didn't sound extremely optimistic.

"Do you go there on business frequently?"

"Not frequently. Two or three times a year."

Trish would have gone with him when she was living. Suddenly it made sense to Polly that he had resigned himself so quickly to her being unable to go. On the one hand, he felt obligated to invite her, since she was his wife now, but he was probably afraid of being swamped by memories and having difficulty carrying off a combination business and pleasure trip.

"If Polly goes with you next time, can I go, too, Daddy?" Jennifer asked.

"No, because we would be doing adult things that you wouldn't enjoy."

Not we *will* be, but we *would* be. It was highly hypothetical.

"Then who would take care of me?"

"Don't worry about it now, honey. I don't even have another trip planned right now."

The atmosphere in the car was subdued for the remainder of the drive. Even Jennifer was affected. She fidgeted, and inquired every few minutes how much longer the ride was going to last.

There were no other children at the formal restaurant where Jonus had made dinner reservations. The maître d' glanced at Jennifer in discreet surprise.

"I was just in my daddy's wedding," she volunteered, as though sensing she needed to substantiate her status as a diner in the exclusive establishment. "This is my daddy and this is Polly, my new stepmother."

The man's eyebrows elevated ever so slightly in mild disbelief that this sober threesome was a wedding party. He recovered himself at once and cleared his face of anything other than professional politeness.

"Congratulations, sir." He inclined his head at Jonus and then to Polly. "Madame. Sir, your table for three is right this way."

Jennifer pointed out in a stage whisper when they were seated, "He didn't congratulate me."

"And he really should have," her father said with a gentle, exasperated irony. "You couldn't have played a more prominent role in today's itinerary."

"What does itinerary mean?" she asked.

"It means schedule," Polly explained.

As she studied her menu, she thought about the deeper truth in Jonus's words. The little girl was the whole reason for his marrying her. He would never have thought in terms of making her his wife if Jennifer hadn't needed a stepmother.

As though there hadn't been enough sensitive discussions already, still another one popped up during dinner, without any warning.

"What's the matter, sweetie?" Polly inquired, when Jennifer lapsed into a thoughtful, frowning reverie. "Don't you like your salad?" The little girl was using her fork to toy with a piece of romaine lettuce.

"It's okay," she replied absently. "It would be better, though, if the garlic taste wasn't so strong."

"I have to agree with her," Jonus said. "I've had better Caesar salad." He looked at Polly for her opinion.

She had been eating her salad without tasting it and had no basis for comparison since she'd never had Caesar salad before, a fact she hadn't mentioned when Jonus had suggested ordering it. There had been few occasions when she and Brad had eaten in the kind of restaurant that had Caesar salad on the menu, and they had never gambled on ordering an unfamiliar fancy salad prepared at tableside. Brad hadn't been a big salad eater, anyway.

"I'm not a gourmet, like you two are," she said evasively.

"I was just wondering..." Jennifer sighed, still off on her own mental track. "What should I call you now, Polly?"

"Why, you should still call me by my name, sweetie," Polly replied.

"But now you're my stepmother."

"I'm your father's wife now, too, but he's still going to call me Polly."

Jonus made a movement, and Polly glanced at him to see an expression of dread crossing his face. Too late, she saw the hazards in her remark.

Right on cue, Jennifer said, "Daddy hardly ever called my mommy by her name. He called her 'darling.' Just like he calls me 'honey' or 'baby' most of the time, and you call me 'sweetie.'"

"Those are pet names," Polly said. "It's the tone of voice that makes them special." Her tone of voice was forced and hopeless.

"Do you want to call Polly 'Mommy'?" Jonus asked his daughter quietly. "Because if you do and she doesn't object, it's all right with me."

"I think that that would lead to a lot of confusion, and Jennifer wouldn't feel right. Deep down what she's trying to say is that she'd like a special name for me, but no one can ever take the place of her real mommy. Right, Jennifer?" Polly prompted gently.

The little girl nodded.

"It makes me very happy to hear you call me Polly. No one else says it in quite the same way." Polly reached over and gave her cheek a tender pat.

"But when I have a little half brother or a little half sister, they're going to call you 'Mommy,' aren't they?"

Jonus and Polly both put down their forks. She felt him looking at her, but kept her gaze on her salad plate, lacking the courage to read what was in his expression.

"Polly and I haven't discussed whether you're going to have a half brother or half sister," he lectured sternly. "That's something that the two of us would have to agree on, and neither of us wants to talk about it now."

"To answer your question, if your father and I were to have children, yes, they would call me 'Mommy.'" Polly picked her words carefully, still avoiding meeting his eyes. "When they are old enough to understand, we would explain to them all about your father having been married before and your having a different mother. So there wouldn't be any confusion in their minds, if that's what worries you."

"Jennifer would see to it that everything was explained, wouldn't you, honey?" Jonus said with weary patience.

The rest of the meal passed without incident, but it wasn't relaxed. Jonus and Polly were both on their guard, prepared for Jennifer to plunge them into another awkward moment. It put them under a strain keeping the conversation flowing along safe channels.

Polly was relieved when they had finished dessert, Jonus had paid the bill, and they could leave. There was a strong sense of anticlimax as they headed home on the interstate.

"I didn't like that restaurant." Jennifer spoke up drowsily from the back seat and yawned. "Did you, Daddy? Did you, Polly?"

Polly let him answer first.

"I'd have to give it another chance," he said.

"I can't find any fault with it," said Polly. She gave her opinion as truthfully and tactfully as she could manage, knowing that the bill must have been exorbitant. "The service was perfect. The atmosphere was lovely. The food looked beautiful on the plates. I just didn't have enough appetite to do it justice." She'd had to force down what she'd eaten.

"I'm so sleepy..." Jennifer yawned again loudly. "Could I sit in your lap up there, Polly?"

"That wouldn't be safe, sweetie."

"Then would you sit back here with me? I can't hold my head up."

Polly met Jonus's glance apologetically, asking him if he'd mind. He pulled the car over, and she climbed in the back seat with his daughter, who went soundly asleep with Polly supporting her small, lax body, both of them strapped securely into their seat belts.

"Poor little darling is all pooped out," Polly reported.

"She's had a big day and a lot of excitement." He sounded very tired himself, as though speaking was an effort. "I'm sorry about the way she put us both through the mill and kept bringing up her mother. But I can't shut her off."

"No, of course not. That wouldn't be right. She has to feel free to mention Trish."

"She'll make fewer references with the passage of time." The prediction held a quiet sadness. "Once the newness wears off and she gets used to our being married, she'll stop comparing the past and the present."

Would he? Polly wondered, her heart aching. "I didn't mind on my account as much as I minded for you. I know how painful memories can be."

"They get less and less painful."

"Don't feel guilty because the grief softens, Jonus. It happens with time."

He was silent for a long moment. Polly bit her lip in the darkness, sensing that he wasn't closing her out of his thoughts, but searching for a kind way of sharing them with her.

"Did you think about Brad today?" he asked.

Polly was so unprepared that she didn't answer immediately. "Yes. But only a moment or two. Not at all during the marriage ceremony itself."

"Thank you for telling me that."

For answering the real question in his mind.

"Maybe it's just as well that today went the way it did," she suggested, seeking her own reassurance. "At least neither of us had a sense of déjà vu."

"That's for sure." His agreement was heartfelt. "I was too much on pins and needles to think about anything except getting you to the church before you backed out. When Jennifer and I arrived, you acted as though you were having serious second thoughts. Then the minister met us with the news that he hadn't turned on the heat. I was afraid from your reaction that you were going to suggest postponing our wedding indefinitely."

"You make it sound as though I got married reluctantly, and that's not true," Polly objected. "It was just against my better judgment. Today when you and Jennifer arrived, you looked so handsome and she was so cute and excited that I regretted that I hadn't planned a bigger, nicer wedding for us. You'd left everything up to me, and I felt as though I'd let you down."

"All I knew was that you were on the verge of tears when we were leaving your chalet. I wish I'd had some insight into your feelings. Any kind of wedding plans were agreeable to me, as long as they didn't require waiting. If we could have lived together in the meantime, it would have been different, but with Jennifer, we couldn't. That one night you slept with me, we let her think that you had slept in her bedroom," he reminded her.

"Once we decided to get married, there was no point in waiting."

"We never arrived at any decision together. You just agreed. I took advantage of the fact that you're a natural mother and I put pressure on you." He was quietly analytical.

"You didn't have to apply very much pressure. I was willing. You sound as though you're having second thoughts, now that it's too late to back out," she ventured.

"No, I'd do it all over again, even go through the ordeal that today was. From now on, though, our marriage is going to be a cooperative venture, Polly. We will decide anything of importance together—what kind of home we have, whether we have more children or not. You won't just agree."

"I'm not that passive a person," Polly protested. "Of course we won't have children unless we both want them."

"It's very selfish of a man to ask a woman to experience all the discomfort of pregnancy and the risk of childbirth."

"A woman can feel very undesirable when she's pregnant, especially during the latter stages. She needs to be very secure in her marriage."

That seemed to be all either of them dared to reveal about their feelings on the subject of having children.

When they arrived at her chalet, Jonus carried Jennifer in, and they put her to bed together. He lit the fire in the fireplace and stayed out in the living room while Polly changed into a nightgown and a warm, fleecy robe. She made a pot of coffee while he took his turn in the bedroom, returning wearing a comfortable sweat suit and heavy socks.

They sat on the sofa, with Polly curled up beside him in the circle of his arm, and sipped their coffee. Jonus breathed a deep sigh of satisfaction, sinking deeper into the cushions and stretching out his long legs to rest his feet on the coffee table.

"This is so cozy," he said, contentment in his voice, but also an undercurrent of seriousness. "After all the strain and tension, it's so good to relax and enjoy the simple comforts of home. My daughter is upstairs sound asleep. My wife is sitting next to me. The two people in the world most important to me are safe, under the same roof. Tonight I'm not even going to think about going off to New York by myself."

"You're only going to be gone for three days," Polly consoled. They'd discussed his business trip on the ride from Burlington after the conversation about having children had died off. "It sounds as though you'll be very busy with appointments."

"During the day. But the evenings are going to be awfully lonely. I wish you were coming with me."

With her along, he wouldn't be able to dwell on memories of past trips to New York when Trish had accompanied him, during the period in his life when he wasn't just deeply content, but truly happy.

"The time will pass. Time always does." Polly tried to sound cheerful instead of forlorn.

"Won't you miss me just a little? At least at night after Jennifer has gone to bed. During the days, I know you'll have lots to do to occupy your mind."

"Of course I'll miss you. It'll be very lonely for me in the evenings."

"If Jennifer was a few grades higher in school, it would be different, although she'd still have trouble accepting that one of us couldn't be there for her play. Otherwise I'd have put up more of a fight, even if I didn't stand a chance of winning."

"My feelings aren't hurt that you didn't insist," Polly assured him, not being really truthful. "Neither of us could enjoy ourselves, knowing how we'd disappointed her."

"No," he agreed. "my main consolation is that I'll be leaving her in your care. Don't start any bad habits, though."

"Bad habits?" Polly looked at him questioningly.

He drained his coffee cup and returned it to his saucer. "Like letting her sleep with you. There are some husband's rights I am going to insist on, you realize." He pushed aside the neck of her robe and slipped his hand inside. "I can tell by the feel of this nightgown you're wearing that I'm going to like the way it looks. Lace and thin silky material. What color is it?"

"It's a cream color. It's really prettier than it is sexy." Polly had shopped for it at great length, too.

"Why don't you let me decide that? With your figure you'd be sexy in a flannel nightgown. Finished with your coffee?"

She gave him her cup and saucer, without taking the last swallow.

"That coffee and a few minutes of peace and quiet with you really did the trick," he told her, slipping his hand back inside her robe. "I feel like a new man. I'm ready for our wedding night now."

His touch was working its usual magic on Polly's body, bringing her alive as a woman.

"This nightgown is part of a set," she confided, slipping her hand under his sweatshirt. "When we got here, I felt chilled to the bone, but I've warmed up. Do you want me to go and put on the robe that matches?"

He was fondling her breast, causing her nipple to tingle and harden beneath the separating barrier of silk and lace.

His fingers tightened as she rubbed her palm across his chest.

"I don't want you to go anywhere at the moment. When you do go into the bedroom, I'll be right behind you. I had some idea about carrying you to bed, but when you use your hands on my body like that I know how Samson felt after his haircut."

His low, intimate lover's tone was as arousing as his caresses. "I'm much too heavy for you to carry me," she protested. "Does it really make you weak when I touch you?"

"That's just one effect. The other is very noticeable. Really impossible to hide even in loose sweats."

"You aren't wearing any underwear." She voiced her feminine deduction.

"You aren't wearing any under this nightgown farther down, are you?" He slid his hand down to discover the answer for himself and reported his findings aloud, "No, I don't feel any elastic or another layer of material. Just warm skin and curves and a patch of soft, curly hair right here. I guess we both were of the same mind—to get comfortable, like a couple of old married people, so that we could turn in when we got sleepy."

"Don't you sleep in pajamas?" Polly rubbed her hand over his taut stomach, just above the waist of his sweatpants. He sucked in his breath, his own hand going still on her hip, as she eased her fingertips down inside his pants.

"No, I usually sleep in my underwear and keep a robe handy in case Jennifer gets up."

"Then you weren't getting ready for bed or you would have kept your underwear on." Polly fondled him intimately.

He closed his eyes and made a sound of male pleasure. "I was getting ready for exactly what we're doing. Weren't you?"

"Yes. Speaking of Jennifer, if she should get up and come to the top of the stairs, she could see us."

"Why do you think I haven't taken your robe off?"

Polly withdrew her hand. "Among my other regrets today, I was sorry I didn't follow up on your mention of a honeymoon. It would have been nice not to have to worry about privacy on our wedding night. If nothing else, we could have taken Jennifer back to the lodge and had a sitter stay overnight with her."

"That thought occurred to me, but I didn't quite have the courage to suggest it." He kissed her, gently and then with passion. "My strength is coming back. Now I'm going to carry my wife into our bedroom."

"I'm a big woman," she protested. "You don't have to do that."

"Trust me, sweetheart. I won't drop you."

The endearment melted every ounce of resistance even while it brought a little pain to her heart. He hadn't called her *darling* and probably never would, but he cared for her as much as he was capable of caring for any woman who wasn't Trish.

It was enough for Polly. She would say the words "I love you" silently, since he couldn't say them back to her.

Chapter Fourteen

"I'm so sorry you had to miss the play, Jonus. She was just adorable."

"I'm sorry I couldn't be there, too." His sigh came to Polly over the line.

"You'll be coming home tomorrow," she reminded him. "You'd better prepare yourself for watching the videotape numerous times. If Jennifer doesn't already have it worn out."

"I can't wait to get home, Polly."

The gravity in his quiet voice filled her with dread. She could visualize his face. He would look the way he had when she had first met him and he was grieving over Trish. As Polly had feared, going away to New York by himself must have caused him to realize all over again the enormity of his loss.

"You sound really down in the dumps. Has it been that bad?" she asked, aching with sympathy, but also with despair for herself. Polly would never be able to make him truly happy.

"Much worse than I was prepared for. Not just the loneliness. I can handle that. I've had serious anxiety attacks. Bad dreams. I woke up this morning in a cold sweat."

"You didn't mention any of this when you called this morning."

"I had pulled myself together. By then I had been up since four-thirty, waiting for it to get late enough to call. Once I heard your voice and Jennifer's, I was okay, and I didn't want to put a damper on your day. But then this afternoon I was walking back to my hotel and saw an automobile accident. No one was badly injured, but the noise of brakes squealing, metal crashing into metal, glass shattering, a woman screaming—" He broke off. "I'm sorry. I shouldn't be telling you all this."

"Of course you should. I should have gone with you, Jonus. You probably needed me more than Jennifer did. But then you'd have been even more anxious about her if I wasn't here to look after her."

"Polly, it's not just Jennifer I've been anxious about. Don't you realize how much you mean to me? I—"

She didn't let him finish, breaking in to reassure him, "I'm fine. Jennifer is fine. We're both all settled in for the night, with Sandy here guarding us." At the moment it would be almost more than Polly could bear to hear him say, "I care about you a great deal," instead of, "I love you."

"Are you planning to drive anywhere tomorrow other than to the lodge?"

"Yes, in the morning I'm going into Waterbury to do some grocery shopping. I thought I'd cook a welcome-home dinner for you tomorrow night."

"I'd like that. Just be careful driving."

"I'm always careful. And I'll be using your car. It has four-wheel drive and it's built like a tank." He had driven himself to the airport in her station wagon and left his car for her to use. "You be careful riding in that airplane. You're not the only one who can have anxiety attacks, you know."

"I'm glad you came into my life, Polly."

"I'm glad I did, too. You mean a lot to me, Jonus."

The silence was taut with emotion. She gripped the receiver hard.

"Good night," he said. "Sleep well and don't worry about me."

"Good night. Don't you worry about us."

I love you, Polly told him in her heart before she hung up.

Halfway home from Waterbury, Polly thought of an item she hadn't remembered to put on her grocery list. Instead of turning around and going back to town, she decided to stop at the little general store that also served as a country post office. It was located right at the turnoff for the mountain highway that came to a dead end at the lodge.

She always took any excuse to shop at the quaint, old-fashioned place of business, anyway. Outside were working gas pumps that were practically antiques. Inside was a potbellied wood stove that provided heat and a conversational center for customers. The weather would inevitably be under discussion.

Polly never tired of hearing the local Vermonters talk. She loved the deadpan manner of speech and colorful colloquialisms. Today she pretended to browse after she'd taken her can of cherries off the shelf, listening to a woman's account to the postmistress about a visit to the dentist for gum ailment. Both women pronounced "gums" as though it were spelled "gooms."

A loud crash outside the store made her jump. "What on earth..." she murmured in unison with exclamations from everyone else inside the store.

"Heavens to Betsy. What was that?"

"Sounded like a car wreck, right outside."

Polly stood there, rooted to the spot, waiting for someone else to go and investigate. *Please don't let anyone be badly hurt,* she prayed.

"Uh-huh. That's what it was."

The laconic discussion of the accident quickly eased her fears. A car had driven into the side of a vehicle parked outside. Her vehicle, or rather Jonus's. The driver and passenger of the car were getting out, apparently unharmed and surveying the damage.

It was extensive, and she probably wouldn't be able to drive home, she was able to surmise even before she went outside to see for herself that the whole driver's side of Jonus's automobile was caved in. She winced at the sight and then tried to calm the couple, who looked to be retirement age. Both were terribly upset and kept interrupting each other, but she managed to piece together that they were from Mississippi, had flown to Vermont and were traveling in a rental car they'd picked up at the airport. They weren't used to ice and snow and had skidded out of control.

"Fortunately there's no damage that can't be repaired—just some inconvenience," she pointed out philosophically and ushered them inside the store, where they could calm their nerves and she could use the telephone. Her main concern was getting her groceries home, which would entail calling the lodge and getting someone to drive a lodge vehicle to her rescue.

After she'd made the call, she arranged for Jonus's car to be towed to the automobile dealership in Burlington where he had bought it. Then she rendered what aid she could to the couple before she left them. When her transportation arrived, a local mechanic was on his way to make sure their rental car was safe to drive to the nearest town, where they could exchange it for another one.

Polly was glad to learn that their final destination, the home of a former neighbor, was only a hundred miles away.

She suggested tactfully that they might be better off stick-ing to interstate travel for the remainder of their journey and then put themselves in the hands of their Vermont hosts for touring the countryside, who presumably would be more knowledgeable about the hazards of New England winter driving.

As she put away her groceries, Polly thought about her phone conversation with Jonus the previous night and felt a shivery, unpleasant sensation as she recalled his descrip-tion of the car accident he'd seen. Normally she didn't put much stock in omens and premonitions, but it was un-canny that she'd had her very first car accident today. She'd been lucky and hadn't ever been in even a minor fender bender before.

Suddenly Polly was struck with anxiety for his safety and with yearning for his return. His plane wasn't due to land in Burlington for another three hours. The drive here would take forty-five minutes. The remaining hours of sepa-ration seemed intolerably long.

She couldn't wait to see him, feel his arms around her, know that he was back home with her, physically safe. She would comfort him, soothe the pain of his remembrance.

And she would voice her love to him. There wasn't any holding back the words any longer. *Jonus, I love you.*

Hearing the squeal of car brakes and then the sound of a horn blaring steadily, Polly headed quickly toward the door, her heart pounding with alarm. There hadn't been any crash, but it sounded as though the driver of the auto-mobile out front might have passed out and fallen forward on the horn.

Throwing open the front door, she saw her station wagon parked in the driveway. Pausing just long enough to note that Jonus was slumped over the steering wheel, she ran down the steps, calling out in panic.

"Jonus! Jonus! What's the matter!"

He raised his head, straightened, and was out of the car before she reached it. She went into his arms, hugging him with all her strength while he squeezed the breath out of her with his tight embrace.

"Polly, *darling*. You're here. You're *okay*," he murmured.

"I'm fine, Jonus." She managed to draw enough breath into her lungs to get out the reassurance. "You gave me such a scare! You're shaking! Are you ill?"

He loosened his hold to stroke her hair with hands that trembled. Polly leaned back to look up at him with deep concern. He gazed down at her as though he was stamping her features in his memory.

"Jonus, what's wrong? What happened to upset you so?" she implored. "I wasn't expecting you for several hours."

"I took an earlier flight. I wanted to have some time with you before Jennifer got home from school." He drew a deep breath, composing himself, and caressed her face with gentle, unsteady fingers. "On the interstate I saw my car being towed in the opposite direction. From its condition, I came to the conclusion... I thought it was happening to me all over again, Polly, that my whole world was falling apart."

"No one was hurt. The car was parked outside Little's General Store, and I was inside the building." Polly filled him in on the details of the accident, giving him a chance to recover. While he listened, his eyes were noting every feature of her face, and his hands were feeling her shoulders and back as though he needed to reassure himself that she was unharmed.

When she had finished, he hugged her tight again and said, "Let's go inside, darling, where it's warm. You aren't wearing a coat."

"Do you want to bring in your bag?"

"I'll get it later. And I came home with an extra suitcase full of presents for you and Jennifer. This trip cost me a fortune."

He was sounding more normal. Polly's heart was buoyant with gladness and relief as she walked with him toward the porch, her arm around him and his arm around her.

"Your next trip to New York, I'll go with you," she promised. "And save you money."

"My next trip anywhere overnight you're going with me—and not to save me money. Hello, old fella. I missed you, too."

Jonus stooped to pat the collie, who came up, tail wagging. Polly had let him out a few minutes earlier.

Inside, her cat approached, meowing.

"Another member of the welcoming committee," Jonus declared and squatted down, holding out his hand. "It's about time you were friendly," he chided in a voice full of satisfaction when the feline permitted him to stroke her.

"Shall I make us some coffee and lunch?" Polly inquired as he stood, took off his topcoat and tossed it across an armchair.

"Not now," he answered, slipping off his tweed jacket and tossing it on top of the coat. For his plane flight home, he had worn a turtleneck sweater, not a shirt and tie. "I just want to get comfortable, hold you, look at you, talk to you." He held out his arms and Polly went into them without any urging. "I want to tell you how much I missed you and hear how much you missed me," he went on, hugging her hard against him. "And once I stop shaking inside, I want to make love to the woman I love."

He loosened his embrace so that Polly could look up into his face. She knew that all her thrilled emotion showed, along with a lingering uncertainty.

"Oh, Jonus, do you love me?"

"With all my heart. I hadn't really realized how much until I went off to New York and was separated from you. I tried to imagine life without you and couldn't bear the thought. Last night I wanted to tell you on the phone that I loved you, but you cut me off."

"I wanted to tell you the same thing. I've been saying the words to you without speaking them aloud because I didn't want you to feel bad about not being able to say them back."

"For how long?"

"Since our wedding night. But I knew I loved you even before that. Actually I knew when you proposed to me the first time."

"Then why did you turn me down? And why were you so reluctant to marry me? You didn't doubt that I cared about you, did you?"

"No. I was just very insecure. I'm not beautiful or chic, and I don't have the social background that a woman married to you should have. I was afraid you would regret marrying me in time. I told you all that, in so many words," she reminded him.

"In retrospect, I guess you did. But I felt on such shaky ground with you that I didn't listen. I thought your main reason for agreeing to marry me was to be Jennifer's stepmother. I wanted you to be my wife enough that I was willing to accept the fact that she would always come before me."

"And I thought your main reason for remarrying was giving her a good stepmother."

"It was originally, and then my motives got more selfish. I've had a struggle with myself, not being jealous of my own daughter because I wanted my share of your time and attention and love."

"You'll have your full share of all three from now on." Polly pulled his head down and kissed him tenderly. "The only reason I've held back is lack of confidence."

Jonus kissed her just as tenderly. "You are beautiful to me, you know. As for not being chic, I would like for you to buy a new kind of wardrobe in a year or two."

"I'll try to be more fashionable. Maybe I can get some help from a fashion expert."

"I'm talking about maternity clothes," he explained.

Polly had to blink at a glaze of happy tears. "Would you like for us to have children, Jonus?"

"At least one, and if there're no problems, then as many as you'd like to have."

"I'd love to be pregnant with your baby. Every time we made love after we were married, I would think about how we could be adding a new little member to our family if I weren't using birth control."

"Before we add another member, we'll need a bigger house. I've been working on plans but I need your input."

"You've been working on a house for us?"

"I started doing sketches when I asked you to marry me the first time and you turned me down. There's a site on our land that I have in mind."

"We have the money in my savings account if we need it, which we can use toward building a house."

"That's your money," he objected.

"You said *our* land just now," she pointed out. "It's *our* money. As far as I'm concerned, it couldn't be put to any better use than being invested in a home for you and me and Jennifer, and her brothers and sisters. I have a husband to take care of me now. I don't need my own nest egg to fall back on."

"And I will take care of you. Always."

"I know you will."

"I love you, Polly."

"I love you, Jonus."

They kissed lingeringly.

"Are you still feeling shaky?" she asked softly.

"I feel strong enough to climb mountains and slay dragons," he replied. "Strong enough to carry my wife into our bedroom and make love to her. Any doubts?"

"None whatever."

* * * * *

Silhouette Special Edition

proudly presents
the long-awaited "prequel" volume of

★ LOVE AND GLORY ★

by
LINDSAY McKENNA

Dawn of Valor

In the summer of '89, Silhouette Special Edition premiered three
novels celebrating America's men and women in uniform: LOVE
AND GLORY, by bestselling author Lindsay McKenna. Featured
were the proud Trayherns, a military family as bold and patriotic
as the American flag—three siblings valiantly battling the threat
of dishonor, determined to triumph . . . in love and glory.

Now, discover the roots of the Trayhern brand of courage, as
parents Chase and Rachel relive their earliest heartstopping
experiences of survival and indomitable love, in

Dawn of Valor, Silhouette Special Edition #649.

This February, experience the thrill of LOVE AND GLORY—from
the very beginning!

DV-1

Silhouette Books

Take 4 bestselling love stories FREE

Plus get a FREE surprise gift!

WRITTEN IN THE STARS

**Star-crossed lovers?
Or a match made in heaven?**

Why are some heroes strong and silent . . . and others charming and cheerful? The answer is WRITTEN IN THE STARS! Coming each month in 1991, Silhouette Romance presents you with a special love story written by one of your favorite authors—highlighting the hero's astrological sign! From January's sensible Capricorn to December's disarming Sagittarius, you'll meet a dozen dazzling heroes.

Sexy, serious Justin Starbuck wasn't about to be tempted by his aunt's lovely hired companion, but Philadelphia Jones thought his love life needed her helping hand! What happens when this cool, conservative Capricorn meets his match in a sweet, spirited blonde like Philadelphia?

FOUR UNIQUE SERIES
FOR EVERY WOMAN YOU ARE . . .

Silhouette Romance®

Love, at its most tender, provocative, emotional . . . in stories that will make you laugh and cry while bringing you the magic of falling in love.

6 titles per month

Silhouette Special Edition®

Sophisticated, substantial and packed with emotion, these powerful novels of life and love will capture your imagination and steal your heart.

6 titles per month

SILHOUETTE *Desire*®

Open the door to romance and passion. Humorous, emotional, compelling—yet always a believable and sensuous story—Silhouette Desire never fails to deliver on the promise of love.

6 titles per month

SILHOUETTE·INTIMATE·MOMENTS®

Enter a world of excitement, of romance heightened by suspense, adventure and the passions every woman dreams of. Let us sweep you away.

4 titles per month